SANTA MONICA PUBLIC LIBRARY
I SMP 00 2223728 B

P9-DNG-224

The ALBUQUERQUE Turkey

Also by John Vorhaus

Nonfiction

The Comic Toolbox: How to Be Funny Even If You're Not
Creativity Rules! A Writer's Workbook
The Pro Poker Playbook: 223 Ways to Win More Money Playing Poker
Killer Poker: Strategy and Tactics for Winning Poker Play
Killer Poker Online: Crushing the Internet Game
The Killer Poker Hold'em Handbook
Poker Night: Winning at Home, at the Casino, and Beyond
The Strip Poker Kit
Killer Poker Online 2: Advanced Strategies for Crushing the Internet Game
Killer Poker No Limit
Killer Poker Shorthanded (with Tony Guerrera)

Fiction

Under the Gun
The California Roll (a Radar Hoverlander novel)

The

ALBUQUERQUE Turkey

A NOVEL

John Vorhaus

Crown Publishers
NEW YORK

This book is a work of fiction. Names, characters, places, and incidents either are the product of the author's imagination or are used fictitiously. Any resemblance to actual persons, living or dead, events, or locales is entirely coincidental.

Published in the United States by Crown Publishers, an imprint of the Crown Publishing Group, a division of Random House, Inc., New York.
www.crownpublishing.com

CROWN and the Crown colophon are registered trademarks of Random House, Inc.

Library of Congress Cataloging-in-Publication Data
Vorhaus, John.
The Albuquerque turkey : a novel / John Vorhaus.—1st ed.
p. cm.
Sequel to: California roll
1. Swindlers and swindling—Fiction. 2. Santa Fe (N.M.)—Fiction. I. Title.

PS3622.O745A79 2011
813'.6—dc22

2010035464

ISBN 978-0-307-71780-1
eISBN 978-0-307-71782-5

Printed in the United States of America

Book design by Lynne Amft
Jacket design by Kyle Kolker
Jacket photograph © istockphoto.com

1 3 5 7 9 10 8 6 4 2

First Edition

To Jim and Nancy, still patiently
waiting for their kid brother to grow up

Every silver lining has a cloud.

The
ALBUQUERQUE
Turkey

1

Boy

It started with a dog, a biggish one loping down the sidewalk with that weird canter some dogs have, the front legs syncopating and the rear legs slewing sidewise in tandem. He must've been running from something specific, because even while scampering forward he looked back, which resulted in his not seeing, and therefore barreling into, me. He hit me square in the knees and knocked me to the ground. This startled us equally, and for a second we both sat still, locked eye to eye down there at dog level.

I vibe dogs. I do. Or let's say that I prize them: Their unconditional love is a love you can trust. I'd rolled with one or two in my time, but the highly migratory life of a con artist didn't really lend itself to long-term canine commitments, so I mostly just admired dogs from afar. Up close, this one was tough to admire, a mixed bag of black Lab and unknown provenance. One ear stood up like a German shepherd's. The other... wasn't there. Looking at the bitten-off stub, I couldn't help wondering how a dog's ear tastes to another dog. He bore other wounds as well, evidence of many fights—maybe not fair fights, for I thought I detected a human hand in some of his scars and mars. I saw it also in his eyes. He feared me. That made me sad. I reached out a hand to comfort him, and he flipped over in submission position, manifesting what every dog dreads and hopes when it submits: dread that it will be kicked; hope it'll be scratched. I opted to scratch, and immediately made a (man's best) friend.

"Get up, boy," I said as I stood. "I'm not the boss of you." The dog—in my mind I was already calling him Boy—obediently rose to his feet. I didn't know if he was that well trained or just felt like following my lead. He wore no collar, only a weathered, knotted rope that trailed away to a frayed end. Something told me this was a dog in transition, and that whoever had been the boss of him was boss no more. Probably if I wanted to, I could keep him, the thought of which tickled me. I pictured me presenting him to my girlfriend, Allie, who had lately shown such determination that we be normal. "Look what followed me home," I'd tell her. "Can we keep it?" If that didn't say *normal,* I don't know what would.

First, though, there was the matter of making sure I was right. I mean, I couldn't just kidnap him—dognap him—so I started back in the direction he'd come, determined to take a stab, at least, at finding his owner. The dog cowered, reluctant to follow. "It's okay," I said, "I got your back." He still wouldn't budge, so I knelt, rubbed his grizzled muzzle for a moment, then took the scraggly end of the rope and walked him down the street. I could tell he still wasn't too keen on the idea, but now he was a dog on a leash, and they have no free will.

I had just turned the corner when I heard the first shouts.

I thought they came from the courtyard of some garden apartments just down the street, but with the way the sound bounced around off those Santa Fe adobe walls, I couldn't be sure. There was a pickup truck parked in front of the courtyard, and its whole grungy aspect seemed linked to the courtyard noises. Bald tires, primer spots and dents, cracked windshield—a trailer-trash ride, or I'm no judge of trucks. The tailgate was missing, and I could see in the cargo bed a litter of empty cans, both beer and oil, plus fast-food wrappers and crumpled cigarette packs.

And, tethered to a tie-down, a severed rope, mate to the noose around Boy's neck.

Boy recognized the truck. He whimpered fearfully as we approached, causing a picture to form in my mind: Enraged driver pulls up to the curb, anger burning so hot that he upsets his dog, who strains against his restraint and snaps the tired line. Dog is off and running, but driver doesn't care. All his anger's focused on whoever's in that courtyard.

More shouts now, and I could hear two voices, no, three: a man and a woman exchanging heated words, and a little girl playing hapless and ineffectual peacemaker. To me it added up to domestic dispute.

Boy wanted to leave and, boy, so did I. After all, there's two kinds of problems in this world, right? My problem and not my problem. But there was a lot going on in my head. There was Allie's need for the two of us to be citizens (and did not, in some sense, citizen equal Samaritan?) and also Boy, for if I left things as they were, he'd likely end up tied back up in that truck, the thought of which grieved me deeply. The kicker was the little girl's voice. I could see the black hole of human trauma forming in the center of her universe. I knew that Allie came from such a troubled vortex, where Mom and Dad never got along and routinely inflicted horrible damage on anyone within range. I couldn't go back in time and salve Allie's pain. It was likewise probably too late to save the little girl from hers—these things start young—but maybe I could douse the present blaze.

And just perhaps talk my way into a dog.

I moved toward the courtyard. Boy resisted, but I patted his head in reassurance, trying to communicate that whatever I planned to sell, it wasn't him out. I guess I got my point across, for he fell more comfortably in step beside me. I paused to gather myself before entering the courtyard. I didn't know what, specifically, I was about to walk into, but it didn't much matter. A top grifter gets good at improvising successfully across a wide variety of situations.

Even ones with guns.

I didn't see the gun at first, just a man at the base of a short set of steps, looking dirty as his pickup truck in tired jeans and sneakers, a stained tank top, and a polyester cap with some kind of racing logo. The woman stood on the top step with the girl tucked in behind her. They wore matching mother-daughter flower-print shifts. In other circumstances you'd have said they looked cute. Now they just looked scared, but the mother was playing the defiance card hard—a card I could tell she didn't really hold, but that's what they call bluffing.

"Andy, now, clear out," she said. "You know you're not allowed here. The judge—"

"Screw the judge," said Andy. "I want Sophie. I want my little girl."

"No, Andy. Not when you've been drinking and God knows what else."

"Oh, and you're such a saint?" Andy practically vibrated with rage.

"That's not the point. I have *custody.*" The way she said *custody* damn near broke my heart. Like it had magic power, but I knew it would cast the opposite spell.

It did. It brought the gun up, a Browning Mark II Hi-Power. Some of them have hair triggers. Andy leveled it at—as I gathered from context—his ex-wife and child. "Sophie," Andy told the girl, his voice gone cold, "go get in the truck. I swear if you don't, I'll shoot you both right now."

The moment froze. I was afraid to speak. I didn't want to spook Andy, not while he had the gun up. I guess Boy felt the same way. I could sense him repressing a growl. Then... the girl moved. She disengaged herself from her mother's clutching hands and edged warily down the stairs. I knew what she was walking into, could foresee it in an instant. Let's say she survived the next hour, day, week, month, year. Let's say she made it all the way into womanhood. Where would that find her? Turning tricks at a truck stop? Up in some spike house with a needle in her arm? Living with a man who beat her just like Daddy did? Talk about your human sacrifice. It may have been the bravest thing I'd ever seen in my life.

I couldn't let it stand.

"Hey, mister," I piped up, applying my most innocent bystander gloss, "do you know whose dog this is?" Three heads swiveled toward me. The gun swiveled, too, but I ignored it, for part of running a good con is shaping the reality around you. Or denying it, as the case may be. By disregarding the gun, I momentarily neutralized it, for what kind of fool doesn't see the obvious? It's destabilizing to people. They don't know how to react, so mostly they just do nothing, which buys you some time to make your next move. At that point, I don't know if I felt supremely courageous or just dumb-ass dumb. Both, probably. But one thing you learn on the razzle is that once a con starts, the worst thing you can do is break it off. Then you're just twisting in the wind. "Because, um, I found her down the street and she seems to be lost."

"Ain't a she," said Andy.

"No? I didn't look." I bent down to check out Boy's underside. "Hey, you're right, it's a boy. Anyway, used to be." I smiled broadly and started walking Boy forward.

Andy aimed the gun. "Stop," he said.

"Oh, look, I'm not trying to get in the middle of a thing here. I'm just trying to return this dog. Is he yours?"

"Just let him go."

Well, I thought I knew what would happen if I did that. Boy would take off running, and probably none of us would ever see him again. I weighed my own selfishness—I wanted that dog—against his needs and safety, and dropped the rope. Boy surprised me. He plopped down at my feet, content, apparently, to let me run the show to whatever outcome I could achieve. You gotta love that about dogs. When they trust you, they trust you all the way.

"Now clear out," said Andy.

Here's where my play got dicey. Make or break time. "Hang on," I said, bleeding avid enthusiasm into my voice. "What kind of gun is that?"

"What?"

"Because it looks like a 1980s Hi-Power. Is it?"

"The hell should I know?"

I squinted at the gun, straining to see detail, which I didn't really need to do, since one of the many things you learn about in my line of work is guns, in detail. "Two-way thumb safeties, nylon grip, tri-dot sights. Yep, that's a Mark II. Bet it's got the throated barrel and everything."

"Get the fuck out of here."

"The thing is," I said, "I'm kind of a collector. Any chance I could buy it off you?" This was the heart of my play, based explicitly on what the mother had said about drinking and God knows what else. I knew what else. Crank. Crystal meth. I could see it in Andy's dilated pupils, his scrunge-brown teeth, and his generally tweaky demeanor. A guy like that's not likely to be long on cash, and addiction is a voice that never shuts up. He might could want to quell it for a while. Very slowly, again not to spook him, I reached into my back pocket and pulled out my bankroll.

Funny. For someone supposedly off the razzle, I still kept my cash in a grifter's roll, big bills on the outside, small bills within. I held the roll lengthwise, between my thumb and first finger, so that Andy could see its Ben Franklin veneer. "I think I have a grand here," I lied easily. "If that's not enough, we could hit my ATM."

Andy licked his lips, imperfectly processing my offer. "Maybe I'll just take it," he said.

Oops. I hadn't considered that. "Sure, yeah, whatever," I vamped. "You could do that. But what kind of example does that set for your little girl?" This was pure bafflegab—nonsense—and I knew it, but that didn't halt my improv. "Look," I continued, "like I said, I'm not trying to get in the middle of a thing, but it looks like you guys have a problem. If you take my money by force, the problem gets worse. If you start shooting, it gets way worse, right?" I looked at the mother for confirmation, silently encouraging her to nod, which she did. "On the other hand, you sell me your gun, you've got a little scratch, you can take your girl out for ice cream, come back later, everybody's calm, you can all work out your business." I knew he'd take "take your girl out for ice cream" to mean *go score,* and hoped his need was such that he'd opt for the line of least resistance.

He seemed to be leaning that way. I could see him mentally converting a thousand dollars into chunks of scud. "What's in it for you?" he asked.

"I told you, I'm a collector. I've got the Mark I and the Mark III, but the Mark II, boy, those are rare."* I dared a step forward, arm outstretched, dangling my bankroll like bait. "What do you say? Deal?"

The ladies and I held our breath. Maybe Boy did, too.

"I'm keeping the bullets," said Andy at last.

"That's fine," I said. "Who collects bullets?"

Then, so slowly it made my teeth ache, Andy lowered the gun, pressed the slide release, and dropped the magazine into his hand. Still manifesting my goofy enthusiasm, I strode over and made the exchange, then stepped back quickly before he could change his mind. "Oh, man," I said, "wait'll the guys in the gun club see this."

The next sound you hear will be Andy saying, "What the fuck?" when he finds out what a grifter's roll is.

"What the fuck?" said Andy. He threw down the roll and took a menacing step toward me.

"Funny thing, though," I said, raising the gun, "didn't you chamber a round?" Andy stopped. I let my voice go hard. "Go on, get out of here." He turned back to grab Sophie, but, "Oh, no," I said. "No." Then he looked at his dog. "Not him, either," I said. "Get."

Andy got.

Was there a round in the chamber? Did it matter? You can bluff with the best hand, too.

The truck rumbled off. I'd memorized the license plate and would soon be dropping a dime, for there's no way that guy wasn't holding. Meantime, I encouraged Sophie and her mother to clear out to a shelter somewhere, which they thought was a pretty damn good idea. We agreed that Boy would stay with me.

---

*Well, measured in millions.

So, happy ending, right? Sure, except for one thing. Someone videoed the whole thing through a window. It was on YouTube by dusk.

It didn't really matter that thousands of people saw Radar Hoverlander in action.

But it sure as hell mattered that one person did.

2

Two Hours Earlier

"Nude models," Vic Mirplo announced. (This was two hours earlier.) "Radar, we're talking undressed, unclad, au natural, bare-ass bare, stark staring stripped, live nude girls, naked and in the buff, right here in my studio any time I want." Vic leaned back on his couch, arms splayed wide and a paintbrush clamped in his teeth in unconscious allusion to Franklin Roosevelt's self-satisfied cigarette-holder chomp. "That, my friend, is the best part of this gig." It occurred to me that where FDR might have struck such a pose upon ending a depression or battling fascism to its knees, Mirplo's triumph was the slim victory of placing himself in the same room as a naked woman who wasn't a stripper.

At a price he considered, well, worth it.

"Ten bucks an hour," he said. "Can you believe it? They come over. They take off their clothes. They stand there. For as long as you want. In any position you want. And all you have to do is paint."

"Yeah, small problem with that," I said. "Vic, you don't paint."

"I paint," he said. "I put pigskin on canvas." He meant pigment, of course, but Vic often missed his intended words by that wide a mark.

"Don't you think there's a little more to it than that?"

"Like what?"

"I don't know, you know, like... training? Vision? Skills?"

"I got skills, Radar. I got mad skills. Watch this." Vic jumped to his feet and attacked an easeled canvas with the fervor of a rabid javelina.

He used the brush, his hands, sponges of various sizes and textures, even a squirt bottle. What Mirplo lacked in aesthetic sense he made up for in fury, and in less than ten minutes he had created something so visually distressing that it made me want to shoot the painting, just put it out of its misery. "See?" said Vic, sinking back down on the couch, exhausted, as if he'd just run a marathon. "I'm telling you, Radar, you gotta get in on this art shit. Easiest goddamn money you'll ever make."

"So you've sold stuff, then?"

"I will," he said. "I'm creating a buzz."

"What you're creating," I said, "is hazardous waste."

Vic smiled indulgently. "Ah," he said, "the ol' Hoverlander sense of humor. It never gets old."

At this point, Vic's latest model walked back into the studio, returning from her pot break. She looked to be about twenty-five, with pallid lips, ringlets of dirty blonde hair, and the hundred-yard stare of someone who'd just come back from a pot break. Shedding her kimono, she struck a standing pose on the low platform Vic had crudely comprised from a couple of wooden pallets and a thrift-store blanket. Here in Santa Fe, you'd expect the blanket to be Navajo. It wasn't. It was acrylic, with figures from *Star Wars.* Vic immediately stood and affected a pose of his own, what I imagined he imagined to be his artiste stance.

"Um, Jena," he said, stroking an imaginary Vandyke beard, "that pose isn't working for me. Let's try another." It took a moment for Vic's request to leap across Jena's distended synapse gaps, but eventually the girl blinked, rolled her neck slowly, and settled into a yoga seat on the blanket. "*Much* better," said Vic, evidently satisfied with the full Sharon Stone–scape the new pose presented. He turned to me and reverently mouthed the words, "What a muff!"

There are times, and this was one of them, when I consider my ability to read lips less a blessing than a curse.

Vic returned to work. I couldn't bear to bear witness to any further crimes against canvas, so I headed out. As he waved a distracted farewell, a great glob of bruise-colored paint fell off Vic's brush and soiled his jeans like the numinous spew of a sick pigeon. I thought this would irk Vic, since he washed his clothes only under grimmest duress and had been known to wear the same pants for seasons at a time, but he just smeared the color into the cloth and said, "What the hell. Makes me more arty."

What had the world come to, I mused as I walked out into the New Mexico sunshine, when a Mirplo could be legitimately concerned with looking more arty?

What, indeed?

I'd been in Santa Fe about a month, and so far it struck me as the sort of place you could get tired of in about a month. Not that it lacked appeal. The climate was good, the people relentlessly friendly—well, friendly the way people are when they make their living off tourists and they know it. The architecture agreed with me—low adobes that blended sensibly into the desert scrub and cactus by design, utility, and civil statute. I'm told that no new buildings in Santa Fe may be over two stories high, unless architected into setback levels, which gives the tallest structures in town the look of taupe wedding cakes. I didn't mind. It kept the scale human. After Los Angeles, the last city where I'd spent much time, a little human scale was a welcome change of pace.

I think what got to me about Santa Fe was exactly how open and accessible it was. I hadn't been in town two weeks when I started to recognize the same faces—and they started to recognize mine. At the coffee joint or the grocery store, they'd nod at me as if to acknowledge, *Oh, you're still here? If you were a tourist, you'd be gone by now.* This there was no denying: Santa Fe was definitely a three-day tourist town. Georgia O'Keeffe Museum, the Plaza, Loretto Chapel, a quick spin through the art galleries, maybe a day trip to Los Alamos, then it's up the road to Taos or down the road to Albuquerque. If you're not outta here, pretty soon you're from here, and in a town this small, that tends to get noticed. Which is when a grifter like me gets edgy.

Check that, I reminded myself. *Ex-grifter.*

It was back in March when Allie and I decided to go straight, about three months after our measured skedaddle from L.A., and just about three months before this moment here. We'd been propping up a *cervecería* at a Mexican beach, amusing ourselves by tapping out lewd suggestions to each other in Morse code,* when the conversation turned to what to do with the money we'd made off the California Roll. That scam, a scheme to rob China through certain banking irregularities (okay, skims), had netted us north of half a million each—not counting Mirplo's cut, which he scrupulously kept to himself, and who can blame him, for when you've been burned as many times as Vic has, you tend to wear asbestos Depends. But Allie and I had made common cause, sharing our resources as we shared our love: with enthusiasm, abandon, and the devil-may-care joie of two lonely, deeply suspicious con artists who, after a lifetime of looking over our shoulders, had finally found someone who'd have our back. This, in part, was why we decided to give up con artistry. Having traveled so far down separate paths, alone and on the wrong side of the law, we had to view it as a sign that our peculiar skew lines had crossed. The universe, we concluded that night, had handed us a second chance, an abundantly funded clean slate, with the cops who'd dogged us through the California Roll either dead or bought off, and the ponderous Chinese banking system we'd ripped off none the worse for wise. Two smart cookies like us (we flattered ourselves) could easily and legitimately manage seven figures of working capital without having to resort to the sort of flimflammery that had been our respective culling cards for so many years. We could start a business. Buy a franchise. Learn a trade. There's nothing we couldn't do once we determined to leave our bent lives behind. And frankly, the prospect turned us on, Allie especially. "When the world is your oyster," she said, "there's no telling how many pearls you might find." Having sold no few bogus pearls

---

*Which we both knew, and yes, that's a measure of how geekishly made for each other we were.

in my time, I had to admit that the chance to chase the real deal held a certain innocent appeal.

Behind and beneath all this, I suspect, was the fact that we two were not well practiced in candor and were both working hard to keep our maturing affection on the fully up and up. To turn our attention to snukes—cons, that is; jivin' and connivin' for fun and profit—would be to place a layer of professional lies atop our attempted personal honesty. It was bound to leave us confused. So that night in Mexico, we decided to accept this cosmic gift and embrace our second chance as avidly as we'd always each embraced the main one. We sealed the deal by making love waist deep in the warm sea, with the rhythm of the waves serving as languid counterpoint to our own and the full moon illuminating our bodies for any creature, land or sea, that cared to check us out. I may have been stung by a jellyfish. I think I didn't care.

Some beer-driven ideas don't make much sense the next morning, but this one took. So we did our research, settled on New Mexico, Land of Enchantment, as our land of opportunity, wired our bankroll to a Santa Fe savings and loan, packed our meager things, and rolled. Vic, as Vic will, rolled with. If we were determined to go straight, he announced, he'd better come along "for mortal support." We flew to Houston, where I bought a used Song Swing, the nimble little Chinese SUV that used to be called the Scat until its makers realized that while scat means "go away quickly," it also means, inaptly, "poop." Vic, in the Mirplovian tradition of naming cars, named it Carol after a (mythical, I suspect) lost love. We headed west till we hit the Rio Grande, then north until we hit, well, here.

And here I was, on a sun-blanched sidewalk halfway between the converted Quonset hut Vic had rented from some down-at-the-heels artist* and the little adobe cottage where Allie and I currently laid our

*Not rented, swapped—for some spurious mining rights in the falsely allegedly gold-laden Sangre de Cristo Mountains. What can I tell you? Especially for a Mirplo, honesty takes practice.

heads. It was about a fifteen-minute walk between the two places, and every time I walked it, I felt a little better about being a citizen for once. I'd never felt guilty about my chosen profession but had become quite accustomed to feeling furtive. Now I was trying to take on board the notion that there was nothing wrong with people on the street greeting me by name. I even used my real one, Radar Hoverlander, rather than any of the dozen disposable slip-ons I'd cobbled up over the years. And why not? For once in my life, I had nothing to hide. It felt great going straight. I had every confidence I could keep it up.

And I did, too.

Until that dog came along.

3

This Relationship Shit

But the dog came later.

First came Allie, who was sitting at the kitchen table studying some catalogs when I got home from Vic's. She looked completely matter-of-fact, with her bare feet, painted toenails, denim shorts, and halter top. But something about her—maybe the way she absently pushed her cinnamon hair off her face or ticked the end of a pen against her perfect white teeth—made me crave her even more than I usually did, which was plenty.

"What are we looking at?" I asked.

"Career paths," she said. She held up a pair of catalogs and asked, "What do you think, mechanical engineering or nursing?"

"Engineering," I said. "Somehow I can't picture Allie Quinn as a nurse."

"Can't you?" She unfolded from her seat, stood, cocked a hip, and dropped her voice into a breathy coo. "It's time for your sponge bath, Mr. Hoverlander." She reached behind her neck. "Sadly, this is my only top. I dare not get it wet." Deftly untying it, she tossed it away, then crossed to me and pressed her chest against my shirt. "Now then, where shall we begin? Tell me where you're *dirtiest*."

"I know what career you should choose," I said.

"What's that?"

"Porn star."

She slapped me a little, but that was okay. It was the start of something great.

Afterward, we sprawled together on the cool tile floor. From where I lay, I could just reach Allie's toes. I gave them the little piggy treatment and thought about how lucky I was. "I'm loving this," I said.

"'Course you are," she said. "You're getting sex in the middle of the day."

"No, not that," I protested. "I mean, yes, of course that. But more than that. This. All of this. This domestic bliss. This relationship shit."

Allie propped her head up on her hand and eyed me sardonically. "This relationship *shit*?"

"You know what I mean. We're...I don't know...normal. I've never been normal before. It's nice. I could get used to it."

"Well, you'd better. Because I'm going to be a nurse—"

"Or mechanical engineer."

"Or mechanical engineer."

"Or porn star."

Allie ignored this. "And what are you going to be?"

"I don't know," I said. "I haven't given it much thought."

"Tick-tock, Radar. Rent's due on the first of the month. We can't live off our savings forever."

"No, just"—I pretended to do a rough calculation in my head—"a decade or so. If we cut back on caviar."

"So you're not going to take this seriously, is that it?"

"Wait, what?"

"This domestic bliss. This relationship shit." I could tell that all of a sudden Allie wasn't having a good time. Were I Mirplo, with his malaproptic bent, I'd say I'd pinched a nerve. "If we're going straight, Radar, we have to go all the way straight. That means going to school or getting a job or finding some sort of purpose, just like straight people do. It doesn't mean coasting."

"Not coasting," I said. "Transitioning."

"I'm sorry," she said, "I can't buy that word. Before, maybe, when I didn't have anything to lose."

"But now you have something to lose?"

"Of course, you numbskull. You. Us. We backslide into a scam, next thing you know we're arrested or worse. I don't want that, Radar. Do you?" I shook my head. "Okay, then, we have to go cold turkey. Man up. Find something productive to do with our lives. Be citizens."

"Why do I have a feeling being citizens means less sex in the middle of the day?" This was intended as a joke, but it landed flat as a karaoke diva. Allie shot me a sour look, a look I'd already come to recognize as *You're not as funny as you think you are.*

This relationship shit is tricky—land mines everywhere you look. Like the sign says, there's no such thing as a free lunch, not in relationships, not in anything. Everyone wants the good stuff: someone to light candles for, curl up next to at night; someone to bring them soup when they're sick. But if you want the good stuff, of course you have to put up with the rest. Moods. Privacy jags. Not being as funny as you think you are. Most of all, the land mines. Everyone has them—Allie and I had them in spades—psychic sore spots that take a lifetime to bury and then a lifetime again to disinter and disarm. That's two lifetimes right there, and I don't know anyone who's got that kind of time. So instead of doing a thorough, safe sweep of the area, sometimes you just blunder ahead.

And sometimes you step on a mine.

"How's it going to be, Radar? I mean, really, how is it going to be? Do you plan to do this thing, actually do it? Or just hold back, play at being citizen like you've played at numismatist, talent scout—God, I don't know—whatever other roles you've played."

"I've never played God." Another badly misfiring joke, this one actually propelled Allie to her feet. She stormed around the kitchen, picking things up and noisily putting them down. Our little bungalow with generous and low-slung windows stood close to a fairly busy street, and I imagined some passers-by getting an eyeful of the unself-consciously naked Allie. I remained on the floor. I didn't see much point in two of us putting on a show.

At last she came over and crouched down beside me. She touched my cheek. It sort of made me melt. "You don't get it," she said. "Radar, I love you, but this is gonna be *hard.* Hell, it's hard enough to say I love you without freaking out. Look, we've been on the snuke all our lives. Both of us. You think we can stop on a dime? We'll get bored, frustrated, thwarted in our ambitions. It's gonna stress us out, and stress our relationship. And why? Because we won't have the comforting demands of the grift to distract us. We won't have all that *noise* in our heads. We're going to have to face each other, face ourselves. I'm not afraid of that, but I know what it means: questions, Radar. 'Is this the right person for me? Can we grow together? Can we become people of substance?' "

"You make it sound like we need a twelve-step program."

"Maybe we do."

I sat up and took her by the shoulders. "Okay, first of all, there's one question I definitely know the answer to. Are you the right person for me? Yes. Absolutely. Case closed."

"What about the rest of it?"

"Uh... don't ask, don't tell?"

"Not good enough, Radar. We've got to figure this shit out. That's what straight people do."

"Straight people don't figure this shit out. *Swamis* don't figure it out. I should know, I've been a few. Look, Allie, there *are* no answers. There's just questions. Questions and more questions. The type of questions that if you keep asking them long enough, of course you freak out. That distracting noise you're talking about? I'm glad for that noise. We didn't have that noise, we'd slit our wrists before breakfast."

Allie stood again. I thought I heard a squeal of brakes on the street. She looked down at me and shook her head sadly. "Not good enough," she repeated. "We have to do better than that." She grabbed her halter top and shorts, and went in the other room.

Like I said. Land mines.

Times like these, I half wished I smoked, because this would have been a perfect moment to say I was going out for cigarettes. Instead, I called, "I'm going out for gum," which sounded as dumb as I thought it would and really just meant that I was angry and confused and had to walk it off. I got dressed, grabbed my keys and cash, and cruised.

Relationships *are* tricky. Even a rank beginner like me knows that. After all, there you are with your One True Love, right? The one person you can count on to accept you, warts and all. But no matter how many of your hidden demons you reveal and how many she accepts, there's still more to reveal and still more to accept. And some of those demons are fierce. Take me: abandoned by my mother and father. Mom at least had the legitimate excuse of dying of cancer. Dad just bailed, leaving nothing but tales of his conny exploits, a trail of jokey postcards, and a fading picture of his face in my mind. I thought it was my fault. Little kids will do that, place themselves in the center of the universe and blame themselves for every supernova that explodes around them. Later we get smart enough to know that each of us is the center of our own universe, and if your father left you or beat you or drank or ran around, it's because of crap in *his* universe, not yours. But no matter how smart you get, that little kid's still in there somewhere, and guess what? When you're being all vulnerable with your OTL, the demons come out. You can't help it. It's just the way things are. Maybe what Allie was driving at, with all this drive to change, was just the need to leave her old universe behind.

I paused to put that thought to my reflection in the window of a corner store, one selling the newly popular Geoid Equipotential, a tablet computer that, it was boasted, could do everything but wash your socks. Ignoring the new toy, I studied this year's model Hoverlander: a young man, reasonably robust, presentable, with shaggy hair consciously cut boyish, a slender frame topping out just south of six feet, and the dress and demeanor of, well, of a guy on vacation.

I *was* on vacation. Son of a gun, Allie was right. I was holding this tantalizing clean slate at arm's length. She and I had been partners in crime. Our successful resolution of the California Roll had proved how we were good together and, in some weird way, good for each other, too. But that was then. Now what she wanted—what I guess she needed—was a partner not in crime but in change. That wasn't so much to ask, was it? Not of your OTL. But she'd asked, and I sure as hell hadn't answered, which dug a trench of a sort between us. What's that phrase? Never kid a kidder. Allie was an expert grifter, which meant an accomplished liar, which meant atavistically aware of the lies around her. I hadn't actually *lied* to her. I'd told her she was the one for me, and that was a truth, the bedrock sort of truth you can lock down and build on. After all we'd been through together—all the myths and countermyths we sold each other while pulling off the California Roll—wasn't that enough? What more did she want? A job? A 401(k)? Jury duty and backyard barbeques?

Yes. All that. Exactly.

And when you think about it, why not? In my life on the grift I'd played all sorts of roles. Why couldn't I play the role of a normal person for once? People adjust. They do it every day. It'd be no different than, say, going vegetarian. A change of habit. No big deal. All I had to do was not be a scam artist and just be me. Next year's model Hoverlander: brand, spanking, shiny new, new as a Geoid, a seat-belt-wearing, salary-earning, grass-mowing, taxpaying citizen. All for my One True Love.

So there I was with a silent promise to Allie to stop running cons. Two hours later, I'd already broken my word.

4

Devil in a Red Dress

It was for a good cause, though, duping a tweaker and saving a child, and Allie understood that. It think it was Boy who sealed the deal, because within about ten seconds of meeting, they were down on the floor rolling around like old best friends. And in the next days' onslaught of police and press inquiries, the question of Radar's life trajectory got temporarily shelved.

I played the police and the press in an uncharacteristically candid manner. They wanted statements, they got statements. Pictures? No problem. I was innocent, beneficent, I had nothing to hide. It made me a little jittery, not traveling dark after so many years of concealing everything about myself—my aims, endeavors, history, talents, resources, even my name. But Allie wanted it, and I wanted her to have it. So every time I played the hometown hero card with the local cops or TV, I was really playing the change card for her.

Vic thought this was the shit. For some reason, it tickled him to see my picture in the paper, standing there with Boy by my side and a look of pure, stalwart citizenship on my face. "You're such a Girl Scout," he said a few nights later after dinner at our place (where he frequently dined, the mooch). "After all the time I've known you, who'd have thought?"

"Wrong place, wrong time." I shrugged.

"You sure you're not setting something up? Celebrity scam? Phony book deal? Reality TV gig? A guy like you could leverage fame pretty hard." He grinned like he knew what was behind door number three. "So what's your hidden agenda?"

"No hidden agenda, Vic. I just did a good deed, that's all."

"Yeah, well, we know those don't go unpunished." He snapped his fingers and pointed at me with a look of pure Mirplovian inspiration. "I should do an installation!"

"A what, now?" asked Allie. She sat on the couch with Boy's big head in her lap, scratching the stump of his missing ear.

"Installation. An art project, celebrating Radar. Like a sculpture, but conceptual. And someone pays you to put it someplace." Vic turned to me. "I'm telling you, Radar, the pockets in this town are de-ee-eep. Cultural funds. Nonprofits. The college. Chamber of Commerce. They've got it sussed. Art drives the tourist trade, and the tourist trade gets everyone fat. More art, more tourists. More tourists, more snacky snacks for us."

"Again, Vic, I have to remind you, you're not an artist."

"And I have to remind you that that doesn't matter. Look, I already look the part." He waved his hands in front of his body, spokesmodel style, showcasing his sweatshirt with the cut-off sleeves, vintage Converse sneakers, and, yes, those paint-stained blue jeans that made him look more arty. I had to admit that he did exude a certain bohemian chic, perfect for Santa Fe, though in any other context he would look more hobo than boho. "Besides, with these installations, all you really need is a sexy name. We'll call it"—Vic paused to compose—"*The Persecution and Resurrection of Saint Radar (on a Tuesday).*" He momentarily switched into his Uncle Joe persona, a basso vapido fantasy sportscaster, one of whose signature lines, "And the crowd goes wild!," he indulged in now.

"And what," I asked, "would this installation look like?"

"Who cares? Doesn't matter. Get some old mattresses, spray-painted cinder blocks, maybe a refrigerator with holes drilled in it. An upside-down Buddha. It's all about symbolism with this art crowd. The more perplexing the better."

I mulled this over. I could feel a certain stirring deep in my gut as the play laid out before me. It had, I had to admit, a certain appeal: Play your cards right, you could do installations everywhere. Then I looked over at Allie. She continued rubbing Boy's head while silently shaking her own.

The problem with living with a world-class grifter is that she almost always knows what you're thinking.

"Well, good luck with that, Vic. I'm sure you'll be the next Paul Klee."

"Who?"

Say this about a Mirplo, they never let ignorance stand in their way.

After a while, Vic departed to make the rounds of bars and boîtes where, according to his dim understanding of the Santa Fe art community's status system, one could advance one's reputation merely by showing up—or getting kicked out.

"There's a poetry slam at Stalacti," he said. "Maybe I'll crash."

"Now you write poetry, too?"

"What can I tell you?" he said. "I'm a Renaissance dude."

The thought of Vic writing poetry sent a shudder through my linguistic orthodoxy, but I clapped him on the back as I sent him on his way. "Knock 'em dead, kid."

"He shoots, he scores!" bellowed Uncle Joe in reply.

That night, Allie and I made love—slow, sweet, and tender, just the way normal people do when their time is their own and their conscience troubles them not. Later she said, "I'm proud of us."

"For what?" I asked.

"Doing this the right way. Trying, at least. I know it's hard."

I basked in her approval but lay awake long after she fell asleep. Being in the public eye troubled me. Too many people now knew my name, and though I had nothing (currently) to hide, it made me feel unsafe, like a squirrel who'd strayed too far from the trees. Boy lay curled up at the foot of the bed. He farted in his sleep, and I found the expanding bubble of noisome fume oddly comforting. *I've got a woman and a dog,* I thought. *A place to live. Fifteen minutes of fame.*

How bad can things be? But the last thought I had before drifting off was Vic's observation about good deeds—"We know those don't go unpunished."

The next day, incredibly, I actually applied for a job. Okay, not a *job* job, not like a greeter at Walmart or something. What I did, I went over to the community college and offered my services as a career counselor. I figured, who better to counsel careers than one who's had so many?* But I couldn't talk my way past the lack of a college degree without flat-out lying, which the current terms of embargo forbade. The human-resources director told me she found me quite qualified. And charming, which struck me as good news, for it meant that I still had my old Hoverlander mojo. Absent that sheepskin, though, her hands were tied. It made me wonder whether the first step in my remedial reconstruction wouldn't have to be education in earnest. I flashed on myself sitting in the back of a civics or an English class, parsing the three branches of government, or a sentence. Somehow, I couldn't make that dog hunt.

Bootstrap education, then? Find a job that requires nothing more than initiative and will—what your granddaddy used to call gumption—and build a career from the ground up? I thought I had what it took to be a self-made man. God knows I'd self-made myself often enough. But again I could forehear the dismal subaudial drone of days. Where'd be the fun in doing over and over again what I'd long since mastered? That seemed a death sentence of sorts.

I went and chased these cheery thoughts through a plate of steak and eggs at a Rudi's Eatateria, lately franchised and spreading like an algae bloom from its Los Angeles roots because even, or perhaps especially, in these troubled times, people take great comfort in a terrific

---

*Embalmer, film editor, able seaman, construction manager, kiln operator, gem cutter, interior designer, park ranger, and urban planner, to name just a few of the fully hypothetical positions I have held.

plate of steak and eggs. It's my habit to sit by windows when I eat, partly to people-watch, but mostly just out of good con hygiene. You never know when knowing what's coming in the front door will buy you a half-step head start out the back. This Rudi's had a southern exposure, and sunlight washed through tinted windows, splashing a silvery yellow glow across the retro Formica four-top at which I sat. People passed by outside at an uneven pace, as if they couldn't decide whether the day was a pleasant one to savor or a hot one to get in out of quickly. Such can be Santa Fe in June: In shadows, you stroll; in sunshine, you stride.

One pedestrian on the opposite sidewalk impressed me as perhaps the most singularly unattractive woman I'd ever seen. From her chunky black kitten heels to her cankles to her shapeless red dress (which even I could tell the shoes didn't go with) to her clownishly made up face and drab blown hairdo in wig-shop brown, this was one saggy citizen.

Who, I noticed, was looking at me.

Well, window-shopping, I guess you'd say, scanning the storefronts as if skimming for just whatever happened to catch the eye. But as she was across the street, the logical storefronts to scan were the ones on the sidewalk over there. Instead, she let her gaze graze along Rudi's facade, and though I doubted she could see me through the tint of Rudi's windows, she seemed determined to try. She covered her eyes with one meaty hand and peered hard in my direction from beneath furred and furrowed beetle brows. Then she reacted to something—the loud growl of a passing car?—and I thought I saw a flicker of fear break across her face. She turned quickly and hobbled off down the street. Clumsy as she looked on those teetery low heels, I wished her a pair of Reeboks for Christmas.

There's a certain sort of tickle I get in the back of my mind when something's not quite right—call it Radar's radar—and I got it just then, big-time. So big that I was half inclined to trail her. But there were these eggs and steak to finish, and besides, I couldn't be a hundred percent sure I wasn't projecting. Allie was right about the difficulty of detox. The razzle's a buzz, the best I've ever found, and if I was going through withdrawal now, in the unwilling company of my brain's understimulated pleasure centers, it was logical to think that my mind might play tricks on me. Perhaps it was playing one now, concocting intrigue for the sake of intrigue by turning an ugly window-shopper into, I don't know, a KGB operative.

I'm saying, if you want to see ghosts, you see ghosts.

I shrugged off the episode, downed the last of my lunch, and headed out to meet Allie at IKEA, for we had determined that some stand-alone bookshelves were an indispensible part of our conventional new lifestyle. Arriving in the midafternoon lull, we worked our way along the giant store's serpentine layout, a yellow-brick sojourn through the spectrum of domesticity, with leather couches left and right, entertainment consoles in our wake, and kitchen treatments dead ahead. And it was fun: all giddy domesticity and this hand-holdy, *look what we're building together out of prefab furniture,* workaday romance. I'd never been to IKEA before, and I was immediately intrigued by the product tags. Fläkig, Kramfors, Flört...who comes up with these names? Now that's a job I could do till the end of days.

Allie had advanced to bookshelves and was already weighing the relative benefits of melamine versus birch veneer, but I lagged behind, distracted by a bin full of tapered plastic cylinders, the Crüst, at $2.99 each. I spent a long moment failing utterly to grasp what they were for, then hustled to catch up. In the nature of IKEA, partitions sliced the space like canyon walls, with punched-out cutouts and archways yielding glimpses of consumer bliss available in other aisles. So it was that as I headed in Allie's direction, I happened to look through a pass-through into the children's bedroom section.

And there sat the lady in red. To her fashion-casualty wardrobe she had added a pair of oversize daisy-frame sunglasses. She bounced heavily up and down on the bottom bunk of a bunk bed. Testing its firmness, I suppose.

She stopped when she saw me. Tilted her sunglasses down and peered over the top of them. Our eyes met.

The story is told of a man who wanted revenge on a woman who'd broken his heart. "Remember me," he warned her. "Remember my face. Because someday, somewhere, many years from now, you will see this face again. And if you don't acknowledge me instantly, I will kill you where you stand." How horrible it must've been for the woman to carry that weight of wariness with her for the rest of her life, fearful lest she forget. I wasn't thus tormented, but there was not the slightest doubt in my mind that I'd seen those eyes before.

"Radar?" Allie had backtracked to find me.

The lady in red held a fleshy finger to her lips, bidding my silence. Then she rose and walked away. I stared at where she'd been. Every part of me felt frozen.

"Hey, lover." Allie waved her hand in front of my face. "Hello?"

"ISS," said a canny fellow shopper with a knowing smile. "IKEA stress syndrome. My husband gets it bad."

"ISS, Radar?" asked Allie. She has a formidable radar of her own and must have known that there was more to my stupefaction than the riddle of the Crüst.

I shrugged. "I guess I just don't have the shopping gene."

Well, what was I supposed to say? That the woman in the red dress was actually a man, one I hadn't seen in over twenty years?

Woody Hoverlander, in fact.

My old man.

5

How Many Solipsists?

If your father walked out on you when you were eight years old, how much of him would you remember? Of Woody I remembered much. The way he always smelled of Old Spice and the panatelas he smoked. The hand magic he could do, like making a quarter disappear (and then not giving it back, to teach me a lesson in credulity). The frequent, unexplained absences, which I realized long after the fact were either undercover stints on the snuke or time in jail. And then the final big disappearance, which he made worse, I think, by perpetrating the false hope of his imminent return. This he did with a string of postcards that, as a sort of running gag, bore portmanteau photographs of that mythical western critter, the jackalope, all furry haunches and grafted antlers. His handwritten messages were usually riddles like

Q: How many solipsists does it take to change a lightbulb?
A: Who wants to know?

The postcard flow dwindled over time, then petered out altogether. Later, when I started on the snuke, word of his adventures occasionally reached me by roundabout means. I'd meet a grifter who knew a grifter who'd worked a government grants thing with him, or a Jake—a cop or detective—who'd note a resemblance and say, "You're not that son of a bitch's son, are you?" I often wondered if word of my exploits ever reached him. Was he proud that his son had followed in his roguish footsteps? Or could he not care less? I tried to track him down once, just for drill, but apart from the aggrieved screeds of several women who'd discovered themselves to be his coetaneous wives, I didn't get close. When you're a master of the vanishing act, it's no trick to stay lost. As to how he'd found me, I didn't bother to wonder. The way I'd been lighting up the media with my name and picture, I was practically on MapQuest.

"Ouch, shit!" That was me savaging my thumb with a hammer instead of hitting the little wooden dowels that connected the kickboard bracket of the Reåd shelving system to the left and right support struts. And that's because I was thinking more about my father than about hammers and dowels—and lying to Allie with my silence, which was making me edgier than I let on.

I don't know why I didn't just come right out and tell her. Maybe I thought she wouldn't believe me, would just tab the revelation as "intrigue for the sake of intrigue." Or if she did believe me, what then? She's supposed to welcome my biggest inspiration and worst influence with open arms, just when we're clinging to so frail a valence of normalcy? She didn't know my father. Okay, hell, I didn't know my father, either, but it seemed unlikely that he'd pack a whole big mess of normal in his Gladstone. That's not how he rolled.

Plus, let's not forget, he was wearing a dress.

But the alternative, I realized as I sucked the sting out of my thumb, was to deny Allie critical information about the goings-on inside my head. Not quite in the class of an alcoholic sneaking a drink, but sneakiness of a sort, just the same. I figured if I was so unwilling to clue in my beloved to the sudden strange appearance of my own flesh and blood, this in itself was a sign that I'd better come clean.

So I did. I was really afraid she'd see it as a setup of some kind, another Hoverlander effort to scrub Operation Citizen, but all she said was, "We'll have to invite him to dinner."

"Not a good idea," I said.

"What, you don't think he'll like me?"

"Did you not hear the part about the dress?"

"So he's trans. I'm not gonna hold that against him."

"He's not trans."

"How do you know?"

How indeed? After all, after all these years, my dad was not much more than a faded and strangely edited VHS tape in my mind, the sum of my recollections and his reputation. Still, there are some things you know in your gut. I didn't know Woody, but I *knew* him. Or let's say that if the apple doesn't fall very far from the tree, then the apple can learn much about the tree just by considering itself. Had I come to town looking for me, so garish a lady costume would not be transvestite plumage.

It would be camouflage.

Because the thing is, when most people look at you, they don't really see you at all. They judge a book by its cover absolutely. Grifters know this, which is why you so often see them in costumes of one sort or another. Business suits. Coveralls with nametags. Uniforms. Whatever helps them sell whatever they want you to buy. Most people looking at my dad in a dress would reach the cursory conclusion I'd first reached: This is one serious frump. Then they'd look away, which would be exactly his goal. How do you hide in plain sight? You thwart the urge to seek.

From this I surmised that Woody was being sought. Not so huge a leap. Even from my dim and distant childhood, I could remember instances of him working very hard to deflect the attention of one irate mark or another, which need will arise from time to time when a grift slides sideways. One whole summer he never ventured out of the house without carefully cloaking himself in the fatigues and demeanor of a disabled Vietnam veteran, right on down to the shrapnel limp and loud colloquies with the voices in his head. I thought it was cool: Daddy plays dress-up. But the strategy was sound, for whoever might be after him would take one look at the post-traumatic stress victim, think, *Well, that sad casualty's not him,* and turn their searching eyes elsewhere.

I didn't need to explain this to Allie. She arrived at the same conclusion once she'd given it a moment's thought. "So we've got Dad on the lam," I said. "From whom and for what we currently have no clue, but he's working the shade and fade pretty hard."

"Why is he even on the street at all?" asked Allie. "Wouldn't it be safer just to lie low?"

"Safer, sure, but a trap of a different sort."

"True," said Allie. "Holing up just puts you in a hole." She settled down onto the living room couch and I paced nearby, each of us doing what a grifter does when presented with a puzzle like this, mentally teasing the pieces into place. Presently, Allie said, "Since he's not lying low, he must really want to see you."

"Not want. Stronger than want."

"How so?"

"We've been estranged forever. Now he gets wind of me on the six o'clock news or wherever, and maybe this sparks some father-son nostalgia in his mind. He can't know how I'll react to seeing him. If he has the time, he tests the water first. E-mail, phone call, maybe a jackalope postcard."

"What kind of postcard?"

"Nothing. Never mind. All I'm saying is, no test, ergo, no time."

"Does he know how good you are?"

"Let's say he does."

"Then he needs help."

"And rates me as the Red Cross."

"So, how do you feel about that?"

"Allie, I don't know. I know I'm supposed to be carrying all these abandonment resentments, and maybe I am. But knowing what I know about him and about me, I figure that to hate him is to hate me. As far as I can tell, we're chips off the same block."

Boy ambled in from the kitchen and taunted me with the tennis ball in his mouth. This particular slobbery brand of tug-of-war, where Boy chomped his ball in a death grip and Allie or I tried to pry it free, had emerged as one of his favorite games. He usually won, too, since the only way to get the ball out was misdirection, and Boy's elemental brain did not respond too quickly to trickery. He was like a certain stripe of mook: too dumb to fool. I grabbed the ball and yanked to no particular avail. We growled at each other. It was fun.

"Part of me is flattered," I said. "My dad was always kind of legendary, you know? I mean, highly regarded in his circles. The two words you mostly heard were *creative* and *fearless.* I guess if he's coming to me for help..."

"Then that's acceptance."

"Acceptance, yeah. But trouble, too." Allie's arched eyebrow encouraged me to continue. No doubt she'd already formed her own hypothesis about what kind of trouble a runaway Hoverlander could cause, but she wanted to hear it from me. "We're supposed to be going straight, right? I have no idea what direction Woody is headed, but I'll bet my bankroll that straight isn't it."

Allie mulled this for a moment, then asked, "What's that stupid thing I've heard you say? 'Make the latest possible decision based on the best available information'?"

"Oh, that's stupid, is it?"

"A little, yeah. But why don't we do that? Wait awhile. See what happens. After all, he may not even contact you. Maybe he just wanted you to know he's out there."

"Maybe he just wanted a bunk bed."

I deked Boy with disinterest. He let down his guard, the ball came free in my hand, and I'd won another round of How Dumb Is a Dog? This, however, left me holding a soggy tennis ball, so who's to say who won? I threw the ball and Boy bolted after it with a dog's abandon, scuttling across the hardwood floor and banging sidelong into the far wall. Then Allie took up the game and I returned to my Reåd. By midnight, I'd wrestled the bookshelf into shape, and it stood upright in the middle of the room. On a handiness scale of ten, I'd rate myself a six; there were pieces left over. But Allie cast approval on my effort. We were just discussing placement options when a knock at the door startled us both.

It was Vic, as nine and a half times out of ten it would be, and he waltzed in with no thought to the hour, for Mirplovian logic held that if *he* was awake, then everyone was.

"It's not like I didn't check the lights," he said. "My only concern was you two randy rabbits might be screwing, and who wants to see that?" At this point he noticed the bookshelf. "I like it," he said, appraising it critically. "Very nice. Very conceptual."

"What are you talking about?" I asked.

"The installation."

"Vic, it's a bookshelf."

"Against the wall it's a bookshelf. In the middle of the room it's art. You should drape it. Drapes are big right now." Then without segue he said, "Hey, check it out," and rolled up his left shirtsleeve to reveal on his arm a paisley-shaped teardrop with a hole in the middle, like the eye on a curvy sperm.

"Vic," marveled Allie, "you got ink!"

"Yeah, I did," he said proudly.

I didn't bother asking why, for clearly this was the next iteration of his artist presentment. See what I mean about costumes? Meanwhile, I thought I recognized the image, but... "Vic," I asked, "where's the rest of it?"

"What rest? That's it. A yin. Half a yin-yang. Totally conceptual."

"Hurt that bad, huh?"

"Like a motherfuck. I couldn't even finish. I thought I was gonna pass out." He cast an admiring glance at his own shoulder. "It is conceptual, though."

"It is," I said. "I'll grant you that. Have you named her?"

"Her?"

"Yin's the female side."

"Huh. Hadn't thought of that."

"I suggest Half Wit."

"Ha-ha," drawled Vic, then danced across topics again. "By the way, who's the dude?"

"What dude?" I asked.

"The one across the street. If he's trying to not be seen, he's doing a lame-ass job." Vic snickered. "About as lame as his drag."

I didn't bother looking out a window to confirm this, for even a Mirplo at his most conceptual couldn't conjure a cross-dressing lurker out of thin imagination. Then again, just how off my game was I that Vic caught on to the gaff quicker than I had? This business of going straight had its downside in terms of staying sharp. I turned to Allie. "New information, doll. Now what?"

Before Allie could reply, the doorbell rang. Allie shrugged. "Now?" she said. "Now we answer the door."

6

Reading His Lines

It's funny what comes back to you. Suddenly I'm seven years old, reading comic books on the living room floor when Woody comes in in the company of cronies. They're celebrating something, doubtless a con gone right. Times like these, Woody'd come in high off the grift. And then he liked to quiz me.

Hey, Radar, he says, *tell me this. What message could you put on someone's answering machine that would get them to mail you fifty bucks?*

Am I my age?

What do you mean?

No one believes kids. It'd be easier for a grown-up.

Woody elbows his friends. *What'd I tell you? Smart kid.* He turns to me. *Okay,* he says, *let's say you're an adult.*

Can I have a list of grandmas? And a post office box?

Anything you want, son. It's your grift.

Then I call the grandmas and tell them their grandson's been popped for shoplifting. No charges have been filed yet, and fifty bucks to the drop box makes it all go away.

They won't all have grandsons.

I shrug. *Some will.*

Again to the cronies, *See, boys? That's what's called casting a net.*

Honest to God, I hadn't thought of that moment in twenty years. As it came back to me now, I found myself wondering, *What else have I learned from him that I don't know I know?* Then Allie opened the door, and here came Woody Hoverlander, pulling off his wig and kicking off his shoes before the door even shut behind him. "I'm sorry, Radar," he said. "I couldn't wait any longer. The ol' bladder's not what it once was." He blew through the living room, found the bathroom by dead reckoning, and disappeared inside. We three exchanged looks.

"Vic," I said, "check the street."

"What for?"

"Probably nothing." I figured if Woody was chary enough to go around in drag, he was also canny enough not to draw a tail. "But check anyhow." Vic went outside to have a look around.

About the time Vic returned, Woody emerged from the bathroom. He'd shed the dress—had gym shorts and a T-shirt underneath—and washed the makeup off his face. "All quiet on the Westin front," Vic reported. "Clean as a baby's behind." I looked at Woody. He seemed to understand that this was not humor on Vic's part, but genuine allusional miscues.

I hadn't seen my father in two decades but hadn't forgotten what he looked like. He was rounder now, balder, too, and though the years had softened his features—turtle-beak mouth and ball-peen chin—they hadn't yet added wrinkles. He was shorter than I, not fat, yet not the rail I remembered. I did the quick math. He was now over fifty, and while he wouldn't get carded buying booze anymore, he seemed to be wearing it well.

And he had that energy. That smile and that energy. I won't say he was impish. I've already called him roguish. Neither word does justice to the casual electricity he generated just by being there. He charmed without words, perhaps because he seemed so relaxed within himself, or maybe that's just how a grifter rolls when he's gotten that good at the game. You're meant to like guys like him, right? Woody made it easy. Even I felt it, and I was supposedly the boy with the twenty-year tantrum to throw.

Still, it was an awkward tableau. Too many years and too many questions built a wall of silence between us. Woody chipped away at it first. "Can we all sit down?" he asked. "And I wouldn't say no to a beer." Because drinking other people's beer is religion to a Mirplo, Vic instantly bustled off to the fridge to fill the order for them both. We others sat. Woody regarded the bookshelf but offered no comment.

"This is Allie Quinn," I said, by way of introduction.

Woody looked her over carefully and said, "Kitten Caboodle, too, yes?"

Allie laughed and grimaced at the same time. "Oh, God," she said. "You know about that?" She looked embarrassed—cute, I mean, schoolgirl embarrassed. I hadn't ever seen that expression on her, but it lit her up.

"Know about what?" asked Vic, returning to the room.

"A dancing school I ran," said Allie.

"Kitten Caboodle's House of Odalisque," said Woody. "In Palo Alto, California."

I was perplexed. "Taxi dancing, Allie? That doesn't seem like your line."

"Well, there was a little more to it than that." Woody gave Allie a look that asked permission. "Do you mind?"

Allie acquiesced. "Not at all. I'm curious to know what you know."

"Well, I know that you recruited smart gals out of Stanford and Cal. And I know that most of their dance partners turned out to be Silicon Valley start-up nerds."

"Industrial espionage?" I asked.

"I think she called it 'proprietary venture capital investing,'" said Woody. "It's amazing what a little strategic pillow talk can yield." He bestowed a generous smile on Allie. "I admired you from afar."

"Can't have been that far," she said.

"Well, there's more than one way to skin the VC cat. I was brokering contact with military clients."

"Influence peddling," said Vic, intuitively grasping the obvious.

"If you like. We moved in the same circles."

A weird feeling washed over me just then, the feeling that I was being romanced. No, not romanced, *seduced.* With deft application of word, smile, and body language, and without a single backward glance at the missing two decades, Woody was easing himself into my life. And my righteous ire at all his sins of omission? I couldn't seem to muster it. He'd vanished it through denial exactly as I'd vanished the threat of Andy's gun the week before. No, not exactly—more so, for he was working on a whole deeper level, the level of feeling, not fact. And here I'd lauded myself as the apple fallen not far from the tree. Let's remember, class, a tree *flourishes* on the ground; an apple just goes bad.

I looked over at Allie, who struck me as similarly ensorcelled. I wondered what impact this would have on Operation Citizen. Not that Woody had asked anything of me yet, but I suspected he would, and when he did, I wouldn't hear the words *hourly employee* or *pension plan.** As far as I knew, my dad had never had an on-kilter moment in his life. Nor did he appear to be staggering beneath the particular weight of any new leaf. As a kid, I'd found him larger than life. As an adult, I found I'd acquired his life. I wondered what to think about that.

Vic, meanwhile, had shifted into pure idolatry mode. He literally sat at Woody's feet, looking up with doe eyes as Woody told a story about a run-in with a crooked cop back in those Palo Alto days.

"He was undercover vice," said Woody, "but old-school, totally lost at sea in the new digital world. He couldn't touch anything I was actually up to, so he decided to do me for dealing drugs."

"Were you?" I asked. There was some challenge in my voice. I suppose I'd decided to assert myself. Adult son and all.

"Never, Radar. I'll snuke drug dealers—as you know, it's a dangerous game, but profitable and fun—but sell that shit? No way." Interesting. I'd put my adult son subtext right up on the surface where everyone could see it, and Woody'd just batted it away, basically say-

*Except perhaps as part of a plot to defraud the former of the latter.

ing, *Don't try to grab status up here, son. The air is too thin for you.* Yet at the same time, thanks to that "as you know," I felt endowed, not defeated. This rattled me, for in most situations, status is the bedrock metric. You have it, you want it, you win it, you lose it, whatever—it's always there, part of every human interaction. But not with Woody. He seemed immune to status. Which gave him lots. Weird.

"He questioned me all night. Tried to bad-cop me into a confession. By morning I had the keys to his Porsche."

"Why?" asked Vic, agog. "How?"

"Oh, it was all bafflegab," said Woody. He shot me a look beneath his woolly eyebrows, communicating communion, and I thought, *So that's where I got that word. All this time I thought I'd made it up.* Then I thought, *And he knows it.* Then I thought, *Shut up, Radar, you're reading his lines.* When you're running a game against tough adversaries, you definitely want to stay on your own script. Once you start reading the other guy's lines, you've let him into your head, and that's a dangerous place for a quality foe to be. I had to rate Woody as a quality foe.

Yet my inner discourse continued.

No, Radar, you've got it wrong. He's not in your head. You're in your head, oversolving the problem as usual. He's not a god. He's not Superman. He's just a snuke, like you, playing all the cards in his deck. So do what you need to do in this situation. Play your deck.

"Radar." Woody looked at me with bland concern. "Are you all right?" Oh, crap, I'd zoned out. Maybe he *was* in my head. *Just be in the moment, Radar, that's all you have to do.*

Woody next turned his attention to Vic's tattoo, which he appeared to be noticing for the first time, but that seemed unlikely, since one of the cards in our common deck was: Check shit out. "Nice ink," said Woody, then—give the guy credit for knowing how to score a point—"What's that, a yin?" Vic beamed, and I thought, *Man, he better not come after Boy like that.* But I decided to play the civilized son.

"What are you...?" I started. "Um, I mean, I guess I'm supposed to ask, What've you been up to?"

"Now there's a subject that could fill a book."

"Which you'd probably pay someone to write and then pike his fee." So much for the civilized son.

Woody reacted with stiff dignity.

"Sorry," I said. "That was uncalled for."

"Not entirely," said Woody. "You've got a right to hold some grudge. Absentee dad, totally in the wind. Let's call a spade a spade, Radar, I was a jerk."

"Pretty mild dysphemism," I said. "So long as we're calling spades spades, I think something like 'bastard' would be in line."

"You want more mea culpa?" asked Woody, letting a sliver of sarcasm show. "I got a whole big bucket of it right over here."

"So you didn't come to apologize?"

"For what, Radar? You've lived your life, I've lived mine. I don't owe you an apology. I don't owe you anything. I got you born. Everything after that's just gravy."

"Nurturing? Training?"

"Nurturing? What I see here is a friend who's dog loyal and a woman who probably loves you. Seems like you've landed on your feet as far as nurturing goes. As for training, you tell me."

"So you got out of my way to make me a self-made man?"

"If that's how you want to put it."

"Wow, I had it wrong. I'm in your debt."

"No one's in anyone's—" He stopped short. "You know what? Forget it." Woody stood up. "I'm sorry I opened old wounds." He wriggled into his red dress and slapped his wig on his head. Glanced at himself in the mirror. "No makeup." He *tsked*. "It'll have to do." He went to the door.

"Hey, Mr. Hoverlander—Woody," Vic called after him. "What's up with the dress?"

But he was gone. I shut the door behind him and turned to see Allie standing there, eyeing me closely. "You want to tell me what that was all about?"

"Best to chase him off," I said, truculently. "He's bad mojo."

"You can't know that. Your data's out of date."

"A leopard—"

"Don't say it," she said. "Don't say anything about leopards and spots. Because if people can't change, then you and I, we're never gonna make it."

"But that's all him," I protested. "It's got nothing to do with us."

"He's your father, Radar. I'd say he's got at least a little to do with us." She took Boy and retreated to the bedroom.

"Man, Radar," said Vic, "you've got people walking on you all over the place."

I looked at Vic. "You want to be next?"

"Naw, man. I want you to buy me a drink."

7

Hey, Aqualung

We went to a bar called Frosty's Home of the Infinite Agave. Bit of a mouthful, but when you're promoting all-you-can-drink margaritas, it pays to put the pitch up front. There was plenty of elbow room at the bar, for the night was getting on. Vic started to seat himself on my right, then abruptly reversed his field and sat left, rolling up his sleeve as he moved. "Might as well air this bad boy out," he said, then ordered something called a Steel-Toed Boot, a silver tequila margarita laced with blackberry Sabroso. I passed. I had enough idiot in my bloodstream already. We watched sports highlights till the bartender brought Vic his drink.

"To dads," said Vic. I clinked an imaginary glass against his.

"What's up with yours?" I asked.

"Dull normal," said Vic. "Glad I didn't take after him." Vic took a sip, and *aahed* theatrically on the exhale. "But you took after yours, though, didn't you? Big-time."

"I think I had to," I said. "He was such a force. And I don't care what anybody says, he was training me. The first time we worked the Pigeon Drop"*—I looked past Vic, which is to say, over his left shoulder. At the end of the bar sat a girl in a self-consciously crinoline dress, spangly earrings and bracelets, thrift-store fishnets, and streaky blue

*AKA Wallet Drop, wherein a found cache of cash squeezes good-faith money from the unsuspecting.

hair. Even using only my background brain, I found her pretty easy to analyze. Single girl, party flavor. Ghost of Cyndi Lauper, trying to sell the "She's So Unusual" tip. And...

She was checking Vic out.

"That girl down the bar," I said. "I can't believe I'm saying this, Vic, but I think she likes your tattoo."

"Of course she does," he said. "I told you: conceptual."

"You gonna chat her up?"

"When the time is ripe. Keep talking."

So I kept talking. I talked about my first Pigeon Drop, how I played the betrayed little boy who *knew* he saw that wallet first, and how Woody played the self-righteous dad, damned if he was going to see his son get cheated out of what he'd found. We whipsawed that poor mark; he never had a chance. Afterward, we had waffles. Not that I needed rewards, either sugar or Dad's company. I carried his same gene and started chasing his same buzz the second I knew what it was. Got good at it right away. Like some kids can surf or play tennis. I was a natural.

"Maybe that's why he thought he could leave you," offered Vic. "He knew you were in your own good hands."

"Oh, no," I said. "He doesn't get off that easy. You think he was thinking about me? You think he was *devoted*? I was cheap labor, that's all. A partner he didn't have to pay. And then just Mini-Me, his whole narcissist's dream come true."

"Wow, be a little bitter, why don't you?"

"What, I don't have a right to be?"

"'Course you do." He lapsed into Uncle Joe and boomed, loud enough to be heard down the bar, "You have the right to remain stupid! Anything you say can and will be used against you!"

"That's ripening the time?" I asked.

"It's a start," he said, bringing his voice back to normal. "Meantime, remind me, what's Radar's First Law of Emotion?" If I was needling Vic over the girl, he was needling me right back over my historic insistence on dispassion in the grift.

"Okay," I said, "I get your point."

"No, no, I forget how it goes. Tell me."

So I did. "Effectiveness and emotion are inversely proportional."

"In other words?"

"Anger makes you dumb."

"Okay, then, have all the anger you want. But you decide what to do with it. I put it to you that barfing it all over your old man is probably not your best play."

"Wow, Vic, when did you get so smart?"

"I've been smart all along. You just haven't been paying attention. Now watch this."

Vic rolled off the barstool and, hand to God, literally sauntered down to the pretty poser at the end of the bar. He leaned in close and whispered an extensive something in her ear. She seemed rapt, and whispered back. They conversed for a few moments, then he left her and walked back to me.

"Her name's Zoe," he said. "She writes software, but get this: Her dad owns an art gallery."

"In Santa Fe?" I asked. "What are the odds?"

Vic just helped himself to a satisfied swig of his drink.

"That looked like a good play," I said. "What'd you tell her?"

"That it's a typo. Should've been a yang."

"No, seriously."

"I don't know, Radar. What do you care? You're off the market."

"For good, you think?" My voice betrayed my hope.

Vic looked at me. "You want it, don't you? The whole cohabitation trip. Pair bondage. Maybe even marriage?"

"Let's not get crazy here."

"Then don't *you* get crazy here. Allie's a good girl. Better than you deserve. Don't piss her off. Show her you can be normal with your old man. It'll make her think you can be normal with her. That's all she wants, Radar. Haven't you figured that out?"

"Damn, Vic, you *have* been smart all along."

"Told you. Now if you'll excuse me, I have to walk a lady home." Quietly adding, "He shoots, he scores!" Vic started away, then paused and looked back. "Your dad," he said. "Don't you even want to know why he's here?"

He left with Zoe on his arm. Vic Mirplo a smooth operator? That was going to take some getting used to.

Vic's question echoed in my mind.

Then in my ear, "Well, don't you?"

I looked to my right, and there, hunched over the bar, was the most child-molesting-looking ancient perv I'd ever seen. With his ratty coat, venous nose, lank greasy hair, and mad-eye stare, he looked like the creep on the cover of Jethro Tull's *Aqualung.* More to the point, he looked like someone you'd rather not look at at all. Thus, of course, Woody.

"You've got a lot of wigs," I said. "What happened to your dress?"

"I had to make a change," he said. "That cover was blown."

"Someone's following that hard?" He just nodded. "You haven't had any trouble following me."

"At first you didn't know. Since you've found out, you've made no effort to shake me. I'm thinking you want me around."

"Well, I don't think I do, but let's let that go for now. So why *are* you here?"

"What? I saw you in the paper. You dusted that guy good. I came to say, 'Nice job.' "

I turned to face him. "Hey, Aqualung," I said. "I know what noise sounds like. If you want the benefit of my doubt, you're going to have to do better than that. Let's start with who's following hard, and why."

Woody paused to gauge the seriousness of my intent. At last he spoke. "There's two teams of two. They know I'm in Santa Fe, but they don't know where. One's been checking the hotels, representing as health officials on the trail of a Typhoid Mary."

"I've worked that gaff."

"Be surprised if you hadn't. The other two just cruise. They saw me outside that restaurant today, but they didn't know it was me."

"So that's why you turned tail. I thought you looked scared."

"Did I? Hmm. I'm surprised I gave that away. Anyway, they're just thugs. You know: knee breakers."

"Working for . . . ?"

"This guy in Las Vegas, Jay Wolfredian. He's sort of a casino boss."

"Who you mooked?"

"In a manner of speaking."

"And now he wants his money back?" Woody nodded, doleful. "What, you didn't give him a VPM?"*

"You don't think I tried for the reacharound? I just couldn't reach, that's all."

This made me laugh. Not because it was funny, particularly, but because it so resonated on my frequency. We spoke the same language. I mean, Allie and Vic voiced my slang, but they got it from me. Suddenly I was drinking from the source. It felt good. Like part of me had been missing. And at least one layer of resentment sloughed off and fell away.

We stayed at it all night, at Frosty's till closing and then on a bench in the Plaza till the sun came up, exchanging memories, grift techniques, and cell phone numbers. I brought him up to speed on some of my doings, including Allie's and my plan to parlay the get from the California Roll into a shot at the level life. I thought the Plaza was a pretty exposed location, but to Woody it was more hiding in plain sight. "They rate me as pretty devious," he said. "They'll be looking for me under rocks."

"And how devious are you?"

"Hell, I don't know, Radar. Used to be, I could get in and out of this kind of guy's wallet without stirring a breeze." He shook his head. "But I made such a hash of this one. I think I'm losing my edge."

"What game were you running?"

---

*Verbal prostate massage: endgame bafflegab to leave the mark smiling when you go.

"You tell me." *How could you make someone send you fifty bucks, son?*

"Past-post team?" I asked, naming a scam of (as Vic would put it) yesteryore, when groups used distraction and sleight of hand to place bets on, say, roulette after the ball dropped into the slot.

"No way," said Woody. "Too many cameras, too much heat. Besides"—and here I thought I heard a glimmer of criticism in his voice—"that's a gambling gaff, not a boss gaff."

I quickly mentally rifled through other possibilities, ghosting Woody—seeing things from his point of view—and at the same time realizing that I really wanted to get the answer right. *So okay,* I thought, *if he's going after a casino boss, he has to be bringing what bosses want: action, money.* "Huh," I grunted. "You high-rolled him."

"You got it!" he said. "I knew you would." He beamed with pride, and I have to admit that I basked a little in that bright light.

High rollers, or whales, as they're commonly known, don't abound in Las Vegas, but when it comes to a casino's bottom line, they're difference makers. Sure, you can survive on the steady earn of small-time slot machine play and the vigorish on sports book bets, but to thrive you need whales, and you land them with all manner of krill: luxury suites, show tickets, five-star wines, ten-star escorts, drugs, obsequity, and generous lending policies. Competition for whales is fierce, but it's considered bad form to poach other casinos' high rollers outright, so when one makes a change, you have to make it look like the whale's idea. Think about trying to seduce a married woman with her husband in the next room: You gain no traction till the lady says yes. As a consequence, there are all these go-betweens, independent operators constantly sweeping the sea lanes for migrating whales. Sometimes they bird-dog pretty aggressively, sweetening the pot with their own resources or whatever the destination casino slips them under the Chinese wall.

That's what Woody said he was doing: bird-dogging, but with a difference.

"I promised Wolfredian a Saudi prince," said Woody. "Very proper, very circumspect. Deep, deep pockets, but he can't be seen on the casino floor until the moment is absolutely right. And abso*lute*ly can't be seen going to the cage for cash."

"So Wolfredian advanced you a stake."

"Against an unimpeachable line of credit."

"Which didn't exist."

"No more than the Saudi prince. Now I've got twenty-three thousand out of Wolfredian's change purse, and he's all bent out of shape."

"Over only twenty-three grand?"

"I know, huh? It's more ego than anything. He hates that I mooked him."

"How'd it go wrong?"

"Excellent question. Do you mind if we save it for another time? I'm beat. I'm not used to these all-nighters." He got up to go, effortlessly affecting the leering, drooling look and demeanor of a man you would not want little Jimmy or Nancy anywhere near.

"Where are you staying?" I asked.

"Elsewhere," he said airily, which I took to mean anything from a bed-and-breakfast under an assumed name to a blanket beneath the stars. "But don't worry, I'll be around. Maybe you can help me figure out what to do with these goons." He paused, then: "Hey, Radar, are we all right?"

"We're better," I said. "I still don't know how I feel about you."

"If it means anything, I know how I feel about you. I love you, son."

I couldn't bring myself to reply in kind, couldn't even guess if it was true, so all I said was, "Take it easy, Aqualung," as he shuffled off into the dawn.

8

Face Value

Half an hour later, setting aside thoughts of goons and stray dads, I slipped into bed beside Allie, who stirred and said, "Boy? Is that you? Remember, we mustn't let Radar find out." Hearing the smile in her voice, I determined that the peeved girlfriend stance had been set aside. It made me glad.

I responded by licking her face.

And I don't care what Vic Mirplo has to say about randy rabbits, this is the woman I want to make love to for the rest of my life. It's not just the body parts—the tight, taut, terrific body parts that have a knack for being so familiar but all the time every time brand-new, too. I'm told the new wears off eventually. It hasn't happened yet, but if so, so what? You love a body from the inside out. When you want someone, really *want* them, you want to wear them like a coat. And every time we had sex, I got this incredible sense of wonder, like *I get to do this again? I get to be with her? How great is that?*

It was just carnal at first. It had to be. We were both a big mess, completely accreted like the bottom of an old water heater. Like grifters will get. The only way past all that accumulated emotional inertia was brute force, the fierce urgency of pheromone whores. We could screw, but we didn't know the first thing about intimacy. Or rather, we did, and it scared us both to death. But after the sex came talk. Hours spent dissecting old lovers, techniques, good ideas, bad ideas, good-bad ideas, hidden treasures, unrequited fantasies. We became open to each other in a whole different way. And that was a terrible terra incognita to us both. We felt brave going there. Felt brave ever since. God knows it's tricky when grifters make love. But Allie and I managed somehow.

And we managed pretty well right then.

Later, over *huevos revueltos,** a Hoverlander specialty, I filled Allie in on the night's events. She seemed pleased that things were better with Woody. Pleased also, and this surprised me, that Mirplo'd hooked up. "That's good," she said. "He needs someone. Artists shouldn't spend too much time alone."

"Wait. Artists? Allie, you're not buying into that, are you?"

"Why not? He's half right, you know. Half of art is marketing, creating a demand."

"Yes, but the other half's talent."

"Well, talent. We'll see. What's that stupid thing you say? 'Keep giving them you until you is what they want.' "

"No, that's a stupid thing *you* say."

"I knew I heard it somewhere. Anyway, I want to see his studio."

"Why?"

"Maybe I'll buy something." She shot me a grin. "Original Mirplos could be worth a ton one day."

On the walk over, I found myself checking out the passing traffic with more than passing interest, as if Woody's cruising pursuers might somehow turn their attention to me. It didn't seem likely, for Woody was no doubt adept at shaking a tail, and his costumes were, well, vigorous. Still, it's kind of a chance to take, potentially bringing collateral damage down on your estranged son just while you're getting unestranged and all. Why would a would-be doting dad do that, even if he needed your help?

And what if he didn't need your help after all?

"Allie," I said, "I think we may have a problem."

*Really just scrambled eggs, of course, but it sounds much fancier in Spanish.

"With what?"

"Woody. What if it's all smoke? All this being on the lam, the disguises, everything. What if it's just a setup for something?"

Allie stopped. She let her head sag down on her chest for a moment, then lifted it and looked at me. "Do you actually think that?"

"I don't know, but we have to at least consider the possibility. I mean, that's only prudent."

"If by prudent you mean paranoid."

"He wouldn't be the first grifter to mook one of his own."

Allie sighed. "Look, Radar, I don't suck at judging people, do I? I mean, I picked you out of the bad-apple barrel."

"Granted."

"Well, your father seems okay to me. I like him. And if he's working to make me like him, let's call that good old-fashioned charm, and just move on, huh? For once, just take things at face value. See how that works out."

"Innocent until proven guilty?"

"If you can stand it."

"And if it turns out he really needs my help?"

"Well, that's a different story."

"What do you mean?"

"Operation Citizen, remember? Done with that life is done with that life."

We walked on. It seemed that Allie was trying to have it both ways, but it took me a moment to put the thought into words. "Let me see if I've got this straight," I said at last. "I'm supposed to have a good, honest, wholesome relationship with my father. Give him the benefit of the doubt, take him at face value. In other words, be a loving son."

"Uh-huh."

"Only, I can't lend the hand he might need."

"Not if it means straying from our path."

"Those two ideas kind of clash, you know. How do you hold them both in your head at the same time?"

"I'm a complex person," she conceded. "We're here."

Here was Vic's Quonset hut, a half cylinder of ancient corrugated steel set back from a narrow street between an auto-body shop and a storefront psychic. The loud drone of something obnoxiously approximating music blared from within. We knocked loudly, but when it became clear that we'd never be heard over the din, we let ourselves in.

The air was thick with a resinous scent I didn't recognize, though I identified its source as a small, shiny brazier, like a pimped-out hibachi, spewing gray-green smoke that swirled and spread throughout the hut, driven by a fan the size of a jet engine. Vic stood nearby in Bermuda shorts, attacking a painted piece of Sheetrock with a compressed-air nail gun. Peering through the smoke, I could see impaled on the Sheetrock various means of killing rats (traps, snares, poison) and, I believe, a smattering of actual dead rats. On the modeling stand stood Zoe, Vic's new best friend, naked, posing. At intervals, Vic would pause, stare at her intently, then unleash a frenzied new burst of nail-gun carnage.

"Vic!" I shouted over the oliated din, but he didn't respond, so I reached forward and tapped him on the shoulder. He whirled, still firing, and I felt a rush of air as a nail whizzed past my ear and clanged off the far curve of the Quonset hut.

"Christ! Be careful!"

"Sorry, man. I was in the zone." Noticing Allie, he said cheerily, "Hi, Allie," then repeated, "I was in the zone." He reached down to a boom box and turned off the audio waterboarding. "Good to see you guys."

I waved a hand at the brazier. "What's with the smoke?" I asked.

"It's sage," he said. "I'm smudging."

"Smudging?" asked Allie.

"Ritually cleansing my environment to make my art more potent." He hooked a thumb in Zoe's direction. "It was Zoe's idea. She's a very intricate thinker." Then he indicated the boom box. "The music helps."

"Is that what you call that?"

"Ha-ha, Radar. I composed it myself, you know. A true artist masters all arts. I've started taking flying lessons."

"How is that art?"

"Everything's art, my friend," said Vic. "I'm surprised you don't know that." He stepped back from the Sheetrock and offered it for our inspection. "Well," he said, "what do you think?"

"Are those real rats?" I asked.

"Taxidermed," he said. "Got 'em at a yard sale."

Allie examined the piece with a critical eye. "What do you call it?" she asked.

"*Nailed You Good, You Rat.*"

"A little on the nose, don't you think?" I asked.

"So far," he said. "But watch." He rummaged in a nearby bin of flotsam, pulled out an empty Pop-Tarts box, and crucified it to the Sheetrock. Then he sprayed the whole thing with aerosol cheese. "See? Now it's a comment on consumerist society."

"Conceptual," I granted. "But kinda grotesque."

"You say that like it's a bad thing. Art's not meant to be pleasant. It's meant to make you think."

My eye caught the lifeless eye of a rat. "I think I want to puke."

"Good. That's good."

"Really?"

"Radar, dude, how many artists you think there are in Santa Fe?"

"I don't know. Thousands?"

"And how many better than me?"

"Pretty much all of them."

"In terms of painting shit that looks like shit, yeah. Flowers, buttes, butts, whatever. I can't compete with that." He drew himself up to his full five-foot-seven skinny magnificence. "Therefore, instead, I shall outrage."

"With dead rats?"

"Dead rats," said Vic imperiously, "is only the beginning."

By this time, Zoe had thrown on shorts and a crop top and walked over to join us. We exchanged greetings and names, and then Zoe headed out.

"She seems nice, Vic," said Allie.

"She poses nude for free."

"Do you think she might be hinting at something?"

"Hinting at...?" The thought filtered down through Vic's brain stem and spinal cord, arriving at last at his joint. "Oh!" he said, genuinely surprised. "Son of a gun. I'll have to look into that." He turned to me abruptly. "Hey, did you talk to your dad?"

"Just all night. Turns out he was in the bar."

"Yeah, no, I mean now, today. He stopped by earlier."

"Here? Why?"

"Search me. Guess he wanted to see the genius at work. He seemed kind of rattled, though."

"Rattled?" I looked at Allie. I could see her suspicion eyeing mine. "Vic, let me ask you a question. Did he *seem* rattled or *was* he rattled?" Allie opened her mouth to speak, but, "Face value," I said. "I'm just confirming it." Back to Vic. "You know, was he stuffing?" I used the grifter's descriptive for representing a hope or fear you do not feel.

"Why would he stuff?"

"No reason. Was he?"

"Gut? No. He's chased. After all, he *was* in disguise."

"What disguise?"

"Santa Fe Trails bus driver's uniform." Vic chuckled. "Wonder where he got his hands on that."

"I think he's got good hands," I said.

"Well, whatever. He said to meet him at Cross of the Martyrs if he didn't catch up with you first."

"What time?"

"When does anyone go to the Cross? Sunset."

"Gotcha. Wanna roll with?"

"No," said Vic contemplatively, "I think I'll visit Zoe, investigate that whole nudity thing."

Allie and I left shortly thereafter, and walked back to our cottage. I was distressed on a couple of levels. The one I could most easily finger was concern for my dad—and concern that I felt concern for someone who, let's face it, hadn't earned it by his track record. The other was the constraint I felt on my freedom, like all of a sudden I had to justify my choices. A guy says meet me in a place, I don't care who he is, your father, the pope, whoever, I'm going into that meeting eyes open, not slackjaw like a rube. Only now that's not an option, 'cause it's not the straight play. But this is a potentially hazardous situation, so which is more important, playing straight or staying safe? I voiced this to Allie. She said the two were not mutually exclusive.

"Of course we have to be careful, Radar. We just don't get sucked up into any schemes."

"You think that's what he wants?"

"I think it's what you want."

"What's that supposed to mean?"

"You tell me," she said. She didn't say it aggro or anything, more like flattery, like *You're smart enough to know your own mind.* It felt again like Woody quizzing me on plays against Vegas or, deep in my past, that telephone snadoodle. Like everyone wants me to figure out everything for myself.

So, okay...

"A grifter going straight," I said, "is like an addict in recovery. He's looking for an excuse to go out. Any one will do, so long as it's, you know, acceptable to interested parties. A valid exception, like saving Sophie and Boy. By that math, I'm actually hoping Woody's jammed up. I want to play hero again, just to keep playing." I could feel Allie mentally awarding me a gold star. "But if that's all true," I continued, "then it serves my interest if his jeopardy's for real. So then, why do I doubt?"

"Because you're a complex person, too."

"Screwed up, you mean."

Allie kissed my cheek. "So aren't we all, honey. So aren't we all."

At a quarter to sunset we hiked up the short set of paved switchbacks that led from Paseo de Peralta to the bluff above, where a twenty-five-foot steel cross presided over the plain of Santa Fe, memorializing the death of some people at the hands of some others. For cover (and on this I insisted) we tricked out as tourists, with cameras, water bottles, guidebooks, and new Santa Fe souvenir T-shirts. At the summit, we joined a handful of fellow travelers taking in the view, 270 degrees of pueblo panorama. The setting sun lit low clouds from beneath, energizing the pink of the adobes below. There wasn't much else to look at up here, just brick paths with handrails circling up to the concrete apron where the cross stood, two unadorned steel girders painted white. Dirt paths ran off east, toward the remains of Fort Marcy, another monument on another bald hill. "Not a lot of cover," said Allie. I knew what she was thinking. If Woody was traveling dark, it made no sense to meet in so open a place.

But sometimes you bring your own cover. We heard the wheeze of air brakes and looked down to see a luxury motor coach disgorging a tour group.

"Bet you anything...," I said.

"No bet," said Allie. We watched the tour group climb the hill. When it reached us, we melted into it and made our way to Woody, whose professor-on-holiday drag included wire-rimmed glasses, trekking hat, chukka boots, and a realistically natty white trim beard.

"You go to lengths," said Allie, her voice pitched low to blend in with the tourists *aahing* at the sunset.

"Sometimes you have to," Woody murmured. "I spent a whole year once masquerading as a Sandinista."

"In that context," I asked, "what's the difference between masquerading and being?" Woody gave me a look like *the stories I could tell,* but the tale went untold for now. As the tour group fragmented, we three took up station on the railing in front of the cross. It offered a clear view of the street below and, if one turned around and leaned against the rail as I did, an unobstructed look across to Fort Marcy, as well. "So what's going on?" I asked.

"I'm leaving," he said. "I've worn this town out. I should never have come here in the first place."

"What about help with your goons?"

"No. That was a bad idea. Sentimental and self-indulgent. It puts you at risk."

"You know, I decide about that."

"Anyway, it's really just a matter of returning some money."

"That's not what you said last night."

"I exaggerated. I... milked the drama."

"And the disguises?"

"More of same. Anyway, it's no big deal. After I get it sorted, I'll come back. Maybe we can hang out." He paused, self-conscious. "Radar, I am sorry about the years. What do you say to take two?"

Before I could answer, Woody froze. "You don't know me," he whispered fiercely, and glided away from us. I heard two car doors slam and looked downhill to see a freshly parked sedan and a pair of men in jeans and Western shirts hustling up the path. Woody buried himself in the clot of tourists and listened with rapt attention to the guide's description of the dead friars and others that the cross commemorates. He produced a notebook from somewhere and hunched low over it, taking fervid notes. Allie and I drifted apart—no set play, just good grift hygiene. She took pictures. I pretended to be bored.

The men ran up and scanned the crowd like men adept at scanning a crowd. They spotted Woody, silently flanked him, and eased him out of the group. As they led him down around a bend in the ramp, Allie and I observed as well as we could without giving ourselves away. I wondered what I'd do if things turned violent. I'm not big on violence; I prefer moves. We think of people as machines, especially in threat situations, but they're still just people, and a bit of unexpected confusion can still put them off their game.

Meanwhile, all of Woody's body language said *surrender*. He held his hands out, palms down, in a gesture of pure placation. Reading his lips, I could see him saying, "I don't have the money. I don't know where it went." The goons seemed not to believe him; they moved in tandem, one using his bulk to block the scene from casual eyes, while the other loaded up a kidney punch. They were about to administer a very quiet, very private beat-down to my old man.

Just then Allie moved in, thrusting her camera in their midst. "Could one of you guys take my picture, please?" She rolled her eyes and added in a goofy, girly voice, "I promised my boyfriend." They looked at her like she was daft—daft being the look she was going for, I'm sure—and distanced themselves from Woody. See? Moves. And this one was a beauty. It let them know there were witnesses. Sure enough, they broke off the beat-down and, after another moment's rough rhetoric to Woody, headed back down the hill.

They even took her picture.

We waited till they were well away, then reconvened. "Thank you, Allie," said Woody. "At my age, things take forever to heal." She nodded acknowledgment, but I could tell by the flush on her cheeks and her bright eyes that she'd gotten off on the move. *What do you know?* I thought. *I'm not the only one chasing the buzz.*

"So much for milking the drama," I said.

"It's not so bad," said Woody. "I've been summoned, that's all. Got two days to get twenty-three grand back to Vegas."

"So, not a problem," I said.

"Wouldn't be," said Woody, "if I had the twenty-three grand."

9

4king Awsum

Woody was gone. He'd taken his stiff upper lip and the $23,000 hole in his pocket and put Santa Fe in the rearview. It wasn't clear to me whether he was heading back to face the music or further out on the lam. I didn't care. When something rings as loudly false as that AWOL money, it tends to drown out everything else, including sympathy, empathy, and any father-son football fantasies I may have entertained.

In other circumstances, and against a lesser mark, I'd have expected the play to go something like this: Woody explains that he made a dumb move with the 23K, lost it, got robbed, whatever. Then, and with great reluctance, he asks the mook for a bridge loan, just enough to buy him out of the bad guys' grip while he waits for some sure (but slow-developing) windfall to get everyone well. But Woody knew I'd never fall for that, so he gave no reason for the missing money nor the slightest hint of wanting a bailout from Radar National Bank. I wonder what he'd have said if I'd offered. Probably be offended that I'd put him on so naked a play. Either that or be disappointed that I bought in. But I kept *stumm* and so did he. We bid our adieus, and he got his stoic ass in the wind. I expected I'd get a postcard of a jackalope someday.

As for Allie's and my postmortem, we didn't see eye to eye at all. She, still taking things at face value, thought Woody just thought better of dragging me into his mess and beat a hasty, one might even say noble, retreat. I said he made the whole thing up: Wolfredian, the phantom whale, all of it.

"Why would he do that, Radar?"

Sensible question. I had no sensible answer, so I offered the one of a hurt little boy. "Just to screw with me," I said. "Just to watch me dance."

"Come on, lover, even you don't believe that."

"Okay, I don't. So then I don't know why he did it. I do know this, though: We haven't heard the last of him."

"But he *left*. He left without asking for help."

"Obviously," I said, "he wants me to take the bait without his having to ask. He knows he can't ease me in. I have to do it myself."

"So he's going to seduce you by not seducing you?"

"That's right."

"Then it was all an act? The disguises, the goons..."

"*Alleged* goons," I amended.

"You're saying he hired them?"

"I'm saying it's possible."

(All of this, by the way, is taking place in the back room at Shabookadook, a wine bar around three corners from the Plaza, where every Wednesday night is Performance Art Night, and for which Vic and Zoe, we've been tweeted, have cooked up something, and I quote, "4king awsum." The mind boggles at the prospect.)

"You should be happy in any case," I said. "Now there's nothing interfering with our merry little citizens' band."

Well, I knew that was trouble as soon as I said it, but Allie, to her credit, let it slide, electing to stick to the logic of the situation and not get sucked into the dangerous undertow of emotion. "Look, Radar, you're the big fan of Occam's razor"—where the simplest explanation that fits the facts is likeliest to be true—"so you tell me, which is simpler? (a) a known grifter gets into the sort of trouble that grifters are known for getting into, or (b) your father goes ten different kinds of devious just so he can *not* ask you for help."

"You don't know my old man."

"Neither do you!" She raised her voice on this, drawing shushes and dark looks from the reverent fans of stand-up art seated nearby. I chided myself for being a dickweed. *Loyalty, Radar. It's Allie who's important, not Woody. So he got in the wind. So what? Maybe he won't come back around. If he does, that'll just prove you're right and she's wrong. And if he doesn't? Then getting to know him is a missed opportunity you never knew you had. Now shut up and watch the show.*

(A frail, pale woman stands onstage, arms outstretched. From her arms hang various lengths of hollow bamboo, which clack somewhat musically as she sways to her inner rhythm. She is a human wind chime. The crowd loves it.)

"Know what I think it is?" said Allie. "I think it's subject-object confusion. You're so used to playing everything three levels deep, you assume everyone else is, too." I started to protest, but Allie overrode me. "I'm not saying he's not capable of it. I'm just saying Occam's razor." She took my hands. "I'm sorry he left a bad taste in your mouth, sweetie. But he *left*. Let it go if you can." And with her hands in mine, I found that I could. I took a deep breath and banished Woody from my mental map. *Farewell, jackalope. So long, Aqualung.*

(Vic and Zoe take the stage, each mummified in tulle of striped bright crimson and green, a disharmonic color combination that vibrates sickly, very hard to look at. They stand in silence for a moment, then Zoe opens her mouth and drones an ugly, warbly, flat monotone, "Waaahhh," until her breath runs out and the sound dies in broken, croaking syllables. Vic, meanwhile, is spraying two different types of air freshener, bayberry and piña colada, and their clashing syrupy smells fill the room. To add a grace note, I suppose, he takes out a urinal cake and smashes it to smithereens with his fist. Zoe repeats her afflicted-cat wail twice more, and in the welcome silence that follows, Vic makes an armpit fart, which inspires weak, uncertain laughter in the audience. He glares at the laughers, making clear the seriousness of his intent. Then he and Zoe start coughing at each other, drawing closer and closer until they're virtually coughing into each other's mouth, and this goes on for some time. It's pretty uncomfortable to watch, which, knowing Vic and his commitment to outrageon, is the whole idea. Next he takes off his shoes and clips his toenails. Then Zoe flosses her teeth, and Vic licks the floss clean. For a grand finale, they make some deformed balloon animals, like the zoo at Chernobyl, and squeak them horribly. Then Vic intones, "Domestic Violence," and they leave the stage to unabashed applause.)

(Emperor's nudity goes unremarked.)

We joined Vic and Zoe later in the front room of the bar, where I shouted a round of Red Man Ale* and congratulated them on a job, well, done.

"This is just the beginning, Radar," Vic said, his eyes bright with excitement. "We have a space!"

"A space?" asked Allie. Was she thinking of the one between his ears? Probably that was just me.

Vic put his arm around Zoe. "It's her father's. He was mounting a show for these artists who got arrested."

"Selling Jimson weed," said Zoe, as if that explained everything. "They couldn't make bail."

"So now it's empty and we get to use it. We're going to blow minds. I've got half a yard of concrete, a crate of paintballs, some old neon signs, this giant-ass block of obsidian, a spool of copper wire, an acetylene torch, and a lateen sail from a dhow." I was wondering how these things could possibly permute into anything even vaguely approximating art when Vic added, "Plus, I've got a line on a crocodile."

"The art community in this town has gotten way too stuffy," said Zoe. "Vic's really gonna shake them up."

"A crocodile will do that," I offered.

I suppose Vic heard the snark in my voice, and he jumped on it. "Man, Radar, why don't you just shut down once and reboot. You're like Mr. Mockery over there every chance you get, you know that?"

I'll tell you what I knew: Vic had gotten laid. You could see it in his

*Original slogan: Drink Like an Indian Drinks—true fact or bar fact?

proprietary arm around Zoe's shoulder, and hear it in his truculent assertion of competence. Well, I couldn't knock him for that. Let the man have his moment. Plus, maybe he was right. Maybe I did need to update my file. He'd come a long way from the rookie mook I first saw running dumb-ass baseball ticket hustles back in L.A. And, really, who's to say where the con leaves off and art begins? Like Allie said, half of it's marketing, and no one markets harder than a true believer. Therefore, even if I thought Vic was running a scam, I could help him most by buying in. It was the least I could do for a friend. Or even a Mirplo.

"Okay, Vic, I'll dial it down. Does this installation have a name?"

"Not yet," he said. "It's still forming in my mind. I've got components, but no controlling idea yet, you know? No g-salt."

"G-salt?" asked Allie.

"He means gestalt," whispered Zoe.

I stifled a chuckle. *Okay,* I thought to myself, *baby steps here. Baby steps.*

Vic had also gotten his hands on a pallet of deformed Barbie dolls. "Someone screwed up the molds," he said. "They've all got, like, three arms and shit." How this particular treasure came to be at the product liquidators outside of town where Vic found it, he couldn't say, but he was terribly excited about it. "Twelve hundred fucked-up Barbies," he said. "There's no telling what you can do with something like that." He invited us back to the Quonset hut to see them. At minimum, he said, we could shoot at some with his nail gun, and that was as good a Wednesday entertainment as anything anyone could think of, so off we went.

The day had been warm, but the desert night sky wicked off the heat, making for a temperate walk. The click of crickets mixed with the not-too-distant wail of sirens. Vic and I ambled along, trading evil things to do to a Barbie. Allie and Zoe followed a few yards back, discussing whatever it is women discuss when men are out of earshot. Not, I'll bet, evil things to do to a Barbie. For a moment, I saw us four from the outside: folks out for a stroll together just like any other people in any other town. Normal people. This was new.

Look at us, I thought. *We're couples. Next thing you know, we'll be having movie dates.*

As we neared Vic's street, he paused and turned back to say something to Zoe. I reached the corner first and stopped. "Vic," I called back over my shoulder, "any chance your Barbies were combustible?"

"What do you mean?"

"Like maybe smoldering within or something? Composting?"

"No, man, they're cool."

I beckoned him forward and pointed down the block, where three fire trucks stood before what had been Vic's art studio, and was now a blazing shell. Vic gaped.

Then he shouted, "He shoots, he scores!"—from my pocket, which I found strange until I recalled how, in a fit of whimsy, I'd lately sampled Uncle Joe for my ringtone. I took out my phone, looked at the caller ID, and saw that it was Woody. I passed briefly through *How did he?* before remembering that we'd exchanged digits that night at the Plaza.

"Radar," said Woody when I answered, "son, I'm sorry. It seems I'll need your help after all." I heard the fear-quake in his voice, but that could've been fake-quake, who knew?

At the Quonset hut, firemen on mechanized ladders poured water from high-pressure hoses down through a ragged blast hole in the roof, beating back a plume of acrid black smoke that rose from within. *That'll be the Barbies,* I thought. But burning plastic doesn't put that kind of hole in that kind of roof. Not without help. Like, explosive help. "Where are you?" I asked.

"The Gaia Casino in Las Vegas. And I need you here by Friday."

"How 'bout that," I said. I scanned the rapidly swelling crowd of gawkers. So Woody was in Vegas, huh? Either that or here among the crowd in masquerade. "What's up with this fire?" I asked.

"What fire?"

"What fire? This fire."

"Radar, I don't know what you're talking about."

Can you tell if someone's lying? Over the phone? When he's a master of deception and your brain is addled by fumes from burning polyvinyl chloride? Me neither.

"Fine," I said, not really meaning it. "What do you need?"

"You know what I need."

"Uh-huh. And what's the 'or else'?"

"'Or else'?"

"There's always an 'or else' in this script, isn't there? What are they going to do if I don't pony up the princely sum of twenty-three grand? Kill you?"

"Yes," said Woody simply. "Probably they will."

"Oh, for Pete's sake."

"Friday in Vegas, Radar. There's no other way."

I crossed to Allie. "Babe," I said, "you gotta hear this." I handed her the phone.

But the line was already dead.

10

Humbo Gumbo

"Of course they're related!" I shouted. "You think it's a coincidence that Vic's studio blows up at the very moment Woody calls with this ridiculous bibble about getting kacked over chump change?" I paced the floor of our adobe cottage, completely freaked out. Boy paced with me, sympathetically freaked. I hated for him to see me like this. I knew it was bad for his psychic wounds.

"It didn't blow up, Radar. It burned down." Allie sat on the couch. Her voice had a dulcifying quality to it that I was unused to. The kind of voice you use for talking a jumper down from a ledge.

"We don't know that! The fire department..."

"The fire department found enough flammable paints and solvents to torch a forest." She shot Vic a gentle look. "Not very well stored."

Vic didn't respond. He sat beside Zoe on the sill of the flagstone fireplace, looking shell-shocked. That studio had housed possibly the first genuinely—albeit perversely—productive thing he'd done in his life, and now it was gone, all up in flames, along with a heavy emotional investment. My heart went out to him. Which may have been why I was so determined to prove it wasn't his fault.

"They'll find out," I said. "If this two-bit town has any kind of decent arson squad, they'll find out the fire was set."

"By Woody?"

"Him or someone else."

"Who?"

"I don't know! Someone trying to scare Vic. Me. You. Us. All of us."

Allie got up and came to me. She put her arms around me and forcibly stopped me from pacing. "Honey," she said, "you're not making any sense. Come on now, do what you do: Break it down. Tell me what you're thinking."

So much of the time on the grift you get caught up in incompatible story lines. Part of this is because grifters lie, and lies and truth tend to diverge over time, confounding a coherent picture of reality. Mostly I think it's just our (my?) helical nature and damn habit of trying to solve the same problem six different ways at once. What Allie was saying was *Untangle the strands.* So I took a deep breath and let my experience and training take over.

A building incinerates at the same instant Woody outs himself for help. He plays dumb on the coincident nature of this, but if it's a coincidence, it's one hell of a one, and someone—no doubt Woody himself—long ago taught me not to believe in those. So then what? Woody's gone back to stalking me, this time with phone in hand, waiting for the opportune moment to place his panicked call? If so, then he's also playing firebug, or paying goons—thus confirmed as confederates—to do it for him. And why? Just to convince me in a highly roundabout and fully convoluted way that he's facing death over a sum so insignificant I could put it on my credit card?

Man, that's a lot of far to fetch.

But if not that, then the Quonset fire is an unhappy accident, the result of Mirplovian carelessness. And the damning hole in the roof is—what?—an oxyacetylene tank gone blooey? Could be. Betting on Mirplovian carelessness is never a bad gamble. So then Woody's phone call is just bad timing, a coincidence I'll have to accept. Which takes me back to the original questions of whether Woody is gaming me and why. Before I can chase that stupid tail, another thought crosses my mind. What if Vic set the fire himself, to enhance his reputation as a tragic figure in the art community?

Did you hear about the guy and the fire? Twelve hundred Barbies up in smoke.

Ooh, conceptual.

Oh, come on, Radar. If that's possible, then why not let's say *you* set the blaze, just to keep the pot of intrigue boiling in your life? You could be that scared of straightness.

But I'm not. And I didn't. And neither did Vic. I knew it in my gut. But I didn't know about Woody. His story was absurd. He must know that I knew that. He wanted me to make a decision, not about his veracity but about whether I'd help even without knowing all the cards. So my choice would eventually come down to this: Harden my heart or get in my car.

All the time I was thinking this through, Allie was still holding me. I didn't see her. I was looking past her, to that place in open space where my mind goes to figure things out. At last I brought her back into focus. I'd never seen her looking so soft, her face showing nothing but concern. Where'd she get all that empathy? It didn't come from her experience, as tough and embittered as mine. Must have been in her nature all the time, dormant as a catclaw seed, just waiting for favorable conditions and a chance to grow.

"Allie," I said, "do you believe he called?"

"What?"

"You didn't actually hear him on the phone. Do you think I made it up?"

"Why would you?"

"Serendipity," I said. "Big fire, big drama. Throw in a desperate phone call, it's the perfect excuse to get in the wind."

"Are you looking for one?"

"No."

"Then no."

"Good."

"So what do you want to do?" she asked.

"Good question. I don't believe him, but what if I'm wrong?" I could see in Allie's face that she knew this was coming, expected it, approved on some level, and yet didn't entirely like it. It was weird. The part of her enamored of Woody couldn't dismiss a death threat out of hand. Other parts of her no doubt feared buying into his play, for that's a move no grifter loves, running someone else's script. Plus, there was the elephant in the living room of whether I was merely looking for an excuse to go off the reservation.

How did I know she had these thoughts? Because I had them, too, exactly. I've always said that the trick of reading people's minds is just reading your own. Ninety percent of everything everybody thinks is the same stuff. Which means if I was worried, Allie was worried, not just about Woody but also about me. About us. "Look," I said, "I honestly don't know if Woody's in trouble or just dragging me into something ugly, but I can't find out from here. So I just need to know that you believe I'm doing all this for the right reasons, and not because I can't hang straight."

Allie wrapped her arms around my neck. "Radar Hoverlander," she said, "you've never hung straight in your life." Was that an endorsement? I couldn't tell.

Vic and Zoe left a few minutes later. She was taking him home. I felt good about that. A loss is a loss, even the loss of something so bogus as your bogus artistic career, and you like to have someone sit shivah with you.

While Allie walked Boy, I spent some time online, investigating both Woody Hoverlander and Jay Wolfredian. Most of the hits on Woody revealed the expected courtroom detritus of dropped charges and bargained pleas. Reading between the lines of court records, I could see the general outline of snaggles he preferred: investment schemes that walked the line between wild speculations and pure pyramids. I particularly admired one called Celebrity Holdings, LLC, which promised to ghost the moneymaking strategies of the Hollywood elite but had no more congruence with reality than Maps to the Stars' Homes.

One oddball datum surprised me greatly, for it contained my picture. Following a link to the scanned newsletter archives of Southern California Keglers, a bowling affinity group, I found a 1986 blurb congratulating Woody on rolling a perfect game. There was a photo of him high-fiving five-year-old me, and a caption that read, "Woody Hoverlander celebrates twelfth strike with son, Randy." I didn't know if "Randy" was a typo or the work of some affronted editor trying to impose normalcy on my name. But in any case, *You bowled, Woody? Where was the percentage in that?*

Wolfredian, meanwhile, came across as a power executive on a steep trajectory. With just ten years in the industry, he'd already held positions of importance in casino security and strategic planning, and had lately joined Gaia Gaming, Las Vegas's first carbon-neutral casino, as vice president of special projects. Gaia's investor relations webpage lauded his achievements—all the right MBA and consulting tickets punched—and occluded in a cloud of PR bafflegab his chief responsibility: keeping Gaia whales happily swimming in Gaia seas. His photo showed him to be shirted, suited, and tied just like the rest of the white-bread Gaia management team. He didn't read heinous or threatening. He read kind of dull.

There was, though, one curiosity. When I ran Jay's name through the same public database that coughed up Woody's arrest record, it likewise coughed, from some dozen years ago, a dismissed charge of criminal misconduct against Jay, which could be anything from carjacking to carnal knowledge of a minor. Since I made him to be in his mid-thirties now, you could chalk it up to youthful indiscretion, but I had a problem with the place, Palo Alto, contemporaneous with Woody's own time there. Another coincidence, and we know how we feel about those. But parsing public records is a bit like reading tea leaves; you think you're reading, but you're maybe just reading in. Best not to make assumptions. Latest possible decision, right?

Allie and I went to bed that night like any other couple, taking turns in the bathroom, reading for a while, then turning out the light.

Boy lay at the foot of the bed, curled up in a ball and steeped in dog dreams. The mundane domesticity of the moment almost moved me to tears. I understand that some people become weary of such routines, but at that moment I couldn't imagine ever taking it for granted.

"It's about a ten-hour drive to Vegas," I said, cradling Allie's head and stroking her hair. "We'll get our gear together in the morning and get gone by afternoon. Think we can trust Boy with Vic?"

"Radar, no."

"Come on, he's not that incompetent. Plus, he's got Zoe to back his play."

"No, I mean no, I'm not going."

"What? Why not?"

"Remember the other day, up at the Cross? When I used the tourist stooge on those guys?"

"Of course I remember. I saw the light in your eyes."

"I know you saw it. And I'll bet you were thinking it changed things."

"Changed how?"

"Changed like I was ready to get back in the game. Like I dug it."

"And did you?"

"I did. But I'm not." She snuggled down against me, talking to my chest. "Part of this business of going straight is for us, but part is for me. I tried once before, you know."

I knew. Back in her late teens, she'd done the whole college coed trip. Might've ended up a flight attendant, but she fell (okay, jumped) in with a bad crowd. "You're stronger now," I said. "You know your own mind."

"Yeah, I do. That's why I'm not going. I'm strong enough to know how strong I'm not." It didn't make much sense semantically, but I understood. "Radar, I don't know if you know it, but I'm a woman of modest ambitions. A man to love. A dog to walk. An honest way to spend my days. Some tranquility to fix my broken parts. Nothing more than that. Really. Give me that and I'm fine."

"Do you want me not to go?"

"No, you have to. I get that." I felt her thigh rub against mine, smooth against rough. "Look, I don't doubt that your father needs help—maybe not the help he represents needing, but something. But I also don't doubt that you're psyched to see if your tools still work. I'm sure they do. You're Radar fucking Hoverlander. I'm just hoping you'll get it out of your system, that's all. I'm hoping it's an interlude."

"But thinking it's a test."

She propped herself up on one elbow and smiled at me. "Radar fucking Hoverlander. Always the brightest bulb on the bush. Yeah, a test. So pass it, huh? Pass it and come back home."

We made love with a special intensity that night, some of the old animal carnality mixed in with the new intimacy. I felt like a soldier getting a send-off. And maybe that's what I was.

Oddly, Mirplo wouldn't roll with, either. He was staying in town to work the victim angle. Or rather, have it worked for him. This he told me as I walked the aisles of a big Smith's supermarket, buying supplies for the road. "They're organizing Vic Aid," he said. "Can you believe that?"

"Who?" I asked.

"The artsy-fartsies. Zoe's friends. Her dad's friends. They're having a charity dinner. Silent auction. Special guest performance by Zoe and me."

"Oh, man, you're not going to repeat that horrible—"

"No, come on, that's yesterday's news. We have to homage the blaze. I've got this Huehueteotl thing worked out."

"Huehueteotl?"

"Aztec god of fire, Radar. Try to keep up. I'm building a volcano. Zoe's going to be a human sacrifice. It's gonna blow their tiny minds. And all proceeds go to the benefit of"—he touched his fingertips to his puffed-up chest—"*moi.*"

"Huehueteotl," I said. "Where'd you come up with that?"

"Duh, Wikipedia. I've figured it out, Radar. You don't have to be smarter than everyone, just a page ahead in the textbook. They'll roll right over for you if you just throw a few details at 'em and dress it all up in humbo gumbo."

"You mean mumbo jumbo?"

Vic cast the knowingest, most self-assured smile I'd ever seen him cast. "Used to be mumbo jumbo," he asserted. "Now it's humbo gumbo. We'll see how long it takes to catch on."

"Oh, so now you control the language, too?"

"Of course I do. Which you of all people should appreciate, Mr. Bafflegab."

Just then I had to admire him. He still couldn't draw a straight line with a ruler, of that I was sure, but he'd caught on to the power of perception. There was growth there. Real, honest to God, grifter growth. But still I had to ask, "Where are you in this, Vic? Do you really want to be an artist, or are you just gaming the rubes?"

Instead of answering directly, Vic drew my attention to a nearby product display, a solid wall of cereal boxes, rows and shelves of them, in perfect rectilinear order. "Is this art?" he asked.

"No."

He took one of the cereal boxes, turned it upside down, and put it back in place. "How about now?"

"Still no."

"What if I took a picture of it and hung it in a museum?"

I paused, then committed. "Not art."

"Are you sure?"

"No," I admitted. "No, I'm not."

"Me neither," said Vic, "but I want to find out."

Okay, so that answered that. Or it didn't.

We hit the checkout line. I had bottled water and caffeinated cola, energy bars, jerky of various dead animals, and my personal undoing, Cheetos. Everything I needed for the haul across the desert.

Everything but company.

It was going to be a long trip.

11

Honey Moon

I'd said a lot of good-byes in my life. All kinds. The kind where "See you soon" means "Not in this lifetime." Where "I'll miss you" means "Later, sucker!" The kind where "I'll remember you forever" means "I forgot you already." They all amounted to the same thing: greasing the getaway, for when the snuke is done, you just run. Without sentimentality and without delay, because usually the roof is about to collapse. Really, since my grandmother died, I'd never said good-bye to anyone who meant much to me, and even with her, she was so far gone before she went, Alzheimer's having perforated her brain, that she no longer knew me, so what did that even mean? In fairness, back then, I didn't know me, either. I was a punk kid, toddler-trained in the snuke by Woody, self-mentored after that. I had a teenager's arrogance and a grifter's gall. I sold beat bags and money boxes, ran rogue moving vans, did self-help and slim-quick tricks, and ran three-card monte games. I was a machine. And like a machine, I was utterly unaware of my own existence. I won't say Allie woke me up. I like to think I was at least half awake before then. She certainly woke me up to the possibilities of real human contact. And on that June afternoon in Santa Fe, she woke me up good to the pain of good-bye.

I'd packed Carol with my travel necessaries, including all that junk food and water, a sleeping bag for car camping, plus clothes of various utilities, and an overabundance of liquid asset—cash—for while it grieved me to contemplate that Woody was putting the paltry, indelicate touch on me, I couldn't dismiss the possibility that maybe he was that hard up. If so, I'd just pay him off and get gone. This was a clumsy play; in other circumstances I would have regarded it as cheap capitulation and failure, but given Allie's and my bloated bank account it augured negligible impact, so whatever. In the upshot, anyone stealing the Swing would find an unexpected payday in the spare-tire well.

And then there was Allie, with Boy by her side, standing outside our little adobe cocoon, and the sight of her engendered in me a new and entirely foreign feeling of forlorn. "Be careful," she said. "Write when you find work." This was a joke, of sorts, but it died in the silence.

I took her hands. "What will you do while I'm gone?"

She looked down at Boy. "Walk the dog."

So, all in all, a clumsy farewell. I guess she was no better at them than I was. I got in the Swing, fired it up, and pulled away from the curb. Glancing in the side mirror, I saw her step out into the street to wave good-bye. A white Song Sharp hybrid veered silently around her. Insane mileage, the Sharp, but a body made of cardboard. This one, I noticed, had a deep, V-shaped dent—a gash, really—in the front end. My mind wandered to the recent ubiquity of the Sharp, how out of nowhere they suddenly seemed to be everywhere. I wondered if there mightn't be a resurgent market for the hundred-mile-per-gallon carburetor scam. *Shut up, Radar. You're out of that line of work.*

I dropped by to see Vic on my way out of town. (Passing six more Sharps along the way—they really were everywhere, especially in a crunchy granola town like Santa Fe.) He'd already set up a makeshift studio in Zoe's garage, and I found him sitting atop a ladder, contentedly glopping layers of native clay onto a huge, cone-shaped lattice of lath and hex netting. He climbed down from his perch to demo the eruption mechanism he planned to use for his volcano, the classic formula of baking soda, dish soap, and vinegar.

"It's great," I said, "but isn't it really just a science project?"

"Not after I apply these bad boys," he said, showing me sheets of butcher paper covered with sketches of primitive glyphs. "I'll carve them in when I'm done."

"What do they mean?"

Again that devilish light in his eyes. "Anything I want."

Credit the man with having fun inventing reality.

So we said our good-byes, and I hit the road, heading southwest out of Santa Fe until I reached the valley of the Rio Grande and followed it down to Albuquerque. More Sharps; I set an over/under line on how many I'd see per mile. I took the under and lost.

It felt odd to be on the road all alone. Made me nostalgic for my first full summer in the grift when I drove coast to coast, hanging bad paper and seeing the sights. I used to go into bars at night and represent myself as a member of whatever state's Alcohol Control Board. That's good for free drinks, but mostly I just did it for company. Now I had company—quality company, with love to boot—that I was leaving behind, but I couldn't deny the rush of all that open space in front.

I scarfed down some Cheetos and didn't worry about my breath.

The drive west out of Albuquerque was a brutal battle against the afternoon sun. Two hours of it left me drained, so I pulled into a rest stop west of Gallup to recharge my batteries. I hit the john, then walked around for a minute, waking up my legs. Returning to Carol, I noticed a white Song Sharp parked beside her. Yet another one; I wouldn't have given it a second look, but for the gash in the hood. Deep. In the shape of a V.

Okay, Radar, don't panic. You said yourself these things are made of cardboard. What's to keep two from being dented? Even as I thought that, I knew I wasn't prepared to buy it. A coincidence too far. My head jerked around toward the bathroom. Had the driver gone in there? Had I noticed? People come and go; you can't notice everyone.

On the spur of the moment, I decided to ping the target: create a situation to gain some information. I opened the hood of my Swing and propped it up on its prop rod. Then I grabbed a bottle of water and dumped it all over the hot engine compartment. A plume of white vapor spewed up, creating the reasonable impression of a cooked radiator. You see this dodge used all the time in gas stations by low-level snukes working the car-trouble scam. I'd long considered such short cons beneath me, but these were special circumstances. I bent over the engine, studying its parts with an air of concern while I waited for the driver of the dinged Sharp to return to his car.

Here he came, smoking a clove cigarette, a black man with closely cropped salt-and-pepper hair atop a high, shiny forehead. Deep smile lines flared out from either side of his broad, flat nose, framing a gray moustache. A white polo shirt clung snugly to his broad shoulders and incipient paunch. He wasn't fat, exactly, but had reached the age, roughly sixty, I'd say, where most efforts to stay in shape are a holding action at best. But with taut muscular arms and legs he looked casually strong and reasonably light on his feet. What struck me most, though, as I glanced at him from the shadow of the car hood, were his barn-owl irises, set against creamy ivory sclera, irises so dark that you couldn't tell where they left off and the pupils began. These were intelligent eyes. They made me think, *This cat's been around.*

I stood up as he walked past. "Shit," I muttered underneath my breath, then backed into him accidentally.

He caught me without giving ground. I uttered some more frustrated obscenities in the direction of the fuming engine. "Engine trouble?" he asked. I'd made the question obligatory.

"No, the engine trouble's passed," I said. "Now I got tow troubles."

"As in..."

"As in how I'm gonna afford one out of this godforsaken hole."

"That broke?"

"That broke." I waved a distracted hand toward the Sharp, not indicating that I thought it was his. "Price of gas...we can't all drive these green machines."

"True," he said, indicating no ownership in turn.

When you're running the car trouble grift for real, you need to string together a few components before you make the pitch. First, you try to bond with the mark, make like you're kindred spirits somehow, so that when you put the touch on him, he'll feel like he's hooking a brother up. Next, you roll out a sob story, something perilous but credible, like employment desperation or a medical emergency. Finally, you have to sell that you're good for the money, and will pay him back as soon as you reach your checkbook. Garb has a lot to do with this; a three-piece suit would be a good deal more assuasive than the traveling clothes I was wearing just then. Not that I was trying to vend the grift, per se. Like I said, I was pinging the target. I wanted to see if he'd out himself.

So I ran the script.

"Where you coming from?" I asked.

"Santa Fe," he said. This disappointed me a bit. I was hoping he'd go fabricat on me right away—start lying, that is—as that would confirm my growing suspicion.

"Me too," I said. "Nice town. Can't swing a dead cat without hitting an artist, though."

"You an artist?"

"Of a sort."

He took a drag on his clove cigarette and blew out a cloud of its characteristically tangy smoke. "What sort?"

"Draftsman, really. I'm on my way to Phoenix. Got a job lined up."

"Yeah? Moving there for good?" I felt good about the way he asked the question. He sounded engaged. Made me think he was buying in.

"Gotta go where the work is," I said.

He peered inside my rig. His eyebrows arched. "You're traveling pretty light," he said. It was a canny observation, for if I were genuinely relocating from point A to point B, I'd doubtless have a few more household goods.

I covered as best I could. "You know how it is," I said. "Pawn shop got half, girlfriend the rest." I essayed to establish a link. "I guess we've all been there."

He nodded solemnly. "That we have," he said. "That we have."

"Anyway, it doesn't matter. I can't get to Tucson now."

"Phoenix."

"Phoenix." I'd made this mistake on purpose to see if he'd catch it. He caught, but didn't seem to mind. "My brother wired some money ahead, plenty, but..." I looked at my car and blew frustration through my lips. "It might as well be on Mars."

He took a last drag off his clovie, threw it down, and ground it out under his shoe. "So, how much you think a tow might be?"

"I don't know," I said, "maybe thirty, fifty bucks."

"How would a hundred set you up?"

Damn. If he was ready to Franklin me on the strength of this weak grift, shot through with intentional errors, then clearly he wasn't in the game. I fretted that my assessment of his intelligence had been so far off. Still, I had to see the thing through. "That...," I said, choking up, "that'd be great."

He thumbed through his wallet for a bill and handed it to me. I took it, intending to disengage as quickly as possible, wait for him to take off and then get my ass back on the road. But when I touched the bill, I almost had to laugh out loud. It utterly failed the fingertip test, and I knew that when I looked at it, I'd find it to be a clownish counterfeit. It was. Some smarmy car salesman grinned out from where Big Ben should be, and on the back it said, IN WALT WE TRUST—SIOUX CITY DODGE. I studied the bill as if taken aback. "I, uh, I don't think this is real."

"Oh, don't you?" I could hear the chuckle in his voice. I looked up to find him grinning at me, like he'd just played the greatest joke in the world. He waved a hand at my car engine. "Any more than your steam-powered breakdown is real?"

"I, uh..." I ran out of words.

"I think you're going to say, 'I'm ready to cut the crap.' "

What could I say? "I'm ready to cut the crap."

"Yeah, you are." He extended a beefy hand, one silver ring on his pinkie. "Honey Moon," he said.

"Honey Moon?" I said. "Really?"

"Radar Hoverlander?" he said. "Really?"

And just like that, we were friends.

12

A Cup of Ex-wife

We convoyed just across the Arizona line to a truck stop in Lupton called Speedy's, where we stopped for a coffee and a confab. I had one eye on the clock, for Vegas was still seven hours down the road and I knew I'd need some sleep along the way. But what I needed more, obviously, was Honey Moon's data dump. He'd gone to some lengths to make himself available to me—to let me discover him, that is—and I had to know why. Fortunately, he didn't play hard to get with me.

Nor with the perky waitress. When she asked him how he liked his coffee, he winked and said, "Like my ex-wife: hot and bitter." She rewarded him with a smile and a wiggly retreat. "Mm-mm," he murmured, admiring her walkaway ass, "like two puppies in a pillowcase." His voice was smooth and creamy, with Southern roots and Midwest overtones, and he pitched it just soft enough that he seemed not to be addressing her, yet loud enough that she might hear. And that's how you deliver a lewd compliment without being offensive. I knew he was ghosting that waitress, getting inside her mind and motivation. Day in and day out, no doubt, she gets groped and grab-assed by every horny trucker within armshot. Annoying? Hell, yeah. But validating, too; the kind of validation that brightens a dead-end day. Honey's approach gift-wrapped all that approval and tied it with a bow of respect. Not run-of-the-mill. Not in her line of work. Some call this charm, but with grifters it's supercharged charm, because it goes deep into the mark's mentality, discerns what she wants and gives it to her. For some it would be the difference between getting slapped and getting laid, but I got the feeling that it was just Honey Moon's standard practice to enchant anyone who crossed his path, because the enchanted are more likely to become allies . . . or marks. I wondered which I was intended to be. "So why were you following me?" I asked.

"Who said I was?"

"You did, when you said my name."

"Now come on, I could—"

I cut him off. "I know: You could have recognized me from my picture in the paper and just wanted to shake a hero's hand. But you didn't. We were in Santa Fe, then we were at that rest stop, now we're here. So, what's that phrase you used?"

Honey smiled, showing teeth stained brown from too much coffee and too many clove cigarettes. "The one about cutting the crap?"

"That's the one," I said.

"Okay," he said. "Crap cut. Your daddy asked me to keep an eye on you."

"See I get to Vegas on time?"

"See you get there at all." The way he said this sent a shiver down my spine. I'd been so focused on the danger to Woody—trying to determine what level of fabricat it was—that I'd basically looked off the possibility of risk to me. But it stood to reason: If Woody was in real jeopardy (granted, an as yet unsubstantiated if), then so might be his succors, i.e., me. This cast Mr. Honey Moon in a different sort of light.

"You're my guardian angel?" I asked. "Is that what you're selling?"

"Not selling anything, amigo. Woody Hoverlander asks a favor, I say yes, and that's from way back. How you deal with it is all on you."

The waitress returned with our coffee. She glanced at Honey and found him making eye contact with her. He communicated much with his look. Another dose of approval, sure, but also a depth of understanding for her lot in life. I saw it pass between them: his blanket acceptance of everything she was and everything she did. I now got that the earlier lewd compliment had just been his way of speaking to her in a lingua franca. His real message was here in his silent look, his intelligent eyes, and his not-half-trying smile. He seemed beatific in this moment, almost religious, and it had an effect. The waitress, surely no giggly girl, giggled girlishly, and withdrew in a fluster, fully seduced by his acceptance.

"You made her feel good," I said.

"Everybody's on their own road, Radar. And every road is hard. No need to strew nails." It occurred to me that this resonant philosophy may have been Honey's means of schmoozing me. But it didn't feel like schmooze. It felt like belief.

I sipped my coffee. It was, according to specs, hot and bitter. I wondered if I'd forever think of bad coffee as a cup of ex-wife. "So, Guardian Angel," I said, returning to the subject at hand, "what kind of danger am I in?"

"I wonder what I could tell you," Honey drawled, "that you'd believe. Your daddy says you're not a credulous man."

"My father doesn't know me," I said, with rather more bristle than I'd intended.

Honey eyed me thoughtfully. "Maybe not," he said. "But I suspect you don't know him all that well, either. I know him well. We've run more games together than you can count. And ever since I met him, he's the one man on God's green earth I trust with everything. So let's start with that and see where we get from there, hmm? I'll tell you my tale, and you decide if it's the truth."

"There is no truth," I said, "only consistent narrative."

Honey smiled. "That there sounds like something Woody would say."

It probably was. That's probably where I got it.

They met in a pool hall, as grifters will, though by that late date, the early 1990s, pool-hall culture was a relic, a shadow of its former self. You could still find a game, even rustle up a hustle, but the big money had disappeared. Neither one of them could quite figure out where the big money had gone. They'd both enjoyed reasonably successful runs through the Reagan years, for deregulation had blown the lid off interest rates, and money market funds had boomed. Putting a Ponzi tap on that vein required little more than some Mayflower names on Letraset letterhead and a quarter-page ad in a metropolitan daily. But Woody and Honey had their vices, and by the time Reagan's trickle-down detumesced into recession, they were down at their respective heels, reduced to a sad handful of short cons and the dwindling opportunity of pool-hall plucks.

"Tried to hustle each other," said Honey. "Believe that? Sandbagged our asses off and were both so good at playing bad that we got ten games deep before we cottoned. So we racked our cues, sat down, got acquainted. Been partners of many sorts ever since."

"And these vices you mentioned?"

"Mine was the powder," said Honey, "of course." He shook his head in mournful memory. "Damn, I must've sucked six Cadillacs up my nose before I got wise. Your daddy helped me with that. Kept calling me stupid, and wouldn't take 'I know' for an answer. One of the reasons I owe him."

"And his?"

"Oh, gambling, for sure. You must know that." But I didn't, and the fact that I didn't struck me with sudden worry. I quickly combed my earliest memories for any resonance of card-room trips or track runs but came up empty. Which meant that Woody'd been more than usually adept at hiding his habit from his near and dear, and if you think it's a piece of cake to pull this off, it's not. Just ask the pothead papa who only ever sparks up in the garage. His kids know. They don't know *what* they know, but they know. Now Honey claims that my dad was disastrously hooked on outcome, but it's news to me, and if I can't backpredict any evidence of it, then that's a hole in Honey's tale.

Check again, Radar. Your recollections are rusty. They'll take some prying loose.

I let my mind slide back to that narrow span of years before Woody got gone. Was there anything? A kitchen table poker game? Church bingo? Powerball tickets? Even scratchers? Nope, nothing. It struck me as strange—an inconsistent narrative—that someone like Woody, who based his life and business model on high-risk, high-reward exploits, should be so devoid of the gamble. No, not devoid. *Cleansed.* I continued to plumb my past. For practical reasons, I wanted to find something, anything, that validated Honey's claim. Why? Simple. If Honey's on the straight, then he's an ally or at least a resource. Otherwise, he's a problem, and I already have enough of...

Wait, problem: There it is. An argument, heard through walls, between my parents late one night. "You have a problem!" says my mom. Woody's saying no, and she's firing back with the fierce rhetorical, "Then what's in the medicine bag?!" What indeed? And at the next opportunity, curious young me checks out the beat-up doctor's satchel Dad keeps on a high closet shelf. Does Woody play doctor? I wouldn't put it past him, but there's no medicine here, just random plastic circles of various colors and kinds.

Chips, I now realize. Chips from all different casinos. Plus dice and cards, cash, and pieces of paper that must've been betting slips. Did I repress this memory, or just consider it unimportant? It's sure as hell important now.

I fixed Honey with a narrow stare. I didn't have to tell him that I'd searched the historical record and found evidence to back his claim. I assumed he could read it in my face. So I skipped to the salient question, "What's he doing in Vegas if he has a gambling problem?"

"*Had,*" said Honey with sudden vehemence. "He got over it. I helped him, like he helped me." Honey spread his beefy hands. "Radar, I've rolled with your daddy off and on for twenty years. Slept in the same fleabag motels. Slept with the same gals more than once. You gotta believe me, when he quit, he *quit,* with not so much as a coin flip since. Now I know what you're thinking: that he took Wolfredian's money and pissed it away in a sports book or such. But that's not what this is about, and if you got *any* capacity to believe, you gotta put it in that. Otherwise..."

"Otherwise what?"

Honey shrugged his shoulders. "Otherwise you can't save his life."

Confirmation, class? Coming from a con man, it could be anything from gospel to overstatement to outright lie. In any case, there's no way I'd rise to such obvious bait, so instead I drew him back to the narrative, still testing its consistency. "How did you roll?" I asked. "You two, all those years. And I'm not really concerned about the gals."

Honey chuckled. "Squeamish, chico? Your pop's a very robust man." But he let it go. "We went to Germany," he said. "Berlin."

"Berlin?"

"I'd served in the Army there in the seventies."

"What, Checkpoint Charlie?"

"In fact, yeah. But that was then. Now it's '92, and the Wall's down. Know what that makes East Berlin?" I shook my head. "The last urban virgin in Western Europe."

"Hence, a *Liebfrau* land rush."

"Oh, yeah."

"What did you do, flip real estate?"

Again Honey laughed. "Nah, man, that's too much work. We opened a local branch of the United States Redevelopment Fund."

"Not sure I ever heard of that."

"Well, it didn't last long." Or exist, of course, outside their imaginings. "We made friends with big developers, guys who held property options on all these old factories and apartment blocks in East Berlin. Then, when word got out that the USRF wanted to invest—"

"Everyone wanted a piece of what your friends had."

"Prices spiked, our friends made a killing, we got our cut."

"Old trick," I said.

"Old to us. New to them."

I was reminded of what Mirplo had said earlier about being a page ahead in the textbook. "So you were one-eyed men in the kingdom of the blind."

"Right on."

"And your joneses?"

"We put 'em away. Europe was good for our heads."

"Why didn't you stay?"

"Why don't our kind ever stay anywhere?" Honey's face went wistful at the memory. "But those were good times, though. We were about your age, a little older." He looked me over as if appraising me for the first time. "You know your youth won't last forever, right?" I nodded. "But they don't tell you how hard shit gets. You don't lose your competence. Hell, you gain competence. I'm ten times the grifter I was back then. But everything takes more effort." He stretched his arms over his head, cracking the knuckles of his intertwined fingers. "And you hurt more. But whatever."

"So you skated the ocean."

"Uh-huh. Back home to America. And find that shit's changed. Now there's computers everywhere, Internet, you don't work in a vacuum anymore. Folks get warned. Folks get wary. I don't guess you give this too much thought, Radar. Having grown up with it, you know how to game it. For old farts like me and your pop, it was a tough transition."

"What'd you do?"

"Tried to go legit, become movie producers. Man, that was a money pit. I tell you what, you want to see a real con artist, lift any rock in Hollywood."

"So you didn't make any movies?"

"Oh, we made 'em. Just couldn't make 'em pay. Studio accounting, see."

"You almost sound affronted."

"Nah. No one to blame but ourselves. We were blind men in a kingdom of one-eyed snakes."

"And after?"

"You know, little this, little that. Eventually we drifted apart. I dabbled in credit card fraud, then went over to the other side and worked in security consulting."

"How to close the barn door behind the cow?"

"Something like that, yeah. Now I'm retired. Semi."

"Semi?"

"I live in Phoenix. Great weather. Couple hundred golf courses. You'd be surprised how many mooks there think a drunk can't putt."

"I'd be surprised if you were drunk."

I sketched a mental picture of Honey running the Wooden Leg hustle up and down municipal links, flamboyantly faux-Irishing his coffee and doubling bets on the back nine. I suppose you could supplement your income with that. Plus, it keeps a man in trim.

Honey set down his coffee mug and measured me with his eyes. "Trying to run the car trouble con past me," he said. "I ought to be insulted. But I like you, Radar. I knew I would, from what your old man had to say. I expect you'll come to like me, too. We're kindred spirits. But your daddy, now, your dad I love. It'll sound too dramatic if I say he saved my life, but he did. We're closer than brothers. I'd do anything for him."

"Then call this woman," I said, writing down Allie's digits on a paper napkin. "Tell her what you told me. If she buys it, we'll meet in the morning in"—I consulted my mental map of Arizona—"Kingman. If not, *vaya con Dios,* okay?"

"Where in Kingman?"

"The Dairy Queen," I said. "It's right off the highway." Which I knew from having once worked Route 66 as a certifier of historical landmarks.*

"I'd rather we traveled together."

"I know: You're concerned about my safety."

"That's right. It's—"

I held up my hand. "Look, if Woody's jammed up like you say he is, then I'm his out, right?" I didn't wait for a response. "And what good is a dead out? Therefore, I think you're overdilling the pickle I'm in." Again he

*Officially licensed. The things people believe.

started to speak and again I cut him off. "I don't hold it against you. You don't know me. I could be a total flake. It never hurts to put the fear on the mark. If I were who you say you are to Woody, I'd do the same thing."

Honey nodded acknowledgment. He tapped the napkin with a beefy finger. "This your girlfriend?" I nodded. "You trust her judgment?"

"More than I trust mine, sometimes."

"You're lucky," said Honey. "Having someone like that. I've had a lot of gifts in my life, but that's one I've missed." He pocketed the paper. "Dairy Queen," he said, then pointed across to the cashier's counter and a prominently placed rack of Swoop 'n' Pummel Energy Blast. "You need one for the road?"

"No thanks." My coffee had reached room temperature, and I drained it at a gulp. "I take my stimulants like my guardian angels," I said. "Cool and black." Honey took this for the compliment I intended it to be. We shook hands. I hit the road.

Half an hour later, my phone rang. I tapped my Bluetooth to answer.

"It's me," said Allie.

"What do you think?"

"Frankly," she said, "I can't tell if he's a funnel or a shield. But he loves your old man."

"Yeah, I got that, too. So do I let him roll with?"

"Not my call."

"If it were?"

She took a breath, then answered, "I would."

"Was I wrong to have him call you?" I asked.

"What do you mean?"

"It kind of makes you part of this."

"I *am* part of this. The anchor part."

Our conversation turned to other subjects. The stunning monotony of desert radio. How Boy cornered a lizard in the kitchen. Mirplo's flying lessons. Then we had phone sex. Thank God for Bluetooth, or I'd have run out of hands.

13

I Come for the Sushi

I slept in a used-car lot in Kingman, a trick of vagabondage I learned long ago. Many places—streets, rest stops, motel parking lots—if you camp in your car, you're asking for trouble, either from police or from smash-and-grab knuckleheads. In a used-car lot, though, you're hiding in plain sight, safe as kittens till the business day begins. Choose, as I did, an eastern exposure, and you have a big yellow alarm clock set to shine in your eyes at sunup.

Fueled by bad convenience store coffee (a jumbo ex-wife with cream), I drove toward the Dairy Queen, which I recalled to be on Stockton Hill Road, just south of the freeway.

It wasn't there.

It looked like it hadn't been there in quite some time. Though a sand-scoured DQ stanchion still stood at the corner of the lot, the rest of the signage had been replaced by emblazonments for Arturo's Fish Tacos. But Arturo was gone, too, and the windows were all boarded up. Another victim of the failed economy; in tough times, fish tacos are the first to go.

I parked at the strip mall across the street, facing the dead DQ. I was half surprised not to find Honey waiting for me. To inject such an air of urgency into the proceedings and then be a no-show was something of an inconsistent narrative. The thought crossed my mind that whatever malevolent forces he'd feared—or wanted me to fear—had caught up to him, but I don't think you can tail an intelligent grifter on the open road if he's looking out for you, nor take him by surprise if he's on his guard.

It did, however, put me in a bind of a kind, for I couldn't wait around all day. I decided to give it an hour, no more. If Honey didn't show, I'd head to Sin City. Of course, what I'd do when I got there I still didn't know. Wander around the Gaia Casino calling, *"Alle, alle auch sind frei!"*? This would have amused Woody, for it was our call sign when I was a kid, smugly trumpeted in authentic German, our way to echolocate each other in crowds, like at baseball games. *Look at that, Radar. You went to baseball games.*

My phone rang. It was Vic. "Radar! I got my first commission! A metal sculpture. Sold it off a sketch of a bird."

"Does it look anything like a bird?"

"Oh, yes," said Vic. "Birdlike, very birdlike. I'm all about things that fly. This woman from Albuquerque wants it. She said she's tired of typical Santa Fe art and finds me fresh."

"Fresh to the tune of...?"

"Man, you don't even want to know. I told you, it's a money tree. Look, finish up what you're doing and get back here. You could be my apprentice."

Every now and then you feel an earthquake, and the idea of me being Vic's apprentice was one. Before I could register an aftershock, I saw Honey's Sharp pull off the freeway, drafting a big-ass Buick, the kind you don't see much anymore because the mileage makes folks laugh.

"Gotta go, Vic."

"Why? What's going on?"

"Tell you later. Gotta go." I snapped off and slouched down low behind the steering wheel. The cars pulled into the derelict Dairy Queen. Honey got out and looked around. If he spotted me, he didn't let on, and I sure wasn't about to start honking my horn. Because just then three heavies exited the Buick and spread out. They had attitude, plus muscles. Not bodybuilder muscles: back-room ones; someone's-going-to-get-hurt ones. These were classic casino sidewheels,* dressed for off-site work in denim shirts, cargo pants, work boots, and brim caps. The two blockier ones took up station at separate corners of the lot. The third, smaller and slighter, circled around to check behind the building—and revealed a shock of red ponytail poking out the back of her cap. Well, what do you know? The sidewheel business goes EEO.

Wolfredian got out next. He matched his website PR photo perfectly, right down to the same bland corporate tie. This struck a discordant note with me, because if he really were a true vanilla functionary, corporate Vegas like Detroit is corporate cars, then what did he need with three sidewheels? That's heavy security for a drive in the desert. I thought it might be for my benefit, just to convey what a player he was. And I'm supposed to cower in the face of this? Well, whatever. Jay scanned the scene in one tempered revolution, taking everything in and, I thought, darkly disapproving. Then he faced Honey, who gave him a shrug and said (as I lip-read), "I guess the kid decided to fade." Wolfredian leaned in the car window and spoke to someone inside.

A moment later, I got a text. *Alle, alle auch sind frei.*

Hmm. Guess I won't be going to Vegas after all.

I spent a few moments deciding how I wanted to play this, settled on feckless, opened the car door and shambled out. Yawning and stretching, I let myself notice the tableau across the street, then held a hand to my forehead, blocking the sun and peering across as if I'd just made an exciting discovery. "Honey? Is that you?" I called. I crossed the street, still devoid of traffic at this hour, essaying another long yawn as I walked. "I fell asleep waiting." I paused at the sidewalk, balked by the sight of the sidewheels. "Who are these guys?"

The redhead returned from around back, and flanked Wolfredian as he stepped forward and introduced himself. "Jay Wolfredian," he said, "Gaia Casino."

*Thugs with job security.

"Hey," I said, and, "Hey," again to the lady sidewheel, who nodded slightly, resisting no urge whatsoever to smile. I turned back to Wolfredian. "I see you know Honey."

"We just met. He says he's been kind of your shepherd."

"I didn't know I needed one. But it's nice of you to meet me halfway."

"Kingman?" said Jay. "I come for the sushi."

This was so unexpected and deadpan that it made me laugh, then let me stand on a platform of pleasant small talk, front-loading the conversation with null signals while I took Jay's measure. What I got off him was a prickliness beneath the veneer. He struck me as the sort of person who'd be totally friendly right up till the moment he wasn't.

Therefore, let's spend as little time with him as possible. "Okay, let's have it," I said. "What kind of muck is my father in this time?"

"Oh, *this* time?" Wolfredian poked his cheek with his tongue, no doubt picturing all the resentment and codependence of our rocky years. I wanted him to have this picture, for it's easier to run your script if your opponent never reads past the clichés. "It's just a matter of money," said Jay. "He hasn't been able to provide it, but he says you can."

My heart sank. Up to that moment, I think I'd secretly hoped that all of this had been some kind of audition, like what Allie put me through before dealing me in to the California Roll. Of course I'd say no to whatever they proposed—Operation Citizen, right?—but at least I'd be flattered at Woody's and this Wolfredian's attention. But all I saw here was a tawdry fake shakedown, jacked up with Honey's humbo gumbo. Which meant that all of them, Wolfredian, Honey, Woody, the sidewheels, and the day-player goons back in Santa Fe, were on a common calling plan. Well, fine, congratulations, you put the touch on Radar Hoverlander. Merry Christmas.

"Money, huh?" I said, projecting weary familiarity with the phrase. "Okay, hang on, I'll go get it."

This seemed to surprise Wolfredian, and as I headed for my car, he motioned to his ponytail sidewheel, who jogged up to fall in step beside me. "What's your name?" I asked. She didn't answer. "Okay, then I'll just call you Red." We reached Carol and I popped the rear hatch. "I suppose you think I'm just throwing good money after black sheep, huh?" I lifted the cargo deck plate and withdrew three banded bundles of hundreds from the spare-tire well. I pocketed two bundles, counted off thirty bills from the third, pocketed that as well, then returned the rest to the wheel well. "I promised Mom I'd look after him." I dropped the deck plate and closed the hatch. "What a bad deal that was. Seriously, what's your name?"

"Louise."

"Hey, that's my mother's name!"

"Joke," she said, mirthlessly.

"Yes," I said. "Yes, joke. Glad you found it funny."

By the time I crossed back over, Woody was out of the car. He looked sheepish, like a kid caught smoking cigarettes at summer camp. I handed Wolfredian the cash. He didn't count it, just weighed it disdainfully in his hand. "What's this?" he asked.

"Twenty-three grand. What he owes you."

Wolfredian laughed. "What he owes me," said Jay slowly, "this doesn't make a dent in."

I looked at Woody, arching my eyebrows in question.

"Son," he said, "I may need more than five figures."

Interesting: a shakedown with an escalator clause. You don't see those every day. "Well, good luck with that," I said, for I was done with this one. "You're as deep into my pockets as you get to go."

I turned to leave. Red Louise blocked my path. Though she kept her expression blank, her nostrils flared and you could tell this was a woman who loved her work.

"No one wants to get into your pockets," said Jay. "It's just that your father needs help."

"Yeah, he needs help, all right. Mental help."

Jay smiled. "I don't disagree with that. All this desert rendezvous bullshit."

If you stipulate for a moment that Woody's actually trying to rope me into something (and not just shake me down), you can easily back-predict a conversation that he and Jay must've had, one where Woody sketched out the script he'd need to run in order to get his boy on board, a script thick with the fake threats necessary to neutralize a truculent girlfriend bent on keeping Radar's nose clean. It may be that when I told Honey to meet me in Kingman, Woody decided to jack up the drama with a road trip. So then Woody was playing Wolfredian by getting Wolfredian to play me.

"He was much sharper back at Stanford," said Jay. (Was this more script?) "Did you know he taught?"

"At Stanford?"

"Continuing education. Business practice. Not a bad class, especially if he liked you. Then he let you in on his private business model. Put your name on a lot of documents."

A certain penny dropped. I knew all about private business models, how when they go keel-up, the name on the papers goes down with the ship. I guessed that could qualify as criminal misconduct. "Mooked you, huh? I'm surprised you're still friends."

"We're not friends. A situation came up. I thought he'd be right for the job. I was wrong. I hope I'm not wrong twice."

"Well, like I said, good luck with that."

"I don't think you get it. He says he needs your help, so your help he's going to get."

"What makes you think I can help him? Everything he says is horseshit. That's horseshit, too. And now if you'll excuse me, I have a life."

I turned to go.

And attacked Louise's fist with my stomach.

I sort of fell down. Jay stood over me. "Your life is on hold," he said. Guess I'd been right about the whole friendly-till-not vibe. He nodded to Red, who aimed a kick and, with evident pleasure, drilled my ribs into the back of the net. And though this seemed like a random act of violence, I recognized it as personnel management of a sort. Wolfredian simultaneously sent me a message and threw his sociopathic sidewheel a bone.

She stepped over me on her way back to the car. "This I find funny," she said.

Then they were gone. With my money. Woody and Honey rushed to me. "I'm so sorry, Radar," said Woody, trying to help me up. "That should not have happened."

I clambered to my feet, angrily shaking off his aid. "Go to hell," I said.

This garnered a strange reaction from Woody: anger; anger and disdain. He put his hands on his hips and said, "Oh, for what, Radar? For trying to deal you into something tasty, just when you happen to be unfortunately and coincidentally tied up in your girlfriend's morality play? And by morality play I mean play for morality, which is fine, you know, some people's choices. I'm just saying: Is it yours? Do *you* want to be out of the game? Because I've always wanted to run a snuke with you. Circumstances didn't allow. Now they do. We can talk about that later if you like, but right now all you have to ask yourself is whether you're going to let some romantic bad timing deny you a major score."

I didn't say anything. Just got in my car and went.

And that was the last time in life I ever saw him, right?

Ha. Not even that day.

14

Repeat Business

For a mark in the grip of a grift, there comes a time when leverage tips, and the guy who thought he was acting as a free agent suddenly finds himself, per the famous oxymoron, voluntarily compelled to continue.

I hated being that guy.

And really hated Woody for making me that guy.

Okay, so how deep was I sunk? *A situation came up. I thought he'd be right for the job.* What kind of job? Another private business model? Could be. Who knew? I needed more information.

I called Allie. We talked the problem through for a hundred eastbound miles, anticipating what we could about what we thought would happen next and planning accordingly. Then my phone battery died, and I just chewed on my thoughts in silence.

When I got home, Boy jumped me at the door, nearly put me on my ass. Allie's greeting was more restrained, with no leaping into anyone's arms. "We've got company," she said in a muted, you've-done-something-wrong kind of voice.

I found Woody and Honey waiting for me in the living room, Woody standing at the window, watching traffic pass, and Honey sprawled out on the couch.

"You drive fast," I told Honey.

"We didn't stop," he said.

"Piss bottles," Woody explained.

"I don't want to hear about it," I said. "Christ, old man, what is it going to take to get rid of you?"

"You can't, Radar. This is serious. Feel your ribs."

"I know what's up with my ribs. Still, why should I make this my problem?"

"That's what I'm trying to tell you. It already *is* your problem."

"Thanks to you," barked Allie.

"Yes," said Woody, "thanks to me. But I was in trouble. When I saw Radar's name in the paper, I grasped at an available straw. I realize now I should have just told him the truth. As you may have gathered, I'm not very good with the truth."

"It runs in the family," said Allie, with enough acid in her voice to take Woody by surprise.

"Any chance we'll get some now?" I asked.

Woody gave the wan smile of a defeated man. "Would you settle for a consistent narrative?"

Woody, according to Woody, had truly been freelance whale-watching for various casinos in Las Vegas. Eventually his path crossed Wolfredian's, as it likely would in so rarefied an industry sector. "I didn't recognize him at first," said Woody. "But he recognized me. Almost instantly offered me a job."

"What kind of job?"

"Casino host, notionally, but really just a bird dog of a different kind. I was to drive high rollers to his bogus investment opportunities. Prequalify the leads, like."

I could see that. Whales bond with their hosts. Be it through craps benders, Jägermeister jags, or sprints up to Pahrump for the legal brothels, you become friends, battle buddies, men with shared secrets. After that, your pet millionaire will no doubt cast a less jaundiced eye on your factitious prospectus. "I gather you took the job," I said. Woody nodded. "Didn't you read him for holding a grudge?"

"Of course I did, but he put that issue to rest. Said he viewed our previous encounter as an initiation of sorts, a valuable life lesson learned." Woody looked thoughtful. "As to why I said yes, I think it was pure pride. He'd reached out to me with a certain amount of admiration and respect."

"Oh, please," said Allie, manifesting frayed patience. "What was he next, the son you never had?" This was borderline rude, and quite uncharacteristic of Allie. Woody seemed to be wondering where all her empathy had gone.

I just wondered how he'd gotten so on Jay's wrong side.

"I told you about the Saudi prince, right?"

"Right, with the bogus line of credit. I should've smelled a rat right there. That line was way too small."

"Yeah, that was a weak tale. I wouldn't have bought it either, I was you." He looked genuinely pained. "The thing is, I never was about finding whales. I was just looking for a new way to pick his pocket."

"Give him another valuable life lesson?"

"Mm-hmm. So I made up this fake Saudi and strung him along for a while. But then I let slip that the Saudi was bogus and..." Woody's face clouded. "Well, yours aren't the only ribs around here, you know."

I could picture a certain moment: Woody getting beaten, saying the first thing that came to his mind—something fresh in his mind because he'd just read the newspaper account. "So you gave him me. What did you tell him I could do?"

"Well, find him a whale, obviously."

"Why would he believe I can do that?"

Woody's smile was bittersweet. "You have a persuasive press agent."

"But all of that was bafflegab, right? He's still the mark."

"Oh, yeah. He's repeat business, for sure." By which Woody meant the kind of mook you can mook and mook again.

"Dangerous business, though. Why didn't you sail?"

"Radar, I'm not going to drop everything and run the first time someone hits me in the ribs, come on. Would you?" I thought about what it means to pull the plug on an operation, a location, an identity. It's a setback. Plus, you could sprain your neck with all the looking over your shoulder. No grifter loves that. It puts a crimp in the future. "Besides," said Woody, "I know I can take him. I just have to find the right gag. I've already found the right partner." He paused, then said, "Well, Radar, what do you say?"

"I say you owe me twenty-three thousand dollars."

"Consider it seed corn."

"I consider it debt," I said, coldly. "Anyway, what makes you think you can button him up?"

"'Button him up'?" asked Honey. He'd been so still and silent there on the couch that I'd almost forgotten he was there. Man, Woody could get me locked on.

"Rip him off clean," I said. "Leave him laughing when you go."

"You kids and your slang," muttered Honey, sinking deeper into the couch.

"I can button him," said Woody. "With your help I can. What do you think about Nana's Attic?"

I snorted a laugh.

Nana's Attic is a vintage—in several senses of the word—con that involves selling certain sorts of nothing for something. It plays in the world of collectibles, driven by something called transaction friction, the natural escalation of prices when pieces change hands. Say you catch a milestone home-run ball, out there in the bleachers. You sell it on eBay, for a price that will never be lower than when starry-eyed you let it go. These virgin items, these treasures of Nana's Attic, exposed to the market for the first time, have a higher long-term upside than almost anything in the collectibles realm. If you happen to be trading in bogus collectibles, as all of us in that room had certainly done at one time or another, you try to come across as the fortunate—and conveniently clueless—heir to such a trove, by way of explaining why your "authentic" home-run ball is so unbelievably cheap. It helps if your mark is as clueless as you're representing yourself to be, but in this instance...

"He'll see right through it," I said. "You'll never make it work."

"Why not?"

I thought about it for a moment, certain familiar wheels starting to turn. The first step to Nana's Attic is discovering what your mark is into. Disneyana? Nazi medals?* Let's use that classic of the Attic, heirloom jewelry. Yours is lovingly counterfeited by Han craftsmen. Now all you need is to find it a home in the mark's display case. This can be tough, though, because the mark, he loves him his heirloom jewelry and knows every last detail of his sad little habit, right down to the standard karat weight of Edwardian gold. But also—and this is your wedge—he wants to believe. Wants to believe that a genuine treasure of Nana's Attic just fell in his lap. So you get your storytelling chops on and feed that belief with plausible provenance. Money changes hands. The mark goes away happy—fully buttoned up—and stays that way maybe forever, but certainly until he tries to resell his prize to someone with a more practiced eye.

"By then, of course, you're long gone." I didn't realize I was thinking out loud. "So no problem. It's a solid scam and it works. Only not this time, because Wolfredian knows you and doesn't trust you. You'd need something he's impossibly wet for, something that trumps all reason."

"I'll tell you what trumps all reason," said Allie.

"What?"

"You. Trying to solve this bogus problem."

"I'm not solving anything. It's just... hypothetical."

"Oh, really? Hypothetical? And if you found the right scam, would you go for it? Hypothetically?"

"Of course not," I protested. "Not unless we discussed it and decided—"

"Decided what? To shitcan all our plans?"

"Not can," I said. "Shelve. Temporarily set aside."

---

*And how weird the collector who's into both?

"Yeah, right," said Allie. Boy trotted into the room. *It got chilly in here. Does anyone need me?* "And not for nothing, but how many times does he have to lie to you before you catch on that that's what he does?" I just blinked. I had nothing to say. "I mean that's *all* he does. Seriously, what in the world makes you think he's telling the truth now?"

"He just is."

"He just *is*?" Allie stared at me incredulously. "Oh, for Pete's sake." She grabbed Boy's leash from its wooden dowel by the door. "Come on, Boy, let's go for a walk." She shook her head sadly. "You're being mooked, Radar. I don't know why you can't see that." To Woody she said, "Don't be here when I get back. I don't want to know you anymore."

She left. I gawked. Honey may have been asleep. The moment opened and poured silence into itself. Then Woody said softly, "Honey, did you ever hear the story of my first anniversary?"

Honey didn't open his eyes. "I believe I did."

"Mind if I tell it again?"

"Knock yourself out."

"Man, was I broke. But it was our anniversary and we needed to celebrate, so I took Radar's mom out to the fanciest place I could find. When she found out I couldn't pay, she threw a fit like you wouldn't believe. Yelling, screaming, right there in the restaurant in front of God and everybody. Chased me out, even. Then she started to cry. They felt so sorry for her, they comped the meal." Woody turned and looked at me from beneath his wooly eyebrows. "You get where I'm going with this, Radar?"

"You staged the fight."

"Of course we did."

"But that's not—"

Woody stopped me with his hand. "Radar, it's fine. She's better off out. Safer, no doubt. And if she feels she needs to cover her retreat with some amateur theatrics, that's fine, too." Woody gave Honey a hand up from the couch. "We'll go," he said. "Don't think I don't appreciate your problem, son. Women make us do all kind of crazy things. Like pretend to go straight. So you're stuck in the middle of what you want for her and what you want for you. What you don't realize is, you can have both."

"How?"

"Bring her around. She's a smart cookie. We'll find her a place in the play."

"That's not going to happen, Dad. You saw her reaction."

"I saw her performance. All that tells me is, what she thinks is out of her system ain't." Suddenly Woody hugged me, then clapped me on the back with two hearty hands. "I'm so glad you're on board, son. We're going to have such a good time."

On board? Who the hell said I was on board?

15

Trapdoor Spider

When Allie came home, she blamed herself for being so see-through. "I'm sorry," she said. "I guess I came on too strong."

"You came on fine. He busted the play, but he still thinks you're out, which is all we need."

This we had decided on the phone during my long ride home, in a conversation that started with Allie asking me did I think my ribs were broken.

"Just bruised, I think. Though from a pain perspective it doesn't make much difference."

"Well, hurry home. I'll kiss them and make them feel better."

"While I don't doubt the salutary effect of your lips on any of my body parts"—

"I love it when you talk dirty."

—"we've got a bigger problem to deal with now."

"I know," she said with a sigh that articulated her disappointment, for if my road trip had been a test, I'd kind of failed. "So much for going straight."

"It's not the end of the world," I said, lightly. "We can always go straight later." Guys do this sometimes, try to sell something they know in advance won't sell. As expected, my airy promise of "future considerations" was met with stale silence. "Allie?"

"I heard you," she said.

"But you don't agree."

"It's our jones, Radar. We can't just take it or leave it."

"Yes, but what if it's not our jones? Or no, yes, our jones, but more, too. Our calling. Our art."

"What, now all of a sudden we're Mirplo?"

"You said it yourself, it's half marketing. What's wrong with marketing how smart we are?"

"That sounds like a rationalization."

"Well, you know what they say: Rationalization is the act of a rational man." Another ugly silence, but I pushed on, for when it came to rationalizations, I had mine stacked and circling like planes over O'Hare. "Okay, how about this? Whatever we make on this snaggle, we'll plough into a... a charitable foundation." I could almost hear Allie's eyebrows arching, and why not? In our world, *charitable foundation* is code for *money press.* "No," I said, "for real. We'll pick a cause, any cause you like. Save the Jackalope, whatever. And we'll—"

"I think we should break up."

The elevator dropped. From the observation deck to the subbasement in a slashed second. My stomach churned. My heart raced. My fingertips tingled. I started sweating. Hyperventilating. I struggled to keep my eyes open—nearly put Carol in a ditch. How could everything change so fast? One second I'm bantering with my baby, the next second my future opens and swallows me whole, hurling me into a grim, gray, solo dystopia. I see it all in an instant, me without Allie, wasting my days on sad, lonely scams, devolving down at last to some bitter old flimflam man running burglar-alarm snukes on baffled housewives and going home to a frozen potpie. *Please, God, no. I can't. I just can't.*

"What?" I said. I may have mewed.

"Oh, poor Radar, I don't mean for real. I mean for the snuke."

The rope breaks. The hanged man falls to freedom, safe and whole. A miracle rescue. Love lives.

Even with the coppery taste of panic still on my tongue, my rational mind kicked in, and I saw that breaking us up made total sense. Not only did it buy Allie a measure of safety, it left us free to reinvent her later as necessary. In the grift, we call this a trapdoor spider, otherwise known as a player to be named later, and they're never not handy to have.

So we break up. Yet the question remained, "On what grounds?"

"These right here. Your backsliding. You won't admit you have a problem."

"I have a problem," I said, still shaky from the adrenaline spike. "You're my problem."

Allie seemed genuinely surprised. "Did I scare you?"

"Yeah, you scared me. I thought you were serious."

"So that was kind of fun. Now I know you love me."

"You knew that before."

"I guess I did."

"Allie, I'm sorry we're still stuck with him. My dad I mean."

"We'll get unstuck. Don't worry, Radar. He's not smarter than both of us."

So that's why Allie went off on me in front of Woody, and that's how it worked out both worse and better than we expected, with Woody seeing through our subterfuge but misinterpreting its intent. Meanwhile, though I didn't trust Woody, did I believe him? Only in the sense that it would not serve him for his partner to make decisions based on bad data. So now I had a filter for whatever he told me. It might or might not be objectively true, but it could be measured against an objective standard. If he saw Jay as a target and me as a means to that end, then the information he now gave me must necessarily help me play my role or he'd be working against his own interest. It's like your basic busted space telescope: If the lens is defective, you write software to compensate.

The next night, I went to see Vic's latest undertaking, the Mirplo Show, a one-act play about Vic, starring Vic, written by Vic, directed by Vic, with music by Vic. His logic seemed to be: Go off in all directions at once, you're bound to get somewhere somehow. At least he was over being horrible in public. In this new work, he told a picaresque saga of his life, all of it myths, of course, but colorful ones, and in the end you got the impression that the storyteller just very much wanted to be liked, and that was Vic, truly. Thus by roundabout means did he arrive at a deeply revealing honesty.

I joined him afterward in the lobby, where Zoe, now firmly embedded as Sedgwick to his Warhol, sold DVD copies of the performance, plus bonus tracks of Vic singing original songs. I waited for the clot of well-wishers to dissolve, then told him how much I liked the show, especially the honesty part.

"But that's what art is," he replied. "Honesty."

"Honesty? Really?"

"I don't know. Maybe. Anyway it's fun. Come on back to my studio." By which he meant Zoe's garage. "We'll hang out. I've got beer." I asked Vic how he was coping with the loss of his Quonset hut. "It's in the past," he said. "They'll put a plaque on the spot one day. 'Mirplo's first studio.' By the way, it's just Mirplo now. Like Bono or Beck."

Of course it was. Why wouldn't it be?

Walking back to Zoe's, I brought Vic up to date on the latest with Woody, and my Hubble Telescope solution to trusting him. It was an ad hoc solution, though, and I worried it wouldn't hold.

"Burn that bridge when you come to it," said Vic, acknowledging what we both knew to be true: that grifters can go through whole complex snukes without ever perfectly trusting one another. You watch your back and figure your partners are watching theirs. Somehow the job gets done, for even if you don't have mutual admiration, you can still have mutual benefit. In a properly designed snuke, it's in everyone's interest to stay the loyalty course, and self-interest will often serve where trust is wanting. If not, you make late adjustments. You burn that bridge when you come to it.

It felt good to share all this with Vic, partly because he was someone I *could* trust, and partly because, in his singular way, he had become something of a touchstone for me. His off-center interpretations always challenged me, or maybe he just had better eyes for my blind spots. For instance, when I told him about how stringing along with Woody was now the only real choice I had, he said, "Yeah, no it's not."

"Come again?"

"For instance, you could get in the wind if you wanted to, but you don't want to."

"Why not?"

"Duh, Freud. It's your father. You want to be a man for him. Make him proud."

"Bullshit. I just want him out of my life."

"And we see how well that's working. Radar, he's got you warped around his finger. And you know why?"

"Why?"

"He's got an ally."

"What ally? Wolfredian?"

"You, nimrod. Man, you are really losing the plot."

"So I'm subconsciously conspiring with Woody against me, is what you're saying?"

"In a nutshell."

"And why would I do that?"

Vic fixed me with the kind of look parents use with slow children. "Because, my demented friend, you don't want to go straight. I'm surprised I have to spell it out for you."

"No, that's not it. He's just sticky, that's all."

"So you *do* want to go straight."

"Yes, absolutely."

"Then you should run. Just fade."

Problem was, running wouldn't work. I mean, suppose we pulled it off. Shaded and faded on up to—randomly selected—Minnesota's Iron Range. We successfully reinvent ourselves as—again randomly selected—Zev and Dusty Yevksy of Main Street, Hibbing. Then what? Settle down and have kids? Live a life and leave a legacy? But what platform do we stand on? One of deceit from the start. Those tend to crumble over time. Worse, our kids grow up Yevksies. Their lives are a lie and they don't even know it. That sort of seemed to defeat the whole point of the exercise.

No, for the time being I was stuck where I was, and if I secretly liked being stuck...it's a thought I put out of my mind.

We reached Zoe's garage. Vic had done a decent job of converting it into a workspace, complete with an ancient La-Z-Boy for contemplative naps and a round-shouldered ancient Frigidaire filled with the necessities of creative inspiration, namely chilled candy bars and beer. He cranked up some tunes (Vic's own and, I had to admit, not half bad), then showed me his work in progress, an elaborate braid of twisted aluminum I-bar that rose from a bed of granite, swirled and jutted ten feet in the air, and then...just...flew. I can't explain it, but I felt like I was flying, too.

"It's nice, Vic," I said. "It's..." I groped for a more expressive word. "Light."

"I know, huh? You get the bird thing, don't you?"

"Yeah, I do. I really do."

"I call it *The Albuquerque Turkey Takes Flight.*" He fired up an industrial airbrush. "Mind if I work while we talk? I've scored two more commissions, and I'm starting to get jammed up."

"You're gonna have to clone yourself soon."

"If only a clone had my vision," said Vic with a serious sigh. "The vision's what they're buying." With that, he started darting and dancing around the piece, spraying it at odd intervals to, so far as I could tell, no effect whatsoever.

"What are you spraying?"

"Aerosolized aluminum and contact adhesive."

"Why are you spraying aluminum on aluminum?"

"Texture," he said, as if that explained everything.

I circled the sculpture, examining it from different angles. I found it completely compelling, not in the grotesque, watching-a-train-wreck manner of Vic's earlier works, but with a palpable soaring glory. And if you looked closely, you saw that aluminum on aluminum did add texture. Vic was getting a clue, and no denying it. "It's really coming along," I said. "You've been working hard."

"Procrastinate later, that's my motto."

Procrastinate later? Mirplo? The world had become strange.

16

Paper-Packing Papa

I met Woody for a hike the next day at a trailhead near Two Mile Reservoir in the foothills east of Santa Fe. He claimed that exercise helped him think, but for me, climbing a steep defile at seven thousand feet seemed to yield no more than oxygen-debt stupidity. Still, I soldiered on without complaint. *Trying to be staunch for your old man, Radar? What's up with that?*

"Keep your eyes peeled for jackalopes," chirped Woody as we passed through bands of sagebrush and Gambel oak. "These hills are lousy with 'em." I didn't reward him with a laugh, for this was less a joke than an attempt to salve old wounds with old microculture. He glanced at me, studied my studied nonreaction, and let it go. A pair of hawks turned circles in the sky, searching for a chipmunk lunch, or maybe baby jackalopes. The trail reached a high meadow that sloped up gently toward the steeper peaks of the Sangre de Cristo Mountains. A lone stand of ponderosa pines stood in the middle distance, and Woody set off for it at a brisk pace. "I like hiking," he said. "Feels good. Holds the wolves at bay."

"Wolves?"

"Of age. You know, infirmity."

"Is this going to be another riff on how you're a feeble old man? Nobody's buying that yarn, you know."

"And I'm not selling. But I'm no springing chicken, as your friend Mirplo would say. I just want you to have reasonable expectations."

"Okay," I said, "here's what I expect. I expect us to work together professionally, button up Wolfredian, and then part company. Understood?"

"Vividly. If that's what you want." We hiked on. The ponderosa pines drew close.

"Suppose you tell me what *you* want," I said.

"But you know that, Radar. The chance to make amends."

"Man, they're made," I said out of sheer exasperation.

"Now who's selling yarns?" He cracked a grin, but I didn't crack one back. "Look, Radar," he said, "I know you've got a book on me, one with old pages, like Where did he go when he left? and new ones, like Why couldn't he just come back clean? They're your pages; read them as you see fit. But at least let it cross your mind, son, that when I say I want to make amends, I'm telling it exactly as it is. And if you're having a problem with that, I would point out two things. First, you've never had a son, or been estranged from one, so you have no idea how that feels."

"And second?"

"For how hard you've been working to get away from me, you're still here."

"You're saying I need you?"

"I'm saying you need answers." We entered the shadow of the trees. Woody settled down on a fallen log, sighing as he sat. "How about you get some now?"

Charles Woodrow Hoverlander, called Woody since childhood, parlayed his gift for hand magic into a nightclub gig at Grossinger's during that Catskill resort's dowager days in the late 1970s. His was a close-up act, and he made lots of new friends that way. Later, he alerted his new friends to a variety of imaginative/ary opportunities, seeding plausible-sounding investment schemes with the latest blue-sky ideas from *Popular Science.* Steam-powered cars, flywheel energy systems, underwater radio, cryonics. Woody's pitch was smooth as his magic act palaver, and he fooled almost everyone. Not my mother, though, Sarah Hoverlander née Blake, the local girl manning the front desk. She kept her keen lavender eyes on everything, including a certain paper-packing guisard long on salesmanship and short on specifics. She saw through him like scrim, but saw him also as just the sort of wild card she'd always wanted to draw. So, with the Borscht Belt unbuckling all around them, she Bonnied his Clyde and they hit the road, wafting across America wherever love and opportunity led them. Hasty nuptials preceded the birth of their only child, named (so one story goes) for the proprietary military technology* that covered the hospital cost of his parturition.

But their essential natures cast a pall across fidelity. Woody worked sweetheart scams to the point of blurring the line between razzle and romance, and Sarah, no matter how many alternatives she sampled, could never satisfy herself that she'd cut to the best card in the deck. The times didn't help: In the golden years between the Pill and AIDS, it was assumed that you'd sleep around, and neither lightly taken wedding vows nor a chubby bright toddler challenged that assumption much. Not even the tacit démarche of "don't ask, don't tell" could keep their relationship from foundering on the rocks of their mutual, and mutually earned, mistrust.

"Then I did a real stupid thing," said Woody.

"What's that?"

"I fell in love." He shook his head in self-mockery, as if that were the daftest move a man could make. "As it turns out, I was also falling apart. Gambling, dope, a few other things. Donna was my church wife. She put me on a path. For my own good, she made me purge my past."

"Made you?"

"We co-conspired." He shrugged. "What can I tell you? I thought it might work."

Radar target enhancers—"Now available for the first time to the investing public!"*

"And did it?"

"Oh, sure. Often for weeks at a time. When I'd polished off her supply of second chances, she kicked me to the curb."

"Why didn't you come home?"

"Home? What home? Your mother had died. You were better off without me. I was still a mess, you know. Not a good influence."

"So now we're back to how you did me a favor by staying away?"

"Who knows, Radar? Who can say? Frankly, I wasn't thinking about you all that much. I was lost in my own shit. Emphasis on the word *lost.* Emphasis on the word *shit.*"

"Which you got out of, eventually."

"Yeah. Honey helped. I guess you know that. Mostly I just grew up. Figured out the difference between my career and self-destructive larks."

"Larks, huh? You make it sound so breezy."

Woody eyed me beneath hooded brows. "I don't have your gift for language, son. If you don't like my choice of words, choose your own, but if that's where you're going to draw your line, I have to say, I think you're being petty."

Which, in fairness, I was. "What about later?" I asked. "Post-lark. You could've come and seen me then."

"Could I? I wonder if I'd have been welcome."

The plain honesty of the thought made us both uncomfortable; rather than open the can of worms of whether he was welcome now, we started brainstorming ways to button up Jay.

Usually on the snuke, it's best to create an identity from whole cloth. Not only does this let you build a consistent narrative, it muddies the evidence trail after the fact. Here, though, we were both known to the mark, so we'd have to build a con on the platform of our true selves and improvise outward from there. It cut off many options. Just the same, I found myself enjoying the exploration and quickly became lost in the comforting pleasure of combating a knotty problem in the company of a like mind. The more we explored various classic and handmade zazzles, the more I realized how much farther down my road my father was. Whatever scam I mentioned—Mozart's Widow, Thai Gems, Rip Deal—Woody knew it, had worked it, and could deconstruct its strengths and weaknesses in intimate detail. He was like a museum of the con.

Most of what we examined we quickly dismissed. Long cons—your pyramids and Ponzis—were just out of the question, for Wolfredian's patience couldn't be counted on to stretch that far. And no short con we could think of suited the twin ends of leading him on while sucking him in. Nevertheless, we dug into these, exploring various high-ticket versions of the Pigeon Drop and the Badger Game. When we'd scraped the bottom of that barrel and discovered nothing more than barrel bottom, we sank into a silent funk. The air beneath the ponderosas, formerly tranquil and perfumed, now took on an oppressive, foreboding quality. I got up and walked around, agitated. I'd taken it as read that once I fell into this thing, I'd be able to think my way out. Now I was not so sure.

High overhead, in the sunlit boughs of the pines, a pair of Western Tanagers flitted back and forth, snatching insects from the air and punctuating the silence with their hoarse, flat calls of *pit-er-ik, pit-er-ik*. The term "free as a bird" crossed my mind (a measure of how runaway my train of thought), accompanied by a mind's-eye action shot of Vic Mirplo happily constructing his *Albuquerque Turkey*. Could he really have it so made? True, trolling for patrons was no day at the beach, but at least his choices were his own, not constrained, as mine were. On top of everything else, he was getting good at what he did. He might really make it big. Yeah, he was definitely on that road. Hmm...

"Know what?" I told Woody, "I think we're oversolving the problem."

"How so?"

"What's Wolfredian after? What does he think he wants?"

"A giant whale," said Woody. "A big, dumb one he can fornicate out of a fortune."

"So let's do that. Let's give him a whale."

Woody shook his head. "You don't know Vegas like I do, son. It's not like in the movies, where planeloads of degenerates fly in with suitcases full of cash. Real whales are rare. Even when you find them, it takes months to build a relationship with them. Sometimes years. No way we have that long a leash."

"We don't need it. We've got Nana's Attic. Fresh meat. New on the market."

"I'm not following you."

"Really?"

"Don't dick me around, Radar." Woody stood up, pulling at his pants to air a pocket of sweat. "Just tell me what's on your mind."

So I did. I told him about Vic, how he was growing as an artist and starting to gain traction. "Suppose he got hot," I said. "So hot, so fast that he suddenly had more money than he knew what to do with."

"That could work," said Woody, thoughtfully. "Jay has a soft spot for artists."

"Really?"

Woody waved it away. "He fancies himself a collector. It's not important. Go on."

I went on. "So suppose Vic drags his newfound wealth into Vegas on the arm of the Gaia's newest casino host."

"Who? Allie?" Why would he ask that? Was he pinging me?

"Me," I said, harshly. "I told you, she's out of the picture."

"Pity," said Woody. "Some of the best hosts are pretty gals." A pause, then, "But you and Vic are friends. What if Wolfredian twigs to that?"

"That's part of the gag. Wolfredian hires me as a host, and I lure in my friend with all the fresh cash. All I have to do is fake a public record that his cash is cash, not flash."

"Can you do that?"

"I'd better can. Without the public record we'll never be able to sell Vic—excuse me, *Mirplo*—as a shooting star." Already my mind was ablaze with the fake websites and fictive press releases I'd need in order to support Mirplo's meteoric rise. I tended the blaze for a few moments, and when I next looked at Woody, he was beaming. "What?" I asked.

"Nothing," said Woody. "Just, I knew you'd think of something."

"How could you know that?"

"You're a Hoverlander, son." That sort of struck me sideways. All my life I'd been Radar Hoverlander, but I'd never been *a* Hoverlander before. It felt rather good. Like joining the Rotary. But I shrugged it off; Woody may have been fluffing me.* "So," continued Woody, "how do we leverage Mirplo into a raid on Wolfredian's mint?"

"We'll burn that bridge when we come to it," I said, in unconscious echo of Vic. "In the meantime, we buy time, because Jay sees us being good boys and running his script. So I'll set up the backstory, and you set up the mark. How does that sound?"

"That sounds just fine," said Woody.

We spent some time sketching out the details of the snuke and divvying up our responsibilities. I had to admit that it felt great to be back working on this sort of thing again.

But the great feeling didn't last.

Because when I got home, Allie was gone.

---

*Inflating my ego to cloud my judgment.

17

True Believers Sell Best

No, I mean *gone* gone. Pots and pans gone. Hangers and hairbrush gone. Gone as grunge. Gone as pay phones. Gone. I called her cell right away. I wanted to lead with "What the fuck?" but all I said was, "Allie? Honey?"

"Hello, Radar," she said, with a timbre of reserve I'd never heard before. "Is Woody with you?"

"No."

"Good. But anyhow we shouldn't talk long. We have to get used to not talking at all."

"What are you talking about?"

"That's funny," she said. "I'm gonna miss the funny." There was a wistful hitch in her voice. "Clean break, Radar. That's what we're trying to sell. You know true believers sell best."

The line went dead.

Imagine you're me, standing in the half-empty living room—half empty because she took the damn bookshelf—of your formerly cozy formerly home. You'd agreed to a mock breakup with your darling con artist girlfriend because it seemed like the smart play, the safe play. But now you're there, turning stuttering circles on shaky legs, wondering where the *mock* in the mock breakup went. "You know true believers sell best," she'd said. Was that a pep talk or a kiss-off? You don't know. Your analytical circuits are blown. In your current state of mind, you couldn't process a knock-knock joke.

Knock, knock.

Who's there?

Who's where?

You stagger to a chair and subside into it. You rub your eyes, run your fingers through your hair; you find you're massaging your scalp. Or maybe trying to hold in your brains. You cast around mentally for a paper bag to breathe into. Then, right in the middle of your panic attack, a sound cuts through the stale air. It's the soothing jingle of dog tags; someone's waking up from a nap.

She loves you! She left you the dog!

Boy ambled in. I took him down to the floor and held him for a long, long time.

"I don't know, Radar," said Vic. "Things are going pretty good for me right now. I've got orders... The Goro-Lubke Gallery wants to do a show, and they're prestigious as hell."

"Do you have enough stuff for a show?"

Vic didn't answer immediately. He seemed lost in his yogurt and cereal. Lost, really, as I was in mine as I sat across from him at the yellow Formica table in Zoe's kitchen. I could hear Zoe in the other room, singing one of Vic's songs. It was hooky, catchy, evidence upon evidence of Mirplo as a Renaissance dude.

This was the morning after the night before, a long and mostly sleepless night I'd spent alone in a big bed, pining for Allie's warmth. Boy had joined me around dawn, hopping up and sprawling out beside me, instinctively trying to fill the void. But a big, prickly mutt with dog breath and restless leg syndrome was no substitute for the woman I loved, not by orders of magnitude. I lay awake watching sunlight crawl up the adobe wall and wondered if Allie was watching the same sunrise. I didn't know where she was staying. Hell, I didn't even know if she was still in town. This was bad. Verisimilitude is one thing, but the thoroughness of her departure suggested something more fervent than mere verisimilitude. Yes, the true believer sells best, and yes, we wanted Allie on the outside for reasons both of safety and of strategy, but I couldn't help wondering, Was there a third reason as well? Had she decided that a Hoverlander (ha! now we're a clan) can never go straight and that it was therefore time for her to cut (A) her losses and (2) me loose? In other unhappy words, was our trapdoor spider plan actually her exit strategy? I didn't know, couldn't know, and had nothing to rely on but my faith in her love and the potentially deflective evidence of a dog left behind. Faith was hard for me to come by—I didn't have a lot of practice in that area. As for Boy, who knew? Maybe she'd cut him loose, too.

Vic, meanwhile, had finally gotten to the bottom of his granola. "Enough stuff?" he repeated. "Enough for a bluff, I guess. It'll have to do."

"Well, that's what I want to do, too. Run a bluff. Take your game to a higher level. Look, when you do a show, what are you saying to the world?"

"That I'm an artist."

"An artist bigger than you are, right?"

"Well, yeah, I mean, that's how you step up."

"Okay, then, so it's all self-fulfilling prophecy. And that's all I'm saying: Think big. You create a market for yourself by saying, 'Well, there should be a market for me,' yeah?"

"Yeah...," Vic allowed.

"So let me pump you up a little. Make you look bigger than you are. Then you'll go to Vegas and splash some money around. What's not to like about that?"

"I lived in Vegas, you know. Back in my poker days." I knew about those days. Vic had decided that his destiny lay in tournament poker; however, unburdened by skills, stones, or the remotest whiff of card sense, he'd quickly sailed the ship of that career onto the rocky shoals of extreme poverty. I understood that when he decamped to Los Angeles he'd left some unhappy backers behind. "Some people," said Vic, "might not remember me fondly."

"I gotta say, Vic, you flatter your past if you think the guy you once were is worth settling a score on."

Vic nodded solemnly, acknowledging the truth of this without suffering it. I had to hand it to him, he had the most straightforward ego I'd ever seen. One could go to school on it. "You're right," he said. "Not that I'm not better now."

"Inarguably," I said, and I wasn't just fluffing.

In the next room, Zoe unsuccessfully essayed to hit a high note. "What about Zoe?" asked Vic. "Can she come, too?"

"Your entourage," I said. "Your call."

"Entourage," he mused. "I'd like to have an entourage. And what the hell, I could even get something going there, artwise. I am ready to step up." He collected himself. "All right, Radar, I'll do it."

"Thanks, Vic. I appreciate it."

"Mirplo," he said.

"What?"

"Not Vic, just Mirplo."

"Oh, right. I forgot."

Mirplo. Just Mirplo. Sheesh.

I've lost myself in my work many times. If you love what you do, this can be a Zen thing, where past and future recede to a vanishing point and leave nothing but the perfect vexing, challenging, beguiling now. I'm told that golf nuts feel this way, that the buzz of golf is really how it lets you (okay, makes you) forget about everything else for the four or five (okay, six) hours you're out there. Well, the grift is my golf, and there's nothing I like better than subsuming myself in the prep and planning of a cool snadoodle. If I lost myself in this one with a rather greater sense of urgency than usual, I think I can be forgiven. I was trying to keep Allie off my mind.

First thing I did was backpredict Mirplo's arc as an artist. I built him a website using 1990s tools (hello, HoTMetaL; hello, Front Page) and filled it with bitmapped photos of the sort of jejune, self-referential artwork you'd expect of a late adolescent. Harsh, earnest self-portraits, charcoal drawings of disproportionate nudes, that sort of thing. I parked the site in a dead-letter corner of the Internet where, if Jay Googled hard enough, he'd find it. This is basic housekeeping. You don't know if the mark will do his due diligence, but you can't assume he won't. So you leave an electronic paper trail. People think the Internet makes it harder to fabricate histories, but actually it's easier. Back in the day, you needed forged documents and live testimonials—hard copy, real-world shit. Now all it takes is a Facebook page and a Wikipedia tap dance. The proof is in the pixels. In fact, I was probably going way the extra mile; when Mirplo hit town, the only thing Jay would likely check was the color of his money. But like I said, I had reasons to get wrapped up in the work.

Stepping forward through the stages of Mirplo's fictive career, I awarded him indifferent stabs at writer, performance artist, sculptor, and musician—the sort of flake's progress you'd expect from someone who took fifteen years to be an overnight sensation. I wrote a backdated grant proposal for something called the Blue/Red River Project, which, had it been funded (or existed), would have placed a flock of ceramic cerulean emus alongside a certain North Dakota watercourse. In the files of the Grand Forks Arts Council—a public database, easily hacked—you'll find a nice letter rejecting Mr. Mirplo's grant request but wishing him well in future endeavors, particularly ones in other states. I likewise inserted into the online archives of a certain literary magazine a turgid short story entitled "Dread Reckoning" about a guy who goes to Jamaica and smokes a lot of pot. And an accompanying poem about lizards. (Poor Vic, what was he thinking?) There was a scathing review of a modern dance thing he tried, and reports of vandalism against an offensive statue he erected in a park somewhere. All of these things taken together notionally led up to the Vic of today: an artist who'd passed through some pretty funky phases en route to finding his groove. You could easily imagine—well, Wolfredian could—that the guy was about to achieve critical mass, and explode.

Next came the exploding part, which entailed planting "real" news stories in legitimate online art sources. Again, not as tough as you might think, for these sources barely spell-check their incoming press releases, let alone vet them. So starting with *The Albuquerque Turkey* and extrapolating imaginatively from there, I gave Vic a sudden spike in popularity and a verifiable (though completely bogus) chain of lucrative commissions stretching into the indeterminate future. A rough calculation of accounts receivable indicated that Vic would soon be quite rich. Now all that remained was to seed a bank account with some crumbs from the California Roll, so Vic could flash appropriate cash at the casino.

Vic balked at this. "I'm not gonna piss away my money at a craps table," he said. "That's not how I roll."

"Don't worry," I told him. "The money's just for show. All your gambles will be high churn, low variance."

"Of course," repeated Vic, "high churn, low variance. Radar, what are you talking about?"

"You place lots and lots of bets—that's the churn—but only on even-money propositions. That's low variance." Of course, there are no true coin flips in a casino; the house always has its edge. If you bet, say, dead red at roulette, you give away 5.26 percent a spin, so you're bound to lose over time. But not much and not fast, and if you place enough bets, the house will note your action and start to rate your play—measure, that is, your betting size and frequency. They're much more interested in how high you play than in exactly how you play, or certainly whether you win or lose in the short run. They know they'll always grind out their cut in the end. Still, someone who bets dead red doesn't look like much of a player, so I'd worked out some mutually hedging complex bets that looked like wild gambles. They essentially canceled each other out, but with enough "action bafflegab" to give the impression of high rolling. The overall effect was rather like a grifter's roll. It seemed like a ton of risk, but really it was not.

Well, explaining this to Vic was a bit like talking to the taxman about poetry, so I drove him down the highway to Sandia, an Indian casino just north of Albuquerque, to demonstrate. There he ploughed through a Saturday night playing my system at $25 a bet. By bona fide whale standards, that's not much, but even at a quarter a throw he caught the eye of the pit boss, who invited Vic to join Sandia's players' club, which was another point of the exercise, for it contributed to the evidence trail of Vic as a gambler on the upslope of his jones. This being Sandia, arguably New Mexico's poshest casino, and therefore not such a much, it would also make plausible Vic's later desire to trade up to something more high-toned. Something like the Gaia.

Vic found the enterprise entertaining. The gambling didn't get him off—he just wasn't wired that way—but he got a big kick out of being the big shot. After so many years of cadging drinks (and everything else) from friends or strangers, he probably liked being the one throwing the party. It made him giddy. Me, I just enjoyed the simple, straightforward, comforting company of a Mirplo. For a grifter, he didn't have a devious—well, successfully devious—bone in his body. So I could relax with him, and that's something I hadn't done much of lately. Truth to tell, the stress was wearing on me. For the first time in my life, I could sort of see the benefits of a life not shot through with duplicity. Such a life would be less intense, for sure, but also less tense.

While Vic banged away at the tables, I called Woody to see how things were going on his end. He had departed a few days prior, heading back to Vegas to alert Wolfredian that I'd hooked a whale and to prospect for a way past Jay's defenses to his cash. He'd told me he thought the fact that Vic was an artist showed promise, and he wanted to pursue that angle. Well, that was the plan, but I couldn't confirm its progress, for Woody didn't answer his phone. Maybe he was still in transit across the desert, out in the wasteland where no cell towers bloom. Maybe.

We rolled back into Santa Fe after midnight, cresting a hill on the Turquoise Trail to see the low-rise lights of the Pojoaque Valley spread out before us, a man-made mirror to the big bowl of stars above.

"Know what?" said Vic. "I'm still kind of wired. You want to stop in somewhere, get a drink? My treat."

Mirplo's treat? For that alone I'd have liked to say yes, but, "I have to walk Boy. He's been cooped up all evening."

"He'll keep," said Vic. "That breed has intense bladder control."

"You don't even know what breed he is."

"Well, neither does he, but I bet he can hold it another half hour. Just one drink, Radar. There's this place you have to try."

The place I had to try turned out to be a basement dive called the Cave, a dimly lit, stone-floor den with a long, varnished burl-wood bar, tables made of cable spools, and enough wall-mounted cow skulls to make Georgia O'Keeffe come. The skulls had been drilled out and implanted with electric candles, the artificially flickery kind, so that the faces of the patrons winked in and out of shadow at odd intervals. Were it not for the fact that the crowd seemed abnormally normal—as if Santa Fe's Young Republicans had discovered the latest hipster hangout first for a change—you'd have feared an outbreak of Santeria, or possibly zombies.

Leaning against the bar while Vic ordered drinks, I noticed one citizen sitting alone at a spool table, opposite an empty chair with a big black handbag slung over its back. Dressed way too business for a Saturday night, he had the arrogant air of someone with all the answers, or at least all the ones that mattered. For his Suit Warehouse wardrobe, his bland complacency, and his smug self-absorption, I kinda felt sorry for his date.

Till she returned from the bathroom.

And it was Allie.

I think I threw up in my mouth.

18

Nuck This

A good grifter plays emotions like a good fielder plays shortstop. You stay on your toes, think ahead, and react quickly. If the moment calls for rage, you rage. If you'd appropriately be showing sorrow, then sorrow's what you show. You give the situation what the situation demands. Not your honest reaction. Not ever. You clasp emotion in the firm grip of self-interest, and you do so automatically, intuitively, like a shortstop backhanding a hot smash faster than even his conscious mind can track. So, though inwardly I felt as though I'd just swallowed a hand grenade, the only outward move I made was to crowd close to the bar and put myself in Vic's umbra, shaded from Allie's view.

"Vic," I said, not raising my voice above the level of bar chat, "how come you chose this place?"

"I don't know, you know. I heard it was cool."

"Really? Who told you?"

"What, you don't think it's cool?"

"That's not what I asked."

I glanced at Vic, who ostentatiously absorbed himself in trying to catch the barmaid's eye. "Man," he said, "who do you have to screw to get a drink around here?" He essayed a smile, which, of course, gave him away.

"You knew she was going to be here, didn't you?"

"Who, this bartender? Tell you one thing, she's not getting a nucking tip from me, no way."

"Vic…"

"By the way, did I tell you? *Nuck* is the new *fuck*. I think it's really going to catch on." He was now officially blathering, the engine of guilt driving the motor of his mouth. "It's a, whaddyacallit, a neolopism."

"Neologism?"

"That's the word. Like calling a reckless driver a pothole or asphalt instead of asshole. Sounds dirty, but it's not."

I turned to face him. Our eyes met. If I was communicating effectively, Vic would understand that I'd seen through this clumsy wall of woffle and that the future of our friendship hung in the balance of what he said next. I, in turn, could plainly read Vic's inner conflict. He didn't care about getting caught—Mirplos are shameless by nature—but what he had to say seemed to pain him so much that he didn't want to cough it up. So I pushed a little. "Vic," I said, "if you don't tell me what's going on, I'm going over to that table and tell Allie that you brought me here just for the drama of it: confrontation, inspiration for your next installation. Then, in all likelihood, Allie will kick your ass, which we both know she's one hundred percent able to do. So what's it gonna be?"

The barmaid finally came to take our order. Vic indicated the draft tap and she poured us a couple of beers. I killed the moment by glancing at Allie's table and reading her date's lips. "So I told my boss that if we wrote it as a floating note instead of a fixed one, we could yield an extra three percent. Awesome, huh? Three percent." By his words and facial expression he betrayed himself as someone who in a million years would never tire of the sound of his own voice. Allie's body language (at least what I could glean from her shoulders and the back of her head) indicated that she was enthralled. Me, I'd be making a cyanide sandwich.

Vic downed half his beer in one gulp, then said, "I saw her here the other night. I asked around. She's been here every night this week."

"With that guy?" Vic nodded. "Why did you bring me here?"

"Duh, to see them. You think you'd believe me if I just told you?"

"No," I had to admit, "probably not. So who is he?"

"I don't know. Just some schlub. Works in a real estate firm. Radar, what's up with you two? I thought she was your trapdoor spider. Is this part of that?"

"Excellent nucking question, Vic. I honestly don't know."

So what to do now? I could confront her, of course, but that seemed like a weak lead. If the con was still on, then I'd be generating unnecessary hysterical public noise. And if it was off? If Allie had genuinely shed me under the guise of seeming to do so, then what purpose would be served by a scene? The best thing, I decided, was to keep cool and scope her out. What I saw distressed me, for all her signals—how she tossed her hair; the way she covered his hand with hers—told me she was into the guy, which I couldn't understand at all, because she used to eat Norms like this for lunch. But it couldn't be an act for my benefit. She didn't even know I was here.

Vic, by way of lame distraction, called my attention to a sports highlights show on the TV over the bar. "Can you believe it?" he said. "This team creamed that other team."

I smiled despite myself. "Do you even know what they're playing?"

"Not sure," he confessed. "Lacrosse? Quoits?"

"What the hell is quoits?"

"A ring-toss game with roots in ancient Greece!" he boomed in his sportscaster voice, but I cut him off.

"Not tonight," I said softly. "No Uncle Joe." Vic nodded, and silently sipped his beer.

I pounded mine and ordered another. Worked it methodically, then started a third. I have a casual relationship with alcohol, as with a distant cousin you only ever see at family reunions. When I do drink, though, I pass through predictable stages, an arc of emotion that takes me from grim and gray through talky and glowy, then back around to morose. I'm not a bad drunk, certainly not an angry or violent one, but I mostly don't drink because it loosens my grip, and for a grifter for whom control is everything, that's anathema. I was just starting to feel the reins go slack when Vic said, "They're leaving." I hunkered down over my beer as they passed behind me en route to the door. The date said something I couldn't hear. I suppose it was a joke, because Allie responded with a lilting laugh.

I'm gonna miss the funny, she had told me. Apparently there was other funny to be had.

They departed. Vic patted me on the shoulder. "I'm sorry, man. Don't kill the messenger, okay?"

"Don't worry," I said. "The messenger lives." I drained my beer and stood to go. I could feel gloom setting in. I wanted to go home and hug my dog. Maybe he could explain where I'd gone wrong.

Just then Allie returned, calling back over her shoulder, "Be right there, I forgot my purse." Looking back at her table, I spotted her bag still slung over the back of her chair. When I brought my eyes back around—a beat slowly, and that was the beer balking—Allie was right up in my face.

"Hello, Radar," she said.

"Allie," I nodded, now realizing that she'd known I was there all along, or at least since Uncle Joe chimed in, and had forgotten her purse on purpose, just so we could have this chat.

"How'd you know where to find me?"

I scrunched my nose. "Loyal friends." She looked at Vic, who gave all his rapt attention to the TV over the bar. "And speaking of friends," I waved a beery hand toward the door, "best not keep yours waiting."

"Radar, I don't want this to be weird."

"What weird? You made a choice. I respect it."

"But do you understand it?"

"Suppose you explain it."

Allie sighed—the patented Allie sigh I remembered from so long ago, when we were just getting to know each other, and every word out of her mouth was one or another brand of bafflegab. But those days were gone, right?

Right?

"Radar," she said, "you are who you are. I thought you could be something else, but..."

"Leopards and spots?"

Her eyes showed sadness. "Yeah, looks like you were right about that."

"I don't know, was I? You're the one who said we could change. Seems to me you bailed on that kind of quick."

"It's called cutting your losses," she said. "I know you know how that works."

Again I waved vaguely toward the door. "And this?"

"Greg's a nice guy," she said. "He's okay. He tells the truth."

"Have I lied to you? Allie, tell me where I've lied."

"It's not me I'm talking about, Radar. You lie to yourself. Look, I wanted you to be something you're not, and that's my bad. But every single move you've made lately has been designed to let you hold on to the thing you can't let go."

"My father..."

"...is just an excuse. If it hadn't been him, it'd be something else."

I mulled that over. For some reason, a boozer's dumb rationalization flitted through my brain. *I never drink before sunset. It must be sunset somewhere.*

"I'm sorry, Radar," Allie continued, "I just couldn't sit around waiting for the other shoe to drop."

"Whatever," I muttered. I suppose I was an easy read, being a little drunk and all, for Allie could see me closing her out. She shook her head, disgusted, and turned to go. "Allie," I said.

"What?" she snapped, preemptively defending against an escalation of conflict.

But all I said was, "Your purse," and pointed to the big black handbag she'd neglected to collect. She went to get it, which gave me a chance to gear up for the last word. "For the record," I said as she passed back by, "if I was lying to myself, you were lying to me, too. You could've just said you wanted to split." I paused, then went too far. "Trapdoor spider, my ass."

She slapped me, hard, with the flat of her hand. At least she didn't use her purse.

I watched her walk away, mourning her. Then something shifted inside me. Alcohol-induced perhaps, but a grim resolution just the same. If a worthy woman deemed me unworthy, then, by damn, unworthy I would be. I'd grip the grift with a vengeance. You can't fight who you are, right? It's stupid to try. Love? That's a comforting distraction, but for a grifter, ultimately a fantasy. No grifter knows love; really, all through our lovey-dovey days, Allie and I were just a couple of mooks trying to mook ourselves. At least I was clear of that now. I got it: Once you walk down our road, you can't unwalk it. Allie still hoped otherwise, apparently, and I knew where it would lead, to a dull normal husband and a dull normal life. But no matter how hard she tried to bury her past in the backyard of her suburban delusion, one day it would rise up to remind her. And then she would be sad. She'd sold herself out of the game. Sold herself cheap, if you ask me. So have a nice life, Allie Quinn. Thank you for cutting me loose.

The thought crossed my mind that cutting me loose was exactly what she had in mind, and for my benefit. I dared to believe that this business with Greg was just another scene in an epic drama designed to disencumber Radar and leave him free to work his magic on the snuke. That would place me smack-dab in the hero spotlight, deeply and deviously propped up by an entire supporting cast. It makes for good drama, but here in real life, you just have to sometimes see things as they are. *Over is over, Radar, and the only hidden agendas are the ones you build in your mind.*

"Nuck this, Mirplo," I said. "Let's get out of here." We left the bar. In my mind, I was already in Vegas.

I hadn't quite figured out what to do about Boy, but when I got home, I discovered that problem to have sort of solved itself. On the tile kitchen floor (where Allie and I'd made love—ack!) I found a note written in crude block letters, like a righty writing lefty, "Sorry, man, she needs me more." And it was signed with a paw print.

Oh, Boy.

19

Martybeth

I was walking through the Gaia Casino in an outfit that did not agree with me. My shoes were too tight, too shiny, too squeaky. My tie was ridiculous—well, all ties are ridiculous, a noose around a neck—and my white-on-white custom suit with the Gaia-green silk shirt made me feel like a revival preacher or a pimp. Or an ice cream man. This sucked. And it sucked worse because when I play dress-up, I want it to be my choice, for my reasons. But this clown suit was Jay's play—one I'd tried my best to talk him out of.

That hadn't gone too well.

Rolling the clock back a few nights, we find Hoverlander and Wolfredian sitting in parked cars in the parking lot of Sunset Park, just south of McCarran Airport's glide path. A beer-league softball game is in progress nearby, the *donk* of aluminum bats on balls cutting through the background din of landing planes.

I had called Wolfredian. Told him about this genius young artist I knew who was suffering from a bad case of sudden wealth. I was surprised to hear that Woody'd not sent advance word of this, but I stumbled past that and proposed that Jay and I meet to discuss the best way to pluck this bird, code name Albuquerque Turkey. I told him I was already in town and could come to his office at the Gaia at his convenience. Instead he directed me here, to this grotty, anonymous ball field, where the Droogs were beating the snot out of Maxx's Tap. I suppose I didn't fit the profile of the sort of associates Jay greeted in his office.

Or maybe Jay was just a huge fan of the Droogs, for just then coming to bat was none other than Red Louise, the sidewheel with the sense of humor. As I eyed Jay eyeing Red, I understood that he was multitasking: having a meeting with me while watching his hot bodyguard play ball. I wondered if they were having an affair.

I also wondered where the hell Woody was, for he'd been tasked to lay pipe for this meeting, which pipe had gone manifestly unlaid. I couldn't ignore the possibility that this was Woody's own exquisite exit strategy: simply paste my picture atop his on Wolfredian's dartboard, then do the shade and fade. I preferred to think not, but who could know? It's not like Woody'd have dropped me a jackalope postcard saying, "Here's my bag of shit, thanks for holding it." Maybe he'd found another angle to pursue, which would put him off script, but at least not off the reservation. Maybe he'd met a mishap, even a premeditated one. I couldn't bring myself to contemplate that dark scenario.

Whatever I wanted of Woody, dead wasn't it.

Wolfredian got out of his car and motioned me out of mine. We slouched against our front fenders, watching Louise take her stance. She toed the dirt, bent her knees, cocked her ass. Her bat, held high and vertical behind her right shoulder, stirred the air like a swizzle stick. She looked off the first pitch, fouled off the second, and drove the third so high and deep into the night that I worried about it getting snarged in a passing jet engine. Her mirthless home run trot brought her teammates to home plate to greet her, and a wry smile to Wolfredian's face. All I could think was, *The damage she could do with a bat.*

Now Wolfredian outlined what he haughtily called his job offer. I was to join the Gaia staff as a casino host. I'd be given a salary, benefits, and a crash course in Gaia guest services. I needn't worry about finagling a casino employee's license, for Jay knew a guy in Gaming Control who could "expedite" (read: totally fabricate) my paperwork. As for my personal history—how I came to work at the Gaia and what I'd done prior—Jay left that to my own natural inventiveness.

"I don't see why I have to jump through these hoops," I said. "I already told you about…"

"The Albuquerque Turkey, yes. Is he ready to write a check?"

"Of course not."

"Of course not. We have to fluff him first. So he'll need his host. Someone he can trust. Can he trust you?"

"Like a brother."

"How about me? Can I trust you?"

"Like my other brother." I saw a segue and slid through it. "Speaking of trust and family relations," I said, "you've been burned by my old man before. Aren't you worried about getting singed again?"

He looked at me. I saw age in his eyes. "I was a kid when he duped me," said Wolfredian. "It won't happen again. Meanwhile, this whale of yours—what did you say his name was? Marlowe?"

"Mirplo."

"Is he any good?"

"Good?"

"As an artist. What do you think of his stuff?"

I answered truthfully, "Getting better every day."

Jay nodded, processing this through some filter I couldn't guess. "Okay," he said, "then let's get him sorted. Bring him to town, show him a good time. But if he's going to gamble in my casino, he's going to be part of my system. Which means *you're* going to be part of my system."

Which led to me crossing the Gaia gaming floor in ice-cream-man mufti, fingering my new photo ID and listening to my shoes squeak. I'd spent all morning in human resources, where I'd (creatively) filled in some personnel forms and selected my choice of health plan. Next came a long trek through the casino's back-of-house, with introductions to my locker, this costume, and a time clock. *Time clock!* I was an employee. A working stiff at last. Against all odds, I'd actually landed a job. I wondered what Allie would think of me now. (Then tried not to think of her now.)

I'd been instructed to report for orientation outside Grēēn, one of the Gaia's three nightclubs. Arriving there early, I studied the club's posted menu of infused waters, energy cocktails, overwrought appetizers, and its signature vodka, Byrd Station, chilled with hundred-thousand-year-old core ice from Antarctica. As I switched my cell phone to vibrate, I mulled the irony of a supposedly eco-friendly casino cooling grain alcohol with heirloom ice.

A lilting voice behind me said, "Mr. Hoverlander?"

I turned and saw a short young woman with a cascade of yellow curls framing her apple cheeks, button nose, and candy lips. Her outfit, the femme version of the Gaia host uniform, strained equally at the bustline of her white blouse and the waistline of her green skirt. Zaftig, that was the word for her; cushiony. The kind of girl who made you want to put your head in her lap and listen for ocean sounds. She extended a hand and smiled, revealing deep dimples and a set of teeth so chemically whitened they practically glowed. "I'm Martybeth Crandall," she said in a voice with the trebly brightness of a talking doll. "Welcome to the Gaia. Mr. Wolfredian tells me you're bringing us a sizable new player."

"Well, I couldn't expect to get this job on my merits, could I?"

This admission, an odd version of the truth, seemed to confound Martybeth, and she tussled with it for a moment before dismissing it and moving on. "Radar," she said. "Well, that's an unusual name. Is it a family name?"

"Yes, I come from a long line of airborne threat detectors."

She looked at me blankly while the joke soaked in, then emitted a tinkly laugh, like falling beads of shatterproof glass. "You're a joker," she said, then repeated to no one in particular, "This one's a joker. Come on, joker, let me show you around."

Martybeth led me on a quick spin through the Gaia's main casino, a grand rotunda filled with roulette wheels, blackjack and craps tables, and bank after bank after bank of every casino's workhorse, the slot machine.

"You won't spend much time here," said Martybeth. "Players at this level don't have hosts. They're all rated and comped through their club cards." She gave me a quick rundown of Club Gaia's point system: For every dollar you gambled, you got ten points. Accrue enough points, you earned a sandwich or a hat. This was beneficence, Gaia style.

We traipsed on, eventually arriving at a discreet door with the word EXCLUSIF emblazoned in raised brass letters across its ebony surface. Martybeth smiled at the doorman there and said brightly, "Good morning, Bob. How's Lawrence?"

"Fine, Ms. Crandall," said Bob as he opened the door.

"Over the flu?"

"Yes, ma'am."

"Well, give him my love. He's a sweetheart." We walked past Bob and plunged into the lounge. "Lawrence is his boyfriend," said Martybeth. "He's cheating on Bob, of course, but I don't have the heart to tell him." This was quite indiscreet to share with a virtual stranger. Poor impulse control. I made a mental note.

The club revealed itself to be an artful throwback, like cocktail hour in the fifties. Leather banquettes faced big windows looking out over a lush botanical garden. Behind the bar stood a tuxedoed barman, honing his invisibility. A single patron sat at a small round table. He was a middle-aged man in a velour tracksuit, nursing a snifter of something and fiddling with a Geoid. Its functionality must have eluded him, for his frustration flowed as he impatiently beckoned Martybeth over. She threw a genial arm around his shoulder and let her fingers dance over the surface of the tablet. In a moment he was smiling and, I noticed, grabbing her ass.

I studied the back bar. The top shelf contained such legendary spirits as Johnnie Walker Blue, Nouvelle-Orléans absinthe, Nun's Tears gin, and several bottles of brandy and cognac whose combined age could be measured in millennia.

There was no second shelf.

Martybeth rejoined me. We crossed to the far side of the lounge and stood looking out at the gardens. "That's Mr. Jarvis," she said. "He's one of my regulars. Never can remember how to transfer more money into his player's account." She leaned in and whispered conspiratorially, "The guy's nose is completely open. Easy as the Geoid makes wire transfers, he's going to give us everything he's got before he's done. Plus, he had me lift his stop-loss."

"What's a stop-loss?" Which I knew, but Martybeth seemed to want to show off, so I let her.

"The limit a gambler imposes on himself. 'Don't let me lose any more than that,' they say. Then they lift their own stop-loss and, boom, it's party time." She hooked a thumb at Jarvis. "His stop-loss is five hundred grand a day."

"Should you be sharing that information with me?"

She squeezed my upper arm a tad too intimately. "There's no secrets here, buddy boy. You're one of us now." Dropping her hand to my elbow, she steered me across the lounge to a dark alcove. "Let's go see the rooms." Inside the alcove was an elevator that opened to the swipe of her card key. "This goes straight to the high-roller suites," she said. "Some of our guests don't like coming in through the front door. They don't want to be seen entering a bar."

"Mormons?" I asked.

"Them, sure. Plus Muslims, movie stars, and alcoholics." As we entered the elevator, Martybeth rattled off a list of famous names, delighting in her naughty indiscretions. A short stab of acceleration later, we were on the top floor.

The suite she showed me was huge and, this being the Gaia, equipped with next-generation everything, including floor-to-ceiling windows that polarized on command or automatically at first light, and a flat-panel TV commanding one full wall of the living room. This, I learned, was independently interfaced with the suite's own satellite dish, in addition to a server loaded with any TV show, archived sports event, or film you could think of, plus hundreds you'd rather not think of unless you're alone or in the company of a like-minded pal.

The sound system was similarly over the top, with a digitized library of over ten thousand titles, and smart speakers that followed you from room to room (including each of four bathrooms) and could mute or damp themselves, should you so choose, at the sound of a telephone or conversation. Apart from three bedrooms, the suite had a pool table, an office equipped with an onyx desk and matching conference table, and six custom leather Think and Leap chairs from Steelcase. On the table lay another Geoid, this one with a distinctive gold shell—the guests' to keep, said Martybeth, so they didn't have to worry about leaving any compromising data behind.

Chefs stood by 24/7, not down in the basement, in the factory-like room service larders—those were for the hoi polloi—but in a private kitchen that serviced only suites like these. There was no menu: if you could name it, they could fix it, from ostrich steak or truffle soup to Black Forest gâteau, made from scratch, on demand, with freshly ground cinnamon and, by damn, authentic Irish butter. Live Maine lobster was flown in fresh every day—and thrown out if no one chose it. Ounce for ounce, it was the most expensive food in the world, but you'd never be charged a penny for it, so long as you kept your downstairs action high.

Certain other delicacies might require a quiet word in the ear of your host. Chronic from Holland. Peruvian blow. Off-label muscle relaxants. Or the latest designer psychedelics. Of course, drugs aren't for everyone. How about a lady? A man? A lady and a man? They'll perform with you, on you, or for you, depending on your taste. And don't feel at all self-conscious, please, about voicing these... ah... exotic requests. Your host is trained to provide and not to judge. You'll find nothing but approval here, no matter how deep into depravity you dive. You are our guest. We want you to feel at home.

All of which Martybeth explained to me while declaring herself a poster child for the concept. “Like this one time,” she said, “with this diva. I probably shouldn’t mention her name.” But she did. “She needed someone to pee on her. At three in the morning! Where do you find someone to do that? Craigslist?”

I couldn’t help asking, “So what did you do?”

“I managed. A good host has her resources.” She shot me a wink and I got the shivery feeling that her involvement had been, as it were, hands on. “She went off very huge. Downstairs in the casino, I mean. I got a nice bonus.” Then she fixed me in the gaze of her pale eyes. “Do you want to know the key to success in this job, Radar?”

“Sure.” I shrugged.

“You can only go so far with amenities. I mean, of course you nail the front-row-center seats or arrange a private meet-and-greet with the big boxer or whatever. But any host can do that. They build up a tolerance for luxury, these whales. They start wondering, ‘Isn’t there anything better than first class?’ ”

“And is there?”

“Only one thing,” said Martybeth. “Personal service. You go the extra mile. Give me a second, I’ll show you what I mean.” Her ample ass followed her into the master suite where, from behind closed doors she called out, “Mr. Wolfredian thinks quite highly of you, you know. He says you’re a *macher.*”

“A what, now?” I went to the window and looked down at the Strip, thirty stories below. The cars looked like crumbs. Tiny, moving crumbs. I wondered how many of them were Sharps.

“*Macher.* A rainmaker. Someone who can land the big whales.”

“I don’t know about that,” I demurred.

“Well, he does,” she called. “So that means I do. Which means that you’re my boy. Okay, come on in.”

I went on in. Behind opaque windows, the big bedroom was dim as dusk. Soft music played. Martybeth had turned down the bed, and now sprawled across it like an overstuffed cat, her staunch bra and panties struggling heroically to stem the tide of her pulchritude. I may have said something. Probably not. Probably I just gawked.

"These sheets," she said, patting them with the flat of her hand, "are thousand-count, long-yarn Egyptian cotton. Each set costs five hundred dollars. And you know what I think?"

She didn't wait for me to answer. "I think we should mess 'em up."

20

5150

There's this thing in my experience called girl logic: a woman's understanding that, in most circumstances, she can have what she wants, when she wants it, just because she wants it, merely by declaring *that* she wants it. It carries some weight, does girl logic. For evidence, just consider the phrase *get lucky* or ask yourself who buys whom drinks in bars.

Or just consider this moment here. Were our positions reversed, with me in my briefs launching this blatant coworker come-on, sexual harassment in the workplace would barely begin to describe the outrage. As things now stand (as Martybeth now stands unsnapping her bra and unleashing her formidable rack), it looks like a moment of classic male fantasy. "Dear *Penthouse,* I never thought this sort of thing would ever happen to me. . . ." Even married men are expected to stand to attention here, their marital vows wilting in the face of a tasty tryst. For someone in my ambiguous situation, it should be a no-brainer, right? Sexy woman say jump, horny man say how high.

But for someone in my ambiguous situation, there are several problems, not the least of which is, hey, I'm really attracted to this chick. I wouldn't have figured her for my type, for I generally don't do Rubenesque, but one look at Martybeth and you know *she* knows she's gonna be a great, sweaty, fleshy, frisky lay. Still, let's not neglect the strategic implications, for what looks like a spontaneous roll in luxury hay is shot through with agenda. Has Wolfredian put her up to this, to see if I can pass a wuss test? Or is this her idea of a strategic alliance with the new kid in town, or just breaking him in on thousand-count sheets? It could be a muscle play: To seduce a man is often to put him in your pocket, in the face of which seduction, the only power a man has is the power to say no. This power is generally well underutilized.

My body, meanwhile, was casting a vote of its own, a vote Martybeth noted and ratified by subtracting the distance between us, and unself-consciously cupping my junk.

I felt a tingling in my pants.

Ah, that was an incoming call. I slithered a hand into the narrow space between us and withdrew my phone from my front pocket. Martybeth craned her neck to whisper hotly in my ear, "Don't answer it."

"I have to," I said. "It might be..." Well, I had no idea who it might be. I half hoped it was Allie, discomfiting though it would be to be caught with this hand on my cookie jar. I glanced at the caller ID.

It was Woody!

Only...it wasn't. As I answered the phone, I heard a woman with a South Asian lilt to her voice say, "Could I please speak to Mr. Hooverlander?"

"I'm Mr. Hoverlander," I said, correcting her on the fly.

"Sir, my name is Dr. Ablasa. I wonder would you happen to know a..." I could hear the flutter of paper, as of pages being turned. "Schyler Colfax?" She butchered that handle, too, pronouncing it *shyler* instead of *skylar.* I knew the name, but as it belonged to a man more than a century dead, I doubted that's the one she meant. I also understood that just as my taste in aliases ran to foreign iterations of *no smoking*, Woody's apparently ran to obscure U.S. vice presidents.

"This Colfax person," I said. "How would he know me?"

"Well, your number was in his phone. Would you please look at his picture, sir? I'm sending it to you now." A moment later, Woody's photo appeared on the tiny screen of my cell phone. He looked distracted, absent, damn near feral. "He says you're his son. Is that true?"

"Yes."

"Great. That's great," said the doctor. "Sir, are you in Las Vegas?"

"Uh-huh."

"Your father has been giving us a rather confusing story of his circumstances. Would it be possible for you to come here, sir, to the Blue Hills Center?"

"Blue Hills Center, huh? Okay, text me the address." I looked at Martybeth and essayed a sheepish smile of What can I do? "Medical emergency," I said.

"So it would seem," she said, sullenly repacking her breasts.

"I can't help it. I have to go."

"There's still more to the tour. I haven't shown you everything."

Nor would she. The moment had broken. There would be neither hanky nor panky between the thousand-count sheets today.

On the drive to Blue Hills, I called Vic and had him do a Google hop on the facility. It turned out to be a treatment and recovery clinic, mostly for teens with depression or adults with drug problems. I couldn't imagine how Woody'd ended up there until Vic said, "It's a 5150 joint."

"Ah," I said, "now that makes sense."

A 5150 is the California Welfare and Institutions code under which a person can be held on a seventy-two-hour psychiatric watch. By association, a 5150 joint is a bedlam sort of place; a loony bin. You could call a bar or a party a 5150, or even your own home on a bad day. I wondered if Woody had abruptly and completely unspooled. It made my heart ache, for getting locked up on a 5150, or whatever it's called in Nevada, was the sort of big trouble I wouldn't wish on anyone, even my problematic old man.

But when I ran this sympathetic scenario past Vic, he just laughed, then bellowed in Uncle Joe's voice, "The chump is in the how-oose!"

"What do you mean?"

"It's a Slurpee," he said. "How could it not be?" Slurpee was grifter cant for a fake fit or seizure one throws to deter an attack or advance a scheme.* It's a useful trick, and one no doubt to be found in Woody's bag of same. Of course, it would have to be an extreme Slurpee to result in a 5150, and what could have eventuated that need? Well, I'd know soon enough, for I'd reached the southern Las Vegas suburb of Anthem, and the Blue Hills Center appeared in the middle distance, sandwiched between a golf course and the dusty cobalt mounds that, I suppose, gave the center its name. It seemed like a pretty place, quiet and placid by Vegas standards. Not a bad spot to stage a recovery. Or a staged recovery.

"We'll see," I said. "Meantime, how's your planning going?"

"Awesome," he said, and stepped out his scheme for taking Vegas by storm.

"Sounds ambitious," I said when he finished. "Are you sure you can handle it? You could scale it back some and still—"

"It's handled, Radar. Don't worry." The confidence in his voice shook me, but I shook it off. We quickly reviewed our respective task lists, and then I let him go.

I was just driving onto the grounds of Blue Hills when a big black Song Segue shot past me going the other way, spewing a blue cloud of imperfectly combusted hydrocarbons. The Segue was the largest SUV in the Song product line, a favorite, in the armored variant at least, of tinhorn dictators and drug kingpins worldwide. This one was an overpowered beast with compression struts and blackout windows, and it damn near put me off the road as it barreled by. I aired my objection with a muttered, "Asphalt," but the Segue was already well past me, hurtling back toward town. It amused me to speculate who might be bundled in back. Some rock star with a blow problem, or a Strip

*So called, I'm told, for being conducted in front of the Slurpee machine at your local 7-Eleven while your compatriot merrily shoplifts through the diversion.

headliner desperately trying to hold his shit together between shows. Then I mentally replayed my glimpse of the driver. Did I see a flash of red behind the wheel?

I suddenly had a sick feeling in my stomach.

Five minutes later, my foreboding bore out when Dr. Ablasa, a studious young Bangladeshi in a lab coat pantsuit, greeted me in her office with the perplexing news, "Your father just left with you."

"I'm pretty sure he didn't," I said.

"No, I mean not you, obviously, but someone claiming to be you."

"You didn't ask for ID?"

"Well, you were expected."

So I was. But who knew that? Recalling my phone conversation with Dr. Ablasa, I realized that I'd named Blue Hills in front of Martybeth. Whom had she told, and why?

"Mr. Hooverlander..."

"It's Hoverlander," I said, with some exasperation.

"I'm terribly sorry, sir, but I'm sure you can understand—"

"Look, let's not worry about that now," I said. "Why don't you tell me how he came to be here?"

"Well, that information is confidential. From a legal standpoint—"

"From a legal standpoint"—I let my voice go cold and hard—"you just turned my father over to somebody who wasn't me. I'm thinking confidentiality might not be your key issue right now." I suppose she agreed, because she opened a folder on her desk and studied its contents.

"Do you want to read it?" she asked.

"Summarize," I said.

Woody had arrived at the facility two nights prior, courtesy of Metro PD. According to the cops who handed him off, he'd made a scene in a pizza restaurant, a scene of the indecently exposive sort. As a result, he'd been apprehended, questioned, determined to be "a threat to himself or others" and dumped here, per Blue Hills' contract with Clark County. Upon intake, he'd presented as troubled, jumpy, disoriented, and, as his interview proceeded, increasingly hostile. The intake doc postulated that he had Pick's disease, but as this cannot be definitively determined short of autopsy tests on the brain, a conclusive diagnosis would have to wait. He certainly showed the symptoms, including memory loss, impaired speech, impaired motion, apathy, antipathy, and abrupt mood swings. But there was nothing on that list a competent grifter couldn't fake.

"Did he get better during his stay?" I asked.

"Well, it was only two days."

"Granted," I said. "But did he improve?"

Dr. Ablasa cast her mind back over the previous forty-eight hours. "He did seem more relaxed," she conceded. "Though that may be a function of reduced stimulation. We pride ourselves on our tranquil environs."

"I'm sure you do," I said. "I'm sure it's all bubble-gum trees and rainbows out here. But why did it take you two days to call me?"

"We, ah, we misplaced his cell phone."

"I see. And when you told him I was coming for him?"

"He brightened considerably. I think he's quite fond of you."

"Was he still happy when the fake me showed up?"

She let her head drop. "No. No, he... well, he became agitated."

"I would, too, if I were being shanghaied." Dr. Ablasa started to bluster a protest, but I put up my hand to belay her. "Never mind," I said. "Just tell me about the guy who took him. What did he look like?"

Now the doc looked truly grim, and the single word she uttered, "Nondescript," rang so pathetically false that I actually felt bad for her.

"You didn't see him, did you?"

"I was busy back here," she said. "The front desk handled your father's release."

"Then let's talk to the front desk."

But by the time we got out there, the incipient shitstorm had sent everyone running for cover, so that the only person remaining at reception was a skinny Honduran orderly who kept saying, *"No inglés, no inglés."* I queried him in Spanish, and he surrendered a terse description—*hombros grandes, sin cuello*—then fled through security doors labeled STAFF ONLY.

Big shoulders, no neck. Could that be anything but one of Wolfredian's sidewheels? Not with a redhead in the driver's seat. They'd snatched Woody right out of his self-contrived protective custody.

And I'd told them where to find him.

Shit.

I was out the door and halfway down the front steps when Dr. Ablasa came running after me to give me Woody's cell phone. I asked her why she hadn't given it to Woody's "real" son, but she just gave me this pained look, like *Please don't sue us too bad.* I let it go. Right now a rehab center's free-range incompetence was the least of my worries. The most of my worries was Wolfredian's decision to escalate things from business arrangement to bag job. The other night he'd been content to let me bring him a whale and help him render it. What had changed?

I sat in my car awhile, ruminating. What if my online evidence hadn't held up? Maybe Jay'd made Mirplo as a fabricat, and this was his ungentle way of saying so. But what good did that do him? If Mirplo's not the real deal, then I'm empty-handed, and snatching Woody is pointless. More likely it was the other way around. He bought Mirplo's bona fides but didn't trust that I'd make good. We Hoverlanders were demonstrably no Boy Scouts, so you could now view Woody as a lien against delivery. Or maybe Wolfredian was just jacking up the pressure on general principle. Con artists do this all the time. It's called rushing the mark, and it makes people act rashly.

Woody's phone rang, and I jumped at the sound, an odd, flat, *blooting* ringtone. I glanced at the caller ID.

Allie.

The phone kept going *bloot, bloot.*

I couldn't bring myself to answer.

21

Bloot

Bloot!

When I was five or six, Woody took me to a carnival. I spent an instructive hour on the midway as he explained how the different games were gaffed, and how the carny barkers preyed on emotions of greed, pride, arrogance, or fear to separate the rubes from their rubles. Later, my lesson complete, he let me go on the Gravitron, one of those centrifugal force rides where you spin around and around in a circle real fast and then the floor drops out. That's how I felt when I saw Allie's name on Woody's caller ID. I'd been going around in circles, and now the floor'd dropped out.

Bloot!

Allie was calling Woody? What could it mean? The obvious explanation spoke to me in a cowboy voice—*"Them two's in cahoots!"*—but my poor addled brain couldn't accept that, and correspondingly grasped at a series of ridiculous straws. Like, maybe she hit a wrong speed dial, though why would she have him on speed dial or even have his number at all? Okay, then, she got his number from Mirplo, and she's calling Woody to reach me because I'm not answering my phone. Sure, fine, except that my phone's right here, forlornly unrung. Then how about this: Allie surrendered her phone number when she broke up with me (so I couldn't phone-stalk her, right?) and whoever got it next, *they're* the ones who dialed by mistake. Yeah, that's plausible. Right up there with "phone snatched by aliens to study our primitive technology." Plus, her *name* came up, not her number. That means her number's been stored in his phone. Why? And for how long?

Face facts, cowboy. Them two's in cahoots, and pro'ly done bin from the git-go.

Bloot!

In a split instant I retraced everything that had passed between Allie and me about Woody. There were inconsistencies, I had to admit. At first she'd wanted me to build a filial bridge, then she wanted me to cut him loose. Next we pretended to break up, but then we broke up for real. Whose idea had it been for Allie to go trapdoor spider? Hers, yes? So now I'm thinking maybe she was trapdooring for the other side.

Bloot!

But why would she do that? For that matter, how? How would she have hooked up with Woody in the first place? Intercepted one of his jackalope postcards and reached out to him with a scheme to squeeze off my half of the California Roll? Had that been her goal all along? I thought she loved me. Maybe she just loved the money, and it offended her deep-rooted grifter's sensibilities that she didn't have the whole roll. All that talk about leopards and spots, was it all just bafflegab in the end?

Bloot!

Okay, what was I going to do about this phone call? Let it go to voice mail? Maybe she'd leave a message, something incriminating or enlightening. But what if she didn't? *Nuck it!* I thought, channeling Vic. *I want to know what's what.*

Bloot!

I flipped open the phone and emitted a guttural grunt.

"Woody? Is that you? It's Allie." So much for *snatched by aliens.* "Woody, are you there?"

I thought I might keep mum, give her a chance to give something away, but I found I couldn't do it. It was Allie. I couldn't not talk to her any more than I could not breathe.

"It's not Woody," I said.

"Radar? Oh, my God." The line went dead.

Hmm, that didn't work so well. Now what?

Bloot!

It was Allie again. I answered again.

"Radar, it's very important that I speak to your father."

"Why?"

"It just is. Please put him on."

"Interesting choice of words, sunshine. Who's putting who on? Who was putting who on from the jump?"

"Radar, *please* let me talk to Woody."

"He's not here."

"Not there? It's his phone."

"Uh-huh. And he and his phone have become separated."

"Separated how?"

"One of them got hijacked."

"Oh, shit."

I read concern in her voice, though not shock, as if Woody being snatched was dismaying but not exactly headline news. That's what I read, but it wasn't like I could trust any of my reads anymore. Hell, that could have been Allie in a red wig behind the wheel of the Segue. Anything was possible now.

Allie, meanwhile, had lapsed into the contemplative silence of processing and evaluating new data. After a moment of this, she said, "Radar, I'm going to hang up. Star-69 me. I'll let the call go to voice mail. Enter my code"—she rattled off some numbers—"and listen to the saved calls."

The line went dead again. I star-69'd her. When her outgoing message kicked in, I punched in her code, and a mechanical female voice said, "You have *no* unheard messages and *four* saved messages. Press 1 to replay saved messages. Press 2 for other options."

I pressed 1, and heard Woody's twice telephone-filtered voice say, "Hey, it's me. A large problem just pulled up outside my place. I'm gonna try to beat it out the back door, but if I don't succeed, that'll mean Jay's holding an ace, so be aware." I heard the distant sound of pounding on a door, then the call ended.

"Second saved message," said the voice-mail gal.

Against a background of street sounds and wind, I heard Woody say, "Me again. I got halfway away, but they're following me. Okay, I see some stores up ahead. I'm gonna try to get arrested." I could hear tension in his voice, but not panic. He seemed, on some level, to be enjoying himself. Well, he would. He's a grifter. We live for this shit.

"Third saved message."

"Sir," I heard a stranger's muffled voice say, "please take your hands out of your pockets."

"What?" said Woody, muffled at first, but then suddenly clearer. "It's not a gun. See? It's just a cell phone."

"Now if you'll just calm down, I'm sure we—"

"I don't have any concealed weapons. I don't have any concealed anything!"

"Sir, please don't remove your—"

I heard a clunk and the line went dead. Apparently he'd dropped his phone along with his pants.

"Fourth saved message."

There was a preamble of ambient noise, including some indistinct radio chatter. Then I heard Woody, muffled again, saying, "Look, you have to believe me, I was faking back there. I'm not a head case. Really, I'm not."

A male voice, young, but full of authority, said, "Just relax, sir. We're gonna take you someplace where they can look after you. Get you the help you need."

"I don't need help! I told you, I was faking. Some guys were after me, so I—"

"Got naked in a pizza joint? That seems like a strange response."

"I had to get away!"

A second voice said, "And I have to get laid, but try telling my wife."

After a little more fruitless back-and-forth, the line went dead.

"You have *no* unheard messages. Press 1 to replay saved messages. Press 2 for other options."

Other options. Well, what were my options? Leave a message? Tell Allie how hurt and angry I was? Ask if she'd been off disporting with Real Estate Greg when these calls came in? There didn't seem to be much point to that. Okay, then maybe I'd take the high road and just tell her I loved her. Again, not much point. Sometimes the truth is just the most useless card in your deck. I tried to imagine a scenario where her and Woody's alliance wasn't anything but a betrayal, but if it was out there, it escaped me. It crossed my mind to wonder if Real Estate Greg wasn't a beard of some kind, and the true object of Allie's affection was a certain vintage model Hoverlander. Could she and Woody be having an affair? The idea was so dismaying that I had to dismiss it. Otherwise my head would explode.

I ended the call and stared at the black clamshell phone for a long, bleak stretch of time. Eventually I came to myself and realized that I was still sitting in the parking lot of the Blue Hills Treatment Center. People probably sat in their cars here all the time, snorking up their last line or popping their last pill before checking themselves in. I felt like checking myself in. I was sure I could use treatment for something.

But the fact remained that Woody had been glommed. However those two had worked me, it didn't feel right just to walk away. I'd see this thing through. Save my father's ass. Then kick it. That was my plan.

It was a long, slow ride back to the Gaia. I felt all alone in the world.

My mind wandered to Martybeth in her underwear. The thought caused me a scrotal tickle, and then a shudder. Though Allie had pretty clearly betrayed me, I wasn't prepared to betray her back.

Yet, Martybeth and her underwear...

At last I had a useful idea.

I phoned Vic. After several rings, Zoe answered. "Thank you for calling MirploCo," she said in a scripted voice. "How may I direct your call?"

"Hi, Zoe, it's Radar. Let me talk to Vic."

"I'm sorry," she said, still on script, "there's no one here named Vic."

This is crazy, I thought. *Allie reappears and suddenly Vic goes AWOL? What's going on?* Then I realized that this problem was purely semantic. "I mean Mirplo," I said. "Let me speak to Mirplo."

"If this is regarding a commission," Zoe continued, on script, "Mirplo is now taking orders for thirty-six-month delivery. If this is about an existing commission—"

"Zoe, it's me, Radar. Let me talk to Mirplo."

Zoe processed this for a long, silent second and then said, "One moment, please; I'll see if he's available."

After a pause, Vic came on the line. "This is Mirplo."

"It's Radar." I filled him in on the latest developments and said, "I'm accelerating the timetable. How soon can you get to Vegas?"

"I don't know, Radar. Right now I'm pimping out the ultralight."

"Vic, this is important."

"And the ultralight isn't? This isn't just about you, you know. It's also about me. My statement."

"Your statement," I repeated flatly.

"Do you begrudge me, Radar? I don't see you as a begrudger."

"I don't begrudge, Vic. I'm not a"—I stumbled over the word—"a begrudger. I just need your help, that's all."

"And don't worry, buddy, you'll get it. Plane's almost done anyhow. It's a dragonfly."

"What's that, the brand?"

"Nah, the motif. It represents—" He cut himself off. "Why spoil it? You'll see soon enough."

We hung up. I jammed the phone back in my pocket and rocketed down the highway toward town. I had to make two quick stops, then get back to the Gaia and talk to Martybeth again.

I suddenly saw her underwear in a whole new light.

22

Special Agent Ysmygu

I went to a business center in a strip mall and spent a productive hour with a computer, color printer, and sheets of plastic laminate. A nearby pawnshop yielded another necessary hunk of verisimilitude, and I returned with these to the Gaia in high spirits—higher than they'd been in quite some time. Granted, Woody was on ice, Allie was past participle, and Mirplo was a shaky (though increasingly arrogant) platform upon which to build a grift, but I was making moves again—snuke moves—and that was like putting on a comfortable old shirt. I felt within myself the same undercurrent of glee I'd heard in Woody's voice on the phone: This shit is dangerous and uncertain, but on some level just fun. I wasn't fooling myself completely, of course. I knew that somewhere deep inside lurked a serious heartache I'd have to address eventually. For the moment, though, I muted it with moves. My imagination was flowing, a cool mental lava that eradicated much in its path.

The perks of a Gaia host's job included a parking space in the employee garage and a room in the old, unimproved part of the hotel. I landed the Swing and thought about going to my room to change but instead went straight to the casino floor, where I found a house phone and had Martybeth paged. When she came on the line, she reacted to my voice about as you'd expect, with a proud cloud of "busier-than-thou" cushioning her hurt. But I'd figured Martybeth out. She was wired to her sexuality. In her mind, she scored points with her body, and I figured her likely to give it a second chance. It's what people do when they're hooked on validation. So I apologized for running out on her, thereby implicitly erasing the stigma of rejection. Then I asked if we could complete the tour, which I knew she'd interpret as "pick up where we left off." She surrendered her reproof immediately, confirming my impression of her as a slave to approval, someone who put ego above everything. She said she was in Aurum, the casino's VIP gaming salon, and told me to come to her there.

Aurum* occupied a giant metal pod mounted on eight steel struts that lifted it high off the gaming floor. Its mirrored surfaces and neon trim gave it the spooky look of a UFO, but the design served its purpose of isolating the salon from the main casino's noise and hubbub, the constant clang of slots, the periodic hoot or whoop of gamblers scoring big with cards or dice, and the undertow lilt of cocktail waitresses crooning, "House'll buy you a drink?" You entered Aurum by climbing a set of cut-quartz steps or taking a short-throw glass elevator. Then, under the frosty gaze of face control, you passed through a polished metal ring (and embedded metal detector) and followed a long, corkscrew corridor, so that by the time you reached the heart of the sanctum, you were physically, acoustically, and psychically separated from the penny public and could enjoy your high-roller lifestyle in appropriate privacy and luxury.

The room held just six tables, two blackjack and one each of roulette, craps, baccarat, and pai gow, but these six tables yielded, on average, almost 10 percent of the Gaia's take. In addition to the gaming tables, there was a conversation pit equipped with marble-top tables and creamy leather couches. Martybeth sat on one of these, chubby legs crossed, showing plenty of thigh and chatting quietly with an ancient Asian millionaire and his young escort. I could read Martybeth's lips as she said, "Don't be silly, Dr. Wu. It's the casino's pleasure. *My* pleasure.

---

*Latin for *gold,* which is weird, because Gaia is Greek for *earth,* and that seems linguistically inconsistent to me, but whatever. I'm not the marketing director around here.

Enjoy your evening." Then she handed him what seemed to be tickets to a show; however, she fumbled the pass, so that I caught a glimpse of a tiny glassine bindle. The escort saw it too, and her nostrils flared.

Martybeth noticed me and disengaged herself from her guests. She crossed to meet me, tugging down her skirt and tucking her blouse tighter against her frame. "I'm glad you came back," she cooed. "I'd hate not to finish my job."

Within the hour, I'd seen all the confidential card rooms, unmarked restaurants, hidden spas, and private lounges that served the Gaia's top-tier guests. I'd seen the exclusive cashier's cage they used, with a safe-deposit room more lavish than five-star hotels. I'd visited the private bell service, concierge desk, and access corridors. And I'd seen Antibes, the Gaia's award-winning topless swimming pool. Did Martybeth measure her roomy self negatively against the taut bodies of all those professionals and avid amateurs? If so, she didn't let on. Perhaps she thought the sight of such plastic figurines in G-strings would inflame my desire. They seemed to inflame hers; she stayed close, and breasted me from time to time, signaling like crazy. Clearly she was at the tipping point.

Time for a nudge.

"That suite we visited before," I said. "Any chance I could get a second look?"

"Not now," said Martybeth. "They're shampooing the rugs."

"Shame," I said, coloring my voice with disappointment and thwarted intent.

"Don't worry, honey," she said, laying her hand on my arm. "This hotel has *lots* of rooms."

Ten minutes later, we're making small talk in a room Martybeth has commandeered. It's no high-roller suite, but plenty adequate for the party we have planned. And there we are, sitting on the edge of a king-size bed. Martybeth fiddles with the buttons of her blouse. As she brazenly pops one open, I reach into my pants...

...and pull out a badge.

By all rights, the fake Jake gag shouldn't ever work. I mean, it's so transparent a play. But if you use it right—a swift strike against a soft target—you can sell the bluff long enough to get what you're after. Martybeth had established herself as a soft target, short on discretion and long on need. Her proximity to Wolfredian (close enough to drop a dime about Woody) implied that she might be long on information, too, so I blitzed her with Special Agent Dim Ysmygu of the thoroughly fictive Nevada Bureau of Gaming Investigation.

The badge, as badges will, stopped her cold. Though naught but a classic generic that I'd picked up at the pawnshop, it engendered the deer-in-headlights reaction that most people have. I handed her my identification card, fruit of my labor at the business center, pure baffle-gab but convincing enough, and laminated, which carries a surprising amount of clout. She stumbled over the name on my paperwork—as she was intended to, for in situations like this, an improbable-to-impossible name rings truer than a common one. John Doe sounds like, well, a John Doe, but who in their right mind settles on Dim Ysmygu as an alias? Its sheer outrageousness lends cred to your credential.

She took a weak stab at pronouncing it. "Dim... Yaz-mig-you?"

"Us-muggy," I corrected. "It's Welsh."*

The first thing most people do when confronted with adversarial authority is try to figure out how much trouble they're in.

Can I cry my way out of this speeding ticket?

Would a blow job unresist my arrest?

Do they know about the Caymans account?

Martybeth, predictably, played the seduction card, the strongest one in her deck. She let the halves of her blouse fall open and looked at me with buttery eyes.

Pocketing my credentials (which had done their job and would now not be seen again), I said, "I'm sorry, Martybeth, we don't have time for that anymore."

---

*For "No Smoking," natch.

I spun her a quick yarn about how the NBGI had inserted me undercover as a casino host to dig into Wolfredian's operation, of which there was suspicion of money laundering, tax evasion, hummery, flummery, and crimes against nature. I had intended, I told her, to run a measured investigation. "But you screwed that up."

"Me? How?"

"By telling Wolfredian about that call this morning. You're going to have to make that right."

"What do you want me to do?" she asked.

"Just tell me"—I spread my hands and smiled—"everything."

Martybeth didn't know everything, but what she did know was enlightening. Wolfredian had assigned her to train the new host—me—but also to stay watchful and report if I did anything strange. I suppose she regarded running out on sex with her as strange, and that's how Wolfredian learned I was off to Blue Hills and got Red Louise there first.

"He doesn't trust you," said Martybeth. She glanced at the pocket holding my badge. "Apparently with good reason."

"You said he thought I was a *macher*."

"I made that up. I wanted you to feel at home." She pouted like a hurt kitten.

"You did a good job," I said, and she brightened. "You're still doing a good job. Tell me more."

This popped the lid on Martybeth, and all sorts of interesting tidbits spilled out, chief among them that Gaia hosts were paid a big bonus for getting Wolfredian next to their guests. "Not even whales," said Martybeth. "Midlevel players. Anyone who might have loose cash in their pocket." It was an open secret that he routinely worked the clientele for investments. "He's really more interested in that," she said, "than even in having them gamble." She became thoughtful. "Which I really don't understand," she said, "since his job has to pay, like, anyhow, seven figures."

"He must have a jones," I said.

"Jones?"

"Habit. If a seven-figure salary's not covering his nut, there must be a big leak somewhere."

"Drugs?" said Martybeth. "Girls? Gambling?" She was trying to be helpful, but it was clear to me that Wolfredian's addiction was simply not in her database. "You might ask his consultant."

"Consultant?"

"You see him from time to time. What's his name?" She scrunched her brain to remember. "Something weird. Harrison? No. Hannibal! That's it, Hannibal Hamlin. Funny name, huh?"

Yeah, funny. Lincoln's other vice president.

"They hang around?"

"Used to," she said. "Not so much lately, at least not the last few days."

Used to hang around, huh? If so, then Woody's tale of his and Jay's adversarial relationship was both less and more than he'd led me to believe. I chased the significance of this information for a moment, but that was a mistake, for it left Martybeth alone with her thoughts, and the light began to dawn that I might not be who I said I was. Her brow furrowed, and I could see the structure of my bluff starting to break down. Any second now, she'd be asking for another look at my tickets.

Time to wrap this up.

Special Agent Ysmygu spent a few hard moments impressing upon Martybeth the seriousness of the situation, then carrot-and-sticked her with promises of immunity but threats of legal hellfire should she breathe a word of this to anyone. I had little hope the lip glue would set, but it was the best I could do on the fly. And, hey, if she took the story to Wolfredian, maybe it would further muddy the waters of my true intent.

In the elevator back downstairs, I sent Vic a long text, outlining some refinements I needed in his script, and ending with: "Time 2 make yr ntrance."

But his ntrance was already under way.

23

The Unbearable Lightness of Being Mirplo

There's a class of pop culture one might call stunt art. Christo's *Umbrellas.* Banksy's graffiti. Big stuff. Impactful. But ephemeral, and soon gone. Christo once said, "I think it takes much greater courage to create things to be gone than to create things that will remain." I think that's a little self-serving, but whatever. The point is that big installations are as much about the artist as they are about the art. With the wave on which Vic—excuse me, Mirplo—rode toward Vegas just then, I shouldn't have been surprised at the magnitude of the stunt art he whipped up for himself. After all, I'd invited his superfueled ambition to town in the first place and inspired him to fire it off in all directions in that supercharged air. True, too, we'd held some strategic consultations, so that what he contrived outside the casino easily conformed to the picture he'd create within its walls. Too easily, in fact. By dint of early success, self-fulfilling self-confidence (my own behind-the-scenes fluffing efforts), and the love of a good woman, Vic was morphing quickly from large to larger than life, no longer the clumsy dumb yutz whose most marketable skill had once been his ability to wheedle free drinks. Maybe the best thing about art is its impact on the artist.

Be that as it may, Mirplo the would-be superstar was coming to town as the superstar he would be. You could read it on all the signs. And I don't mean signs like portents or tea leaves. I mean signs like giant temporary billboards placed along Las Vegas Boulevard—the

Strip—at hundred-yard intervals from the Stratosphere at the north end all the way down to Mandalay Bay.

"Think big," I had advised him, and think big he had.

The colors were electric: reds and greens that shimmered in the sun, vibrating hard, clashing loud, yet somehow harmonizing into a test of visual acuity that, if you passed it, emerged as Mirplo's face and the words BE THE SHOW! Each billboard housed a huge video monitor, with streaming images from the camera feeds of tiny, radio-controlled helicopters flying lazy loops over the Strip. The baby choppers fed to the crowds below liberal and extensive shots of themselves, so that folks looking up at the screens saw imaginatively manipulated shots of folks looking up at screens, a fun-house mirror effect that was (like all of Mirplo's art, I would say) at once refreshing and subtly disturbing, equal parts You are here and Where are you? The billboards formed the centerpiece of a viral marketing campaign for something big, arty, and conceptually Mirplovian coming very soon to an undisclosed desert location near you.

With advance word of Mirplo the phenomenon in place, all that remained was the arrival of Mirplo the man. For this grand entrance, I stationed myself in the Gaia's porte cochere and kept an eye peeled for his limo. I was still fretting about Woody, of course, still trying to quell my anxiety by the following logic: Woody would be safe (I tried to persuade myself) unless and until Mirplo tanked as a whale. Of course, merely succeeding as a whale wouldn't entirely do the trick either. He had to be—I coined a phrase here—a value-added whale, one worth more to the Gaia than his earn and churn, one worth more to Wolfredian than just his deep and seemingly easy pocket to pick. All of a sudden, I had a lot riding on the performance (in many senses of the world) of a man I used to not trust with a dry-cleaning ticket. How things had changed. Well, at least I hoped they had.

And now here he came, his limo sliding to a stop at the VIP entrance, a section of the valet area set apart by stanchions, velvet ropes, and an honest-to-God red carpet. A young Gaia employee in upmarket livery opened the passenger door for Vic, who stepped out grandly, and struck a pose like Columbus landing on Hispaniola. A growth of new beard graced his face, giving it an unexpectedly rugged aspect. His hair, gelled, spiked, and frosted, betrayed the handiwork of some high-priced stylist. This from a guy who used to attack his own greasy locks with kitchen shears rather than part with ten bucks for a Supercuts. He wore big tinted glasses, like something from the bottom of Elton John's prop closet. Matching linen shirt and slacks. Versace black leather Chelsea boots.

And a cape.

It swirled as he moved, and the word MIRPLO! glittered in sequins and LEDs. The overall effect was that of Mick Jagger by way of Siegfried or Roy. And did I see a tiny flashing © after the word MIRPLO? My God, he's copyrighted.

Vic reached back into the limo and offered a hand to Zoe, who alit, resplendent in a shimmery lime jumpsuit—hair dyed to match—accessorized with a feather boa, stacked platform heels, and substantial crystal earrings that refracted the headlights of passing cabs and cars. She took Vic's hand, queen to his king. Say this for them, when they sold a thing, they sold it hard.

More entourage disgorged. Next out was a familiar face in a completely unexpected context. Wearing Western drag—leather shitkickers, Levi's, snap-button shirt, tan cowboy hat, and a silver-tipped bolo tie secured with a chunky turquoise slide—stood none other than Honey Moon. Since when did he roll with Vic? I tried to catch his eye, but he looked right through me; from his point of view, I was just another face in the crowd.

And that was nothing to who came next.

Allie.

Stepping out of the limo, she bent to straighten the lines of her perfect white business suit skirt, then looked up and surveyed the area. She wore librarian glasses, with her hair secured in a French twist, and a Gucci briefcase tucked under her arm. As with Honey, I tried to make eye contact, but as with Honey, I seemed to have become transparent.

At this point, Vic saw me (allowed himself to see me, I'd say), and greeted me with a brassy, "Radar!" He came over and hugged me with the sort of *Hail, fellow, well met* bonhomie you'd expect between old frat brothers or country club cohorts. "It's good to see you, man. I've missed you."

"Vic—"

"Mirplo," corrected Zoe.

"Mirplo," I said, "it's only been a few days."

"But it seems like longer, doesn't it?" I paused to absorb the moment: Vic's attitude, his costume, his crew. And let's not forget the PR efforts in full swing out there on the Strip and elsewhere. He was right. It did seem like longer. He was growing fast, like summer squash. "Come on," he said, "meet the team." First he brought me to Zoe. "Zoe you know," he said. I offered Zoe a hand, but she waved it away, for she'd withdrawn a Geoid from its rubberized case and was completely absorbed in it. Vic just laughed. "Work, work, work," he said. "She never quits." He threw a convivial arm around Honey and said, "This is Cookie Carter. He's kind of my muscle."

"You won't need muscle when you're here," I told Vic. "We're pretty well equipped in that area."

"You never know," he replied. "My fans are off the hook. Your security could be overrun." He turned to Allie. "And here we have Ms. Miriam Plowright. She's my guilty conscience."

"Financial manager," Allie corrected.

"Yeah," agreed Vic. "It's her job to tell me when I've gambled too much, and my job to ignore her." He emitted a laugh that fell just short of the boisterous guffaw of a self-satisfied prick.

"Hello, Mr. Hoverlander," said Allie.

She extended her hand. It was cold and dry as snakeskin. I looked deep into her eyes, trying to find some spark of connection, but she maintained her million-mile stare. I didn't bother trying to deconstruct whether this was part of Mirplo's play or Allie's real reaction to seeing me again. At this point, I didn't have a logical leg to stand on. So I just kind of teetered. "I assume you'll be handling Mirplo's house account?" I said. She nodded. "I'll have someone get with you for the paperwork. It shouldn't take more than a few minutes." I turned back to Vic. "In the meantime, maybe you'd like some food? I've made a reservation at—"

"Nuck that," said Vic. "I didn't come here to eat. Let's gamble!"

It turned out that the Gucci briefcase held a fair amount of cash, most of which Allie placed through the casino cage into a prearranged safe deposit box, and the rest of which she gave to Vic, banded packets of Franklins that he tucked into his pants pockets or, in the case of one bundle, slipped down the front of Zoe's jumpsuit. "For luck," he insisted.

Zoe, buried in her Geoid, barely noticed.

Over the next few hours, Vic established his bona fides as the type of whale who spews money—and attitude—all over a casino. He didn't stray far from the betting system we'd used at Sandia, but slathered every bet with a giant sense of entitlement, quite effectively creating the image of a megalomaniac on a meltdown. Playing blackjack, he'd berate the dealer for putting him over 21, though even a Mirplo (even in his heightened state of self-aggrandizement) knows that the dealer has no control over what card comes off the deck next. Similarly did he take it out on the craps stickman who "psychically poisoned" Vic's roll with bad attitude, and caused him to seven out.

Such superstitious nonsense was not unusual for high rollers, but Vic ran it much hotter than that. Everything he did seemed less about gambling than about *being Mirplo* gambling. I knew that casino surveillance, the so-called eye in the sky, would be tracking this new whale and that Jay was likely somewhere up in security country, his eyes glued to the feed. Would Vic strike him as a guy with his head shoved so far up his own ego that he ran the real risk of—I coined a neolopism—assphyxiation? That was the script, but Vic was far beyond the script. Simply put, he went over the top, admired the view, and settled in for a stay.

At one point, running bad at roulette, he felt the need for some lucky money and put his hand down Zoe's jumpsuit to pull out his stash of cash. This drew a dark look from a pit boss, which triggered Vic's rage, fueled by the combustible mix of grim fortune and overblown arrogance (with just a hint of scripted accelerant). "What?" demanded Vic. "You got a problem with this?"

"It would be better if you didn't—"

"Didn't what? Touch my girlfriend?"

A confrontation loomed, and while such a confrontation would further cement Vic's shambolic reputation, it was my job as casino host to prevent such unpleasantness, so I intervened, cooling Vic out with soothing words, and steering him off the casino floor into the tranquil confines of a nearby sports bar. There, his nose still out of joint, Vic started arguing with Zoe over which team was a better baseball bet, the Cincinnati Reds because red is a power color, or the Milwaukee Brewers because they have beer mojo. I couldn't tell whether this was improvisational theater or the daft logic you sometimes see in, for example, rookie horse players who bet the steed called Steamboat because they went skiing there once and had fun. Allie offered no clues. She just sat there sipping mineral water and thinking her private thoughts. God, I wanted to get her alone for ten minutes, have a frank exchange of views. Because here's the thing: Although Vic was running my script, he was so deeply in character that I couldn't tell whether he was in character at all. And while you do this on the grift—play a role and don't ever let on that you're role-playing—I'd never known Vic to be that accomplished an actor. He'd either gotten tremendous game while I wasn't looking, or else he'd drunk his own Kool-Aid and bought into the Mirplo myth.

And Allie? I simply had no idea where she stood. She was in on the snuke, manifestly, for here she was, part of Vic's entourage, but was she on my script, hers, his, Woody's, or whose? All I got when I looked at her was the empty gaze of someone passing time by trying to remember, say, all the state capitals in alphabetical order. *Albany, Annapolis, Atlanta...*

Nor was Honey—Cookie—any help. While not neglecting to keep scanning the crowd for real or imaginary threats, he set out, with great enthusiasm though no apparent success, to explain to Vic and Zoe what an over/under line was. "The bookmaker predicts how many total runs the teams will score, and then you decide whether the real outcome will be above or below that number."

"So then it doesn't matter who wins?" asked Vic, vaguely grasping the concept.

"That's right."

"Why would you bet on a game if you don't care who wins?"

"That's the bet," said Honey. "That's the over/under line."

"I'm not betting on a line," Vic declared definitively. "I'm betting on a team." He turned to Zoe. "Any of them wear purple? Purple's lucky."

And that was Vic that night in a nutshell: a proto-pompous, self-important clown, the last float on the clueless parade, all ignorance and arrogance, with the high likelihood of going off for a very large number. Not to mix metaphors, but if casinos are sharks, then this whale was chum.

Apparently attracted to the scent of blood in the water, Jay Wolfredian soon arrived. I was not altogether surprised to see him here, given Martybeth's revelation about his pressing need for investors. And Vic had been hamming for the cameras with the awareness (mine, anyway, if not his) that Jay would no doubt be watching the new whale perform. Given all this, I would certainly have expected the Gaia's VP of special projects to introduce himself to a new high roller and offer him the hospitality of the house. That's just good business.

But that's not what happened, exactly.

Playing the dutiful casino host, I facilitated introductions, and Jay wasted no time in schmoozing Vic, who wasted no energy pretending he wasn't lapping it up. Each was on script, of course, with Wolfredian massaging the mark and Vic promoting the Mirplo brand in all its twisted glory. Yet beneath the scripted exchange, I detected something unguarded, something authentic from both. The fan and the man. It was weird.

Jay made a point of mentioning that he'd just come into possession of a couple of Boggs notes—hand-drawn currency created not as counterfeits but as art and traded by the artist, J.S.G. Boggs, for whatever goods or services his traffic would bear. The way Jay eased this into the conversation, patently fishing for Vic's approval, reminded me of a cat laying a dead mouse on his master's doorstep. Vic, though, contemptuously rejected Boggs as a "ballpoint loser."

"His thing is a parlor trick," Vic declared. "It's not art."

"So then what's art?" asked Jay.

"Something that moves you."

"By that logic, a train is art."

Vic graced this comment with a laugh, which seemed to please Jay—delight him, almost—and again I got the sense of something going on here beyond a Gaia guy doing his job. Jay was tapping into something, with a surprisingly deep-dwelling sense of urgency. Vic, meanwhile, cantered on down his path of his self-importance. "Now if it's art you want," he said, "you're going to want to see Mirplopalooza."

"Mirplopalooza?"

"My installation out in the desert. You've seen the signs. BE THE SHOW?" Jay nodded. "I'm telling you," said Vic, "when people get a load of what I've got planned..."

"They'll be moved?"

"Just like a train." Vic clapped a convivial hand on Jay's back—and then proceeded to pimp Mirplopalooza, its grand design, musical guests, diversions and divertissements, things with balloons, kites, and ultralights. Vic pitched it like a fever dream, and though I'd been on the ground floor of the planning stage, those skeletal proposals lacked the weight of authenticity—and courage of conviction—with which Vic pronounced them now.

Especially when he started talking numbers. "I'll have five, ten thousand people there, easy. Next year, twice that."

"You're already thinking about next year?"

Vic leaned in close, conspiratorial. "I pulled a long-term-year lease on the site. Bureau of Land Management. They sell cheap. I'll be doing Mirplopalooza till I die."

This brought Allie—Miriam—into the conversation. "We've done revenue projections through 2025," she said. "Over that time span, the event will net—"

Vic cut her off. "Big money. Who cares? Money's only important to people who don't have anything important in their lives." He gave Jay a knowing look. "Like art, right? Like Boggs bucks." He turned to Zoe. "Hey, do we got any sponsorship slots left?"

Zoe consulted her Geoid. "A couple," she said. "A silver and two platinums."

Vic turned back to Jay. "You want a hospitality tent?" He asked. "For the Gaia, I mean. There'll be awesome foot traffic. Plus you can hang out. I'll throw in some back-row seats to the show."

"You mean front-row."

"Don't tell me what I mean. It's my show. I know the best seats."

Jay and Vic exchanged more art talk for a time, then Jay took his leave, wishing Vic luck at the tables, which is the single most disingenuous thing any casino functionary can say to a guest. Not that Vic cared. Once Jay departed, he declared himself tired and pulled the plug on the party. I delivered the group to their suite, then straggled down to the hosts' office, where I punched out for the night. As I engaged in this prosaic act, it occurred to me that I'd attained, in a sense, the worst of both worlds. I had a straight job that I didn't particularly want or like, and I was running a snuke over which I seemed to be losing control. On that cheery note, I headed back to my room. This involved a long trek down grotty corridors to the far reaches of the hotel, a good fifteen minutes' walk from the main casino floor. Reaching my room, I slotted in my card key, waited for the green light, then opened the door and stepped inside. At this point, something dark and metal swung out and hit me flush on the ear. I spun around and sat down. In the ambient light spilling in from the window, I saw Red Louise standing over me, brandishing brass knuckles with a self-satisfied smirk.

"What was that for?" I asked.

"Fun," she said. "Just for fun."

24

Choose Your Lies

People have existential crises when they least expect it. Guy shoveling snow in Des Moines feels his chilblains and decides the time has come to buy that houseboat in Marathon. College girl crashes and burns in biochem and discovers that, hey, prelaw's not such a crap choice after all. Man on the floor of a hotel room rubs ache from his ear and understands definitively that the merry of his merry-go-round is gone. The man likes to think he has an effect on women, though *violently negative* is not necessarily the one he's going for.

Red Louise pocketed her knuckles and pulled out a Glock.

"Oh, what?" I muttered. "A gun? What for?"

"Maybe to shoot you," said Red.

"Here in the hotel? No. Nope, sorry. I just can't see that."

"Then maybe just to scare you some."

"Okay," I said. "Let's take it as read that I'm some scared."

"I don't think you're anywhere near enough scared." She grabbed me by the scruff of whatever, dragged me to my feet, and held the gun close to my face. My nose twitched to the odd conflation of her lemon chiffon shampoo and the gun's sharp tang of Cosmoline. "So let me be clear. I'm going to ask you some questions. Choose your lies with care, because if I don't like them, I will shoot you dead right here. Don't worry about it being a hotel and all. The cleaning staff can be very discreet."

Then she kidney-punched me. I expelled the pain on a whoosh of sour-tasting breath. I admire strong women. Always have. But when they're holding me at gunpoint and punching me and whatnot, I'm not so big a fan. Times like these, I wished I'd put more effort into bulking up, but that was water under the bench press now. There was no thought of getting the upper hand, or the drop, or whatever it is that the buff guys get. No, I'd just have to ride it out.

Choose my lies with care.

"Fine," I said. "What do you want to know?"

"First of all, what's with the bogus cop routine?"

"Dim Ysmygu? It means 'no smoking,' you know."

She gonked me with the gun on the top of my head. Just a tap, really, to demonstrate her not-so-frivolous mood. "I don't give a crap what it means. Why'd you mess with Martybeth's head?"

"To find out why you snatched my dad."

"I didn't—"

"Please," I said. "You plucked him from Blue Hills five minutes before I got there. You almost ran me off the road. It wasn't necessary, you know. I mean, what does it change? I brought Jay a deep pocket. The rest is up to him."

Red clouted me again. I fell down a little. "Man, stop hitting me," I said. I may have only thought it.

She straddled me. "This deep pocket," she said. "How deep? How real?"

Let me start by saying that I have a fairly high tolerance for pain. It doesn't make me panic, and it doesn't really cloud my thinking all that much. So as I lay there on the floor, slugged four times in three minutes, I understood without doubt that the snuke hung by a certain thread. Trouble was, I wasn't sure which thread. Like if you're James Bond dismantling a bomb and you don't know whether to clip the yellow wire or the blue. What was Red telling me? That Wolfredian didn't buy my whale? He'd certainly seemed engaged earlier, but now here was Louise very nearly calling Vic a fraud. So should I stick with my story, keep calling my spade a spade, or bail on the tale and jump to a new one?

What's it going to be, Mr. Bond? Yellow wire or blue?

Choose your lies with care.

I studied Louise in the half light. Who was she in all of this? I'd had her pegged as Jay's right arm, but this visit felt very freelance, unsanctioned. Of course, Wolfredian could have sent her here with a nod and a wink, to present me with a disunited front, your standard misdirectomy. But this didn't feel like that. It felt like a legitimate difference of opinion. Jay, I believed, made Mirplo as the real deal—the weak-minded mook whose fortunes Jay could Ponzi off at will. His view, however, may have been colored by his infatuation with Mirplo the artist—at least that's what cynical Louise seemed to think. So here she was, independently attempting to confirm her doubts, with coercive outrages against tender Hoverlander flesh as the lie-detector of record if required. Like I said, I have a high tolerance for pain. I'd regret to have to test how high.

So okay, Radar, all you need is an answer that meets her needs, Jay's needs, and your needs. Happen to have one of those handy?

Time to dance out on the high wire of improv. I've been there before. The trick is to not look down.

The first move was obvious: feed Louise the expected narrative. So I stood up and took a deep, confessorial breath. "You're right," I said. "Mirplo's smoke."

"He's not an artist?"

"He's an artist on the come. Most of his accounts are receivable. He's jacking up his image for the sake of future hires."

Louise clenched everything it's humanly possible to clench. "You asshole," she growled. "You fucked with me." Notice she didn't say "fucked with my boss."

"I didn't fuck with anyone," I said. "I brought you a deep pocket. It's real. It's just not his."

"Whose, then?"

"The woman he's with."

"What, that thing with the green hair? Come on."

"Not her. The other one. Plowright."

"She's his flunky."

"No," I said forcefully, "she's his financial manager. And he's not her only client. She controls..." I stopped. "Well, I guess you know what she controls." This was a bluff, and a key one, because if Louise or anyone had done diligence on Plowright, I was toast. I could only hope that they'd been too focused on Vic's bright and shining colors to pay too much attention to his roll-withs. Well, they'd be paying attention now, and investigating Ms. Miriam Plowright at the first opportunity to determine whether my story held water.

That story, hastily stitched together, presented Mirplo as a borderline whack-job earnestly trying to parlay a couple of lucky commissions into a full-blown career. "He's all self-fulfilling prophecy," I said. "Act like someone, you're someone." I offered Mirplopalooza as evidence of that. She might or might not have known how Vic had pimped it to Jay, but she would have seen promotional evidence of it on the Strip and elsewhere. "He's trying to bootstrap himself to stardom."

"And how does Plowright figure in?"

"That was his one smart move, hiring her." I vamped an explanation about how Plowright specialized in dim bulbs like Vic, closely controlling her clients' money to keep it, and them, out of harm's way. As such, she held investment authority over portfolios that aggregated to millions. "He likes to come off as a high roller, but he's not. She won't let him be. It's not in their interest. But they know you can't sell flamboyant rock star from the ten-cent keno lounge, so tonight was his big show. After this, he won't gamble high at all."

"So Mirplo's no whale." She said this smugly, just delighted to be right in her guess.

"Hell, he doesn't even like to gamble."

"Then why is he here?"

"I told you: self-promotion."

"That's stupid."

"He's stupid. But also, there's no such thing as bad publicity."

So here's what I figured would happen next. Louise would kill at least a quarter hour getting someplace she could check out Miriam Plowright online. She wouldn't expect to find much, for I'd painted Plowright as ultradiscreet. Meanwhile, within that narrowest of windows, I'd have to whip up a digital history fast and full enough to fool her inspection. In my mind, I already had my laptop open, plucking what I needed from the Web. Preexisting templates, fake financials; I'd have to pull Miriam's résumé and backstory out of my ass. It was going to be tight. After that, more improv and...

Whack! Something hard and cold slammed into my hairline. The brass knuckles had staged their second act. As the carpet rushed up to meet my nose, I thought to myself, *This is going to play hell with my schedule.* Then I didn't think anything at all.

The turndown service in this hotel rocks.

I woke to the cool, soothing relief of a wet washcloth on my forehead. Clearly, some housekeeper had turned Florence Nightingale. Then I heard an angel's voice saying, "Take it easy, Radar, everything's going to be okay," and my world spun upside down again.

Because the angel was Allie.

Allie stroking my brow. Allie feeding me calm assurances. Allie bending over me, the curve of her breast visible down her blouse. Then Allie raining little kisses along my jawline. Allie lying down on top of me, splayed comfortably along my length. Allie, my angel, where did you come from?

Allie, my angel, are you really here?

Mmm... muscle memory took over. I wrapped my arms around her, stroking her skin through her shirt. My fingers traced the familiar bumps of her spine like tiny skiers jumping moguls along the ridgeline of Mount Back. Our mouths met. Her lips were dry, a little chapped—desert air will do that to you—but they opened to mine, and our tongues slid against each other, an avid pink reunion. To muscle memory add chemical confirmation—this was the mouth I was meant to kiss.

Allie sat up and languidly unbuttoned her blouse, taking her time, as if each button were a tiny personal challenge to be cherished, met, and mastered. She smiled at the task, and I engaged in a brief game of compare-and-contrast, measuring Allie's easy ecdysiasm against the desperate carnality of a Martybeth. Then I shoved the image aside. I had Allie, and if that underscored any point at all, it's that the last thing I wanted was a Martybeth.

I reached up and twirled my fingers in Allie's hair, soft and fine to the touch. My hand dropped to her shoulder, then her breast, and I felt the comfortable fit of it in the cup of my palm. Her stiffening nipple nudged between my second and third fingers. I saw a familiar flush spread from her chest to her collarbone, felt the heat of it almost, and knew that her body remembered mine as mine remembered hers. I could see into the near future, with the two of us naked, melded, rocking together to the silent rhythm of an unsung song. I saluted that song; stood to attention to it. Allie must have felt this, for she placed her hand in the space between our jeans, its warm and solid bulk transmitting delicious pressure back and forth between our goods.

I ached to surrender to the moment, but part of me held back, the damned self-interested and self-protective part which just couldn't trust that what was happening was happening. Like I said before, it's tricky when grifters make love. And it's not like Allie was some sort of blushing flower. After all the times we'd made love, what would one more intimate iteration matter to her, if doing me was something that had to be done for reasons unknown? Part of me said *Don't care,* just take cookies when cookies are passed. But I knew I had to know, and risked destroying the moment by asking the question that had to be asked.

"Allie, are you here?"

"Right here, lover."

"I mean *here* here."

"*Here* here," she assented. She pushed my shirt up to my neck and settled her weight upon me. "I've been here all along."

"That's not how it looks."

"Forget how it looks. Think how it feels."

I knew she wasn't speaking of the limbic stuff. She was telling me to go deep inside myself, inside our history, the totality of it, what Mirplo called the g-salt, review everything that had ever passed between us, and decide if it added up.

I did the math as best as I could—difficult, given the frictive distraction of Allie's breasts against my chest. Two equally plausible narratives emerged. In one, she'd been trapdoor spider from the start, just as we'd planned (though with a few more distressing wrinkles than I'd liked), and was now coming in from the cold. The other had Allie just dragging me around by my dick, a possibility so heartbreaking, so miserably cruel that I decided it couldn't be true. It's ridiculous to speak of a grifter's code. There's no such thing, and we only ever invoke its fiction if it serves some devious end. Nevertheless, I knew Allie, knew her as well as one human can know another across the infinite gulf that separates soul from soul. I knew her bedrock integrity. She wouldn't come back to screw me just to screw with me. She would have just stayed away.

But she was here.

Which meant she was *here* here.

But how? "How did you get into my room?"

" 'Mrs. Hoverlander' locked herself out. A maid let her in."

"I have a lot of other questions," I said.

"And I have a bunch, too, but they can wait. Sweetie, I have *missed* you." She underscored the point by undressing us both with the kind of urgency you see in porn. Entering her was bottled bliss, a bliss made more poignant by my dashed fear that we'd never be together again. Boy meets girl, boy loses girl, boy gets—

"Boy," I said. "Who's looking after Boy?"

Allie laughed out loud. "Are you really asking me that now?"

"I can't help it," I said. "It crossed my mind."

"If you have room in your mind for Boy," she said, salaciously grinding her pelvis against mine, "I fear I've lost my touch."

"Trust me," I said, "your touch is... Wow!" And now I think I was just being bratty. "But where's Boy?"

"He's with Zoe's dad. He's fine." She caressed my head. "But what about you? You've got a couple of pretty big lumps here."

It was nothing to the one in my throat. Allie was back, and the only thing that mattered was that she never go away again. Consequently, I blurted these words: "You should marry me."

She kissed me so gently. "That's not just the lumps talking?"

"You should," I repeated, more forcefully. "Make an honest man of me."

"That's funny on so many levels," said Allie.

"Is that a yes?"

"Of course it's a yes." Again she ground her groin against mine. "But no Elvis."

"What?"

"Just because we're in Vegas doesn't mean you get away with a cartoon wedding. We'll do it right and proper. Someplace splendid."

"Anywhere in the world, honey. You name the spot."

"I will."

Then we made love. Honeymoon love. It didn't last long. That was okay. Considering how long the foreplay had been—weeks and weeks—it all evened out in the end. But in the back of my mind, I couldn't help wondering what Allie meant when she said she had a bunch of questions, too.

25

Back-Channel Jackalope

"He shoots, he scores!"

Uncle Joe cried out in the dark. I sat up and looked around for Vic, caught in that first moment of wakefulness when things don't make sense. Then the phrase repeated, tinny and distant, and I shook away enough sleep to recognize my ringtone. Crawling out of bed, I found my jeans on the floor and groped for my phone. A glance back over my shoulder revealed Allie likewise shrugging off sleep and watching in attentive silence as I connected the call.

It was Red Louise. "Your story checks out," she said. "You'll get a text later where to meet. Bring Plowright. If we close, you're off the hook."

"What about Woody?" I asked.

"He's off the meat hook," she said. "For now. Just make sure Plowright understands that it's a seller's market." The call dropped, and my phone went dark in my hand.

Allie sat up in the bed, eying me with a questioning look, a look that reminded me of Santa Fe and quieter times. Wherever Allie had been, she was back. I knew it to the core of my being, and I knew that I trusted her with my life, by the simple math of: If a trust so firm could be so wrong, then who would even want to live, anyhow? Of course, there remained the questions of why she'd checked out and why she had now checked back in. And the rather more pressing question of what online insights had mollified Red Louise.

"I'm off the hook," I told Allie. "My story passed muster."

"Which story?"

"Yours, actually. Miriam Plowright's."

"Of course it did. Why wouldn't it?"

Well, let's see.... There was the distracting matter of getting whacked upside my pudding head, and then the equally distracting, though much more pleasant, matter of making love to you, my love. "No support," I said. I told Allie how I'd improvised Miriam's involvement with Vic, hoping to find a moment to pastcast her Internet essentials. Not having had that time, I could only assume that when Louise searched for Plowright, she'd come up empty, and angry.

I shared this assumption with Allie.

Who just laughed.

Really, now?

"Of course she didn't come up empty, Radar. Miriam Plowright is platinum. I built her myself."

"Wait, what?"

"Fake website, client lists, celebrity endorsements, the works." Her face flushed with pride. "You're not the only one around here who can wield a mouse, pretty boy."

I felt a little punch-drunk. "So when Louise left here last night to check out Miriam..."

"Out she checked."

"Still doesn't add up," I said. I told Allie how Louise had tabbed Mirplo as a flake and a fake and how I'd thrown her the emergency bone of Miriam Plowright. "But that was just improv," I said. "Spur of the desperate moment."

"Then why did you have me invent her in the first place?"

"*I* did?"

"Of course. Through Woody. You said you were deep undercover and couldn't get to the Web. Told me I had to pinch-hit."

"I said that?"

"Yeah, of course."

"Through Woody?"

"Well, didn't you? He said you did."

The light dawned. We looked at each other and laughed. Then we started exchanging information and comparing notes. Soon one thing was clear: No matter how devious we thought Woody Hoverlander was, he was a thousand times slyer than that. He wasn't just a world-class snuke; he was king of this world.

It began right after Allie moved out. Woody reached out to her, first through Mirplo, then directly himself, by phone. Naturally, she'd been reluctant to talk to him—her pose was still that of active antagonism—"But he wouldn't take no for an answer," said Allie.

"He's like that," I agreed. "But you don't usually get that dewy."

"Nor did I this time. But understand, Radar, he didn't convince me; *you* did."

"How so?"

"He knew it all, everything we'd talked about. Our fake fight, the trapdoor spider, the rebranding of Vic as Mirplo, all of it. I figured he couldn't have all that information without your blessing."

"Or a few deft guesses."

"Yeah, I see that now. He's a clever old jackalope. But look, it seemed like you'd decided to trust him, so I had to decide whether to trust him, too. I talked it over with Vic. He said you probably knew what you were doing and we should just play it as it lays."

"And you?"

"Honestly? I was afraid you might be breaking up with me for real."

"On the back of your own trapdoor spider?"

"Well," said Allie, "you did tell me to date other people."

"No, I didn't."

"No, I know that now. I mean then. Through Woody. He said you said Wolfredian had eyes on you, and we needed to reinforce how really broken up we were."

"Hence..." My heart was in my throat. "Hence that fling with Greg?"

"Fake fling, yes." Allie's eyes became moist. "Radar, I *hated* that."

"I was no fan myself."

"But I thought it's what you wanted. I thought you needed a scene, some theater for whoever'd followed you to the bar that night."

"And Vic thought so, too? That's why he brought me there?"

"I guess." Allie shook her head to clear it. "You know," she said, "looking at it now, it doesn't make any sense. I mean, how could Vic and I have been so snowed? We were both sure you were back there somewhere, pulling Woody's strings."

"Credit the master," I said ruefully.

Then it struck me that the master had made a mistake, for if a Wolfredian operative witnessed the fight that night, what would keep that same operative from later pegging Miriam Plowright as Radar Hoverlander's explosive ex-girlfriend? But Woody doesn't make mistakes like that. Therefore... "Wolfredian never had eyes on us. Woody just had us stage that scene so we'd look broken up for sure—not in the bad guys' eyes, but in our own."

"Why would he do that?"

"Keep us off balance. Keep us from making a separate peace. Maybe that's what he was most afraid of: that if we compared notes too closely, we'd realize we weren't as messily enmeshed as he wanted us to believe."

"Man, Radar, he really had us played."

"Not completely." I rubbed Allie's arm, so glad to have her within arm's reach again. "Why'd you break cover now?"

Allie blushed. "Horniness, lover. Being with you all evening, I just couldn't not be with you last night. I figured if anyone looked at us sideways, it would just seem like Miriam and Radar had hit it off."

"She's not my type," I said.

"I should hope not," said Allie. "She's a bitch."

"But the right bitch at the right time."

The right bitch at the right time. Indeed she was. And how lucky to have her handy when I made my desperate heave to Miriam Plowright under the duressive shadow of Louise's gun. Then again, where had I gotten that ad hoc idea in the first place? Well, it was Miriam at first sight, wasn't it? The moment Allie stepped out of that limo. Her own introduction—*"Financial manager," she corrected*—had told me how to pitch her if need be. Then, when need was, my natural gift for baffle-gab grabbed an available resource and put it in play. Of course I kept the details sparse, not wanting to have to support too complex a lie after the fact. Could Woody have guessed before the fact that I'd know what to do with Miriam when I saw her, his confidence born of the fact that I was "a Hoverlander" and therefore capable of everything? Wily old dog, it was possible. He was that many moves ahead.

And if he was that many moves ahead...

"Allie, what about those phone messages? Were they real?"

"I thought they were," she said. "Now I'm not so sure."

"We should go look for him, maybe retrace his steps."

"Or maybe stay here, retrace ours," said Allie, seductively. "We're engaged now, remember?"

"And you believe in sex before marriage?"

"I believe in sex before breakfast."

So we ordered room service and beguiled the time till it arrived.

I know, I know: so many unresolved questions. So many potentially disastrous outcomes. In the middle of a life-or-death crisis, where do we get off getting off? I have no answer. None. But look, it wasn't just animal fun. It was the consummation of conviction: the first sex of the rest of our lives. Absent an engagement ring, this was how we sealed the deal between us. The deal thus sealed, everything else seemed to recede into unimportance. Life? Death? Whatever. She's mine, I'm hers, and the rest is a ridiculously distant second to that. So bring it on, room service. Bring it on, morning sex. Whatever dangerous connivances waited for us beyond that hotel door... nuck it—let 'em wait.

Breakfast came and went. The day aged. Allie and I took a spin to the pool, I in slow Speedos and she in Miriam Plowright's idea of casual swimwear: a no-nonsense one-piece; severe sunglasses; black, broad-brim hat. She did not look cute. How Allie Quinn could look not cute was a bafflement to me, but she managed. I think it was more a matter of character than costume. When she was in Plowright mode, she oozed bad vibe.

As for the two of us having hooked up, we decided to run that as a mutual setup for a mutual double cross, predicated on the notion that creeps like us will sleep with anyone if we think it yields an edge. Then, in extremis, we could plausibly turn on each other like a couple of quislings with privileges. By roundabout means, and thanks to Woody's devious machinations, we had fortuitously repositioned ourselves as each other's backdoor trapdoor spider. It was a play. Not much of a play, but a play.

"Excuse me, señor, you dropped your wallet."

I must've been dozing in the sun, for it took me a moment to register that the voice—a soft lilt with a Mexican accent—was addressing me. I opened my eyes to find someone kneeling at the foot of my lounge chair, wallet in hand. He wore the uniform of a Gaia groundskeeper: khaki pants and shirt, lug-sole boots, and an engineer-style khaki cap jammed down over his unnaturally (because artificially) cordovan face. The cap shaded his face, but I could see that it was badly (and again artificially) acne-scarred. Looking at him, you'd want to look away, so you probably wouldn't notice that the man behind the makeup was...

"Woody," said Allie, sitting up on the adjacent chaise.

He just smiled and held out the wallet.

"It's not mine," I said.

"Let's pretend it is," he said. "*Una fantasía.*" He handed it off, stood up, and, quietly humming a *narcocorrido,* walked off to pluck dead fronds from a line of potted palms. I followed with my eyes until I lost sight of him among the scantily clad tanners, then turned my attention to the wallet.

It was empty but for a plastic card key and a yellow sticky note with the words Villa 23.

"Well, Miriam," I told Allie. "It looks like we got an upgrade."

26

Pitch and Switch

We waited a decent interval, then made our way down the undulant length of the pool to the broken horseshoe of private-courtyard cabanas at the far end of the Gaia's grounds. Villa 23 was a postage stamp of paradise behind whitewashed walls, complete with plunge pool, Jacuzzi, teak patio table and chairs, gas grill, and two thickly padded gliders with their own shade awnings. A babbling low waterfall fed a koi pond framed by sword ferns and bonsai boxwoods. Sliding glass doors led into a cozy little dayroom with a bed, hammock, and wet bar. Woody stood at the bar, mixing drinks. Eschewing the house options, he poured amber liquid from a hip flask into a highball glass. "Tequila Brain Death, anyone?" he asked.

"Little early in the day for me," said Allie.

"Oh, there's no alcohol in a Tequila Brain Death. Just grenadine, lime"—he waggled the hip flask demonstratively—"and apple juice. The tequila is entirely rhetorical."

"To what end?" asked Allie.

I answered for Woody. "To the end of appearing drunk when you're not."

Woody nodded. "Handy for all manner of hustles." He smiled broadly at me, all proud papa. "As I knew you'd know."

"Yes, could we stop marveling at how clever I am? Since manifestly I'm not or I wouldn't be here now." The frustration in my voice summed up my ire at all the ways I'd been tricked, misled, manipulated, cornered, juked, snuked, and sock-puppeted since this whole enterprise began. From front to back, not Radar Hoverlander's finest hour, particularly considering that by now I was supposed to be on the high road to normalcy as a high school algebra teacher or some such. Fine role model I'd make. *What's the square root of deception, class?*

Woody cut through my bitter reverie. "Don't sell yourself short, son," he said. "I'll grant I've played things a little loose around the edges"—his eyes shifted back and forth between us—"as you and Allie have no doubt discussed at length by now. But you've pulled a few threads, too. Some admirable ones, I'd say. Right now, I hazard to guess, Jay and Louise are in a great state of confusion about where Vic's money really is and how it's to be had. They'll be improvising now."

"And if you're not particularly good at improvising . . . ," I said.

"Things can come rather quickly unspooled. Now all we have to do is unspool them further."

"Still," I said, "that thing with Miriam Plowright was a lucky audible."

"Not lucky," said Woody. "Inspired."

"Lucky," I insisted.

"Well, lucky or not, it was well done. Congratulations."

"I bask in your approval. That said, and if it's not too much trouble, would you mind filling me in on the Pitch and Switch you've sent me to such wearisome lengths to set up?"

"Pitch and Switch?" asked Woody, blankly.

"You're really going to play that dumb?"

"Let's imagine I am," he said. "You say you're not that clever, I say you are. Let's test it. Tell me what I have in mind."

And why did I rise to his bait again? I guess with Woody so successfully ghosting my every thought, I wanted to show that I could get inside his head, too. So I told him what he had in mind.

There's a gaff the old-timers used to run called the Fiddle Game. In that snuke, a short con good for maybe a hundred bucks or two, some down-and-out old folk musician comes up short for the price of his restaurant meal. A conveniently expired credit card usually does the trick, and our honorable minstrel collaterals his sentimentally beloved instrument while he goes to get some cash. Now here comes his confederate, masquerading as a stranger who recognizes the modest fiddle as an undiscovered masterwork—a genuine Flapdadivarius!—and essays to buy it for some goggly multiple of its real worth. As it's not the restaurateur's to sell, the disappointed buyer can only leave behind his contact information, "should the situation change." When the old folkie returns, meager dosh in hand, he's entreated to sell the tool of his trade for a fraction of the above-mentioned multiple. The geezer reluctantly relents, and the Midan proprietor eagerly awaits the buyer's return. Naturally, neither buyer nor geezer is ever seen again, and repeating the scam awaits only their purchase of more pawnshop catgut* and another restaurant meal. The Fiddle Game is such a trope, of course, that no one in the know falls for it these days. But you can dress it up in different clothes. Represent an old book as a rare first edition or fake bling as real. Plus don't forget that in this life those in the know are never in even the bare majority.

The Pitch and Switch is essentially a scaled-up version of the gag. You invest more time, energy, and evidence in cementing the false value of the item in question, but the scam remains the same: Put something of seeming value in the hands of the mark, jack up the value in his mind, get paid, and get lost before he twigs. The first half of our snuke had been to install Vic as a high roller. The second half, predicated on the notion that Jay was repeat business, had to be a Pitch and Switch. But switch to what? It had been Woody's job to determine what would push Jay's "buy" button. Had he done so? Probably. And withheld the information from me, as usual, just to see if I could tease it out on my own. Really, Woody, after all these years, I don't need homeschooling. Still, if I had to hazard a guess...

---

*Catgut is 100 percent not cat. True fact or bar fact?

"What's going to happen," I said as I finished telling Woody a dozen things he already knew, "is that Miriam Plowright will turn out to have something she grossly undervalues, something for which you'll be on hand to set the proper price."

"Already done," said Woody.

"And that something is...?"

Woody gave me that same blank look, but by this point it didn't even bother me. I figured the answer was already staring me in the face. So I mentally scanned Plowright's clients' portfolios, which, given that they were entirely fictive, could arguably contain anything. Antiques. Baseball cards. Solid gold meteorites. Pieces of the True Cross. But how could fake assets be made real enough to snuke a man so manifestly on his guard? Wolfredian was a hard case. Always. Well, almost always. Last night...

Wait...

Last night...

I said it softly. "Mirplopalooza."

"And you say you're not clever."

"Yeah," I said ruefully, "I'm the head of the nucking class. But would you mind telling me why you think it'll work?"

"But, Radar, you've been working on it all this time. You must've figured it out. Are you really going to play that dumb?"

"Let's imagine I am," I said. I glanced at the bar. "And I believe I'll have a Brain Death after all."

Woody began the discussion discursively. "Do you remember," he asked, "a fellow named Clifton Greenwald?"

"No," I said. "It doesn't ring a bell."

"He was an artist. About fifteen years back. Called himself Kagadeska."

That bell rang. "He did those Japanese cartoons, right? Manga?"

"Cartoons," scoffed Woody. "That's like saying Mozart wrote ditties." He recounted Greenwald's career, an asymptotic upslope from greeting cards through graphic design to his big breakthrough in American manga. "Did you know he went to Stanford?"

"You...," I couldn't help asking, "you weren't him, were you?" It seemed impossible, but at this point, I wasn't putting anything past the old man.

"No, I wasn't him," said Woody. "Especially after he died."

"Oh, that's right." Allie snapped her fingers. "Rode his bike off a mountain."

"And that, dear friends, is the slender thread by which we all hang. One random patch of gravel...poof, you're posthumous." He eyed us keenly. "And if you're an artist of some note, your works start to appreciate. The story goes that someone broke into Greenwald's studio just after he died and stole hundreds of unpublished one-sheets."

"And you know this story because...?"

"I started it, of course. And made sure it reached Wolfredian's ears. He'd sold a start-up, had some money, was splashing it around."

"Was this before or after you snuked him with your private business model?"

"Oh, during. I worked him from all kinds of angles. In this case, I hired a beard, a gallery gal who introduced him to the market and helped him corner it. He was an avid buyer."

"So he never saw your fingerprints?" asked Allie.

"And still doesn't know he bought fakes."

"Or the other fakes you've sold him," I said.

"Excuse me?"

"Over the years. Through beards. He's repeat business, right? I assume you didn't establish that fact by accident."

Woody shrugged. "It's true I've kept tabs on him. Even steered a few items his way, by roundabout means. But he's grown. He tracks bigger targets now."

"Like Mirplopalooza," I said. "Which I thought was Vic's idea."

"Let's call it a collaboration," suggested Woody. "Purpose-built to appeal to a man of Wolfredian's taste."

"And supported by all the shills and ancillaries I've been pumping into the event for... well, I have to say right now I don't even know what for."

"Need-to-know basis, Radar, that's all. No time for every tiny explication."

"Hey, lack of data's one thing. I can live with that. But why all this keeping us in the dark? Sending Allie instructions 'through' me. Engineering our breakup—that was just cruel. And working with Vic on your own. Look, if you didn't think you could trust me..."

"Well, did *you* think I could trust you? You haven't had both feet in this snuke since the start." He turned to Allie. "You may find this hard to believe, but I honor your goals. Your life is yours to live as you see fit. You want to be a professional. Scientist. Save the world, I don't care. But you've put my boy in a place of ambivalence, caught him between two things he knows he loves.

"Where I come from, there's a saying: 'The truth is revealed under pressure.' What you call misdirection and manipulation, I call just an attempt to arrive at a certain truth. Radar's truth. The thing that's in his heart."

"I know what's in my heart," I said. I put my arm around Allie.

"Yes, but now, unfortunately, she's not so certain of hers. Because loyalty goes both ways. She wants what's best for her but also what's best for you. It forces choices." He looked at Allie. "Isn't that right, Miriam?"

"Don't call me that."

"You adopted a role," said Woody, simply. "You made a choice."

"Doesn't mean I can't unmake it."

"True," said Woody. "Everything is fluid."

"Okay, that's great," I said, "but this conversation is netting us nothing. Let's review what we know."

"Very well," said Woody, "This much is gospel: Wolfredian sweet-talks whales into bogus investment schemes."

"And uses those proceeds to fund his art jones?" asked Allie.

"*Jones* is too weak a word," said Woody. "It's an obsession."

"Which makes Mirplo a kind of harmonic convergence for Jay. Which you must've recognized the minute you met him: the perfect tool to crack Wolfredian's safe."

"With just a few complications like Miriam Plowright and Red Louise to keep things salty."

"Speaking of Red Louise," I said, "weren't you kidnapped? Or was that staged for my benefit?"

"No, no, not staged. Jay wanted me on ice. I think he finds you less formidable than me. In that, of course, he is wrong. But he's also thinking of another move to make."

"What," I asked, "hold you hostage so I'll ransom you back?"

"You've done it before," said Woody, referring to the money I gave Jay in Kingman.

"And said I'd never do it again."

"Which Wolfredian obviously read as 'protests too much.'"

"How do you like that?" I said, almost chuckling. "Jay thinks *I'm* repeat business."

"Funny old world," said Woody.

"I can't help noticing," I said, "that you're no longer on ice."

"What can I tell you? Ice melts." He was thoughtful. "But it would certainly be better if Jay continued to think otherwise. So you might reinforce your concern for me next time you talk to little Martybeth. Did she try to seduce you, by the way?"

"Who's Martybeth?" asked Allie.

"She's frisky, that one."

"Who's Martybeth?" Allie asked again.

"No one," I said.

"Oh, do I let cats out of bags?" asked Woody, a twinkle in his eye.

"There's no cat and no bag," I said. "Stop making trouble." I turned to Allie. "Martybeth is a girl whose ample charms I resisted. I flipped her. She confirmed that Woody once had Jay's ear, but now Jay can't decide whether he likes Woody better as a partner or a stashed asset. Or," I added thoughtfully, "a revenge tip."

Woody waved that notion away. "Honestly, you have to like the play from Jay's point of view," he said. "He's eyeing Mirplopalooza for an investment and working Miriam Plowright for the angel fund. If everything goes according to his plan, he'll be using Vic's own money, through his own investment counselor, to buy his own crown jewel."

But just then it occurred to me that things might not be entirely on Wolfredian's script. A snippet of Louise's conversation came back to me. *"You fucked with me," she said. Notice she didn't say "fucked with my boss."* I shared this observation with Woody.

"You think she's going rogue?" he asked.

"Maybe it's just improv," I said. "I don't know."

"Yeah, me neither." It struck me that this was the first piece of information I'd handed Woody since...ever?...that didn't lay flat in the groove of his expectation. It seemed to rattle him. Which kind of rattled me. "Can you deal with that?" he asked.

"What?"

"Deal with that problem. Make it go away. Find some counter-improv."

I looked at Allie. "We've still got a couple of trapdoor spiders," I said. "I suppose we might."

"It would be best if you did. A little conflict there, a little bad blood...it could help in the endgame—maybe rush the mark some." I heard distress in Woody's voice, and that distressed me. Unsettling as it was to have Woody outthink me at every turn, I realized I'd come to rely on him. Now here he was telling me he didn't have complete control over the snuke and was counting on me to hold up maybe more than my end.

"Are you sure you can rule out revenge?" I asked.

"One can't entirely ignore that scenario," he said. "However, in my experience"—he quickly swept his doubt back under the rug of his confidence—"greed trumps revenge every time. Go sort out Louise. Best case, she's not even around for the endgame."

"Worst case?"

Woody smiled. "We'll burn that bridge when we come to it."

Just then a text message arrived, including a street address and a cold warning concerning Woody's fate—well, *someone* thought he was still on ice—if Miriam and I didn't show. I turned to show Woody the text.

But all I saw was a hole where he'd been.

The jackalope had bounded off again.

27

New ow Taver sino

Half an hour later, Allie and I were plunging past desolation row houses into the near North Las Vegas neighborhood known as the Alphabet Streets, an arid wasteland of vacant lots and dirt parks sequestered by freeways and railroad tracks from the downtown casinos (themselves a big step down from the glitz of the Strip). This was the part of Vegas the happy gamblers never see, bar those unlucky enough to be led astray by their onboard navigation systems or the need for crack at two A.M. Bulletproof mini-marts and sad window-barred Pentecostal churches bookended blocks of aging immobile homes and apartment buildings gone to demon seed. Permabums littered the sidewalks, pushing shopping carts of hoarded jetsam, or sprawled on bus benches swilling King Cobra from forty-ounce cans in paper bags.

If you're ever wondering where *down and out* hits *rock bottom,* visit the intersection of F Street and Jackson Avenue in North Las Vegas. It's there. Right there.

We stopped at a stoplight. A Metro PD car pulled up beside us, and the cop riding shotgun looked us over with a smug, How lost are you? look. The cruiser turned left and rolled on, its occupants confident that if we were here by accident, we were too stupid to be helped, and if we'd come by design, then we deserved whatever evil fate we found.

I looked at Allie, trying to get a shared laugh off the cop vibe, but she'd changed into her Miriam Plowright daywear—stiff white blouse with matching taupe jacket, skirt, and shoes—and her Plowright mood had come along for the ride. Where her sunny smile should've been, a scowl had seized her face.

"You okay?" I asked.

"'Course I'm not okay. I'm Plowright. I hate me like this."

"I'm no fan myself."

"Plus, Radar, what are we even doing here? This whole play is so ragged. I gotta tell you, I'm pretty lost right now."

"Confusion is the soul of understanding."

"What's that, a fortune cookie?"

"No, I'm just saying, we're trying to solve a puzzle, right? Make all the pieces fit."

"But the pieces *don't* fit."

"Exactly. And the fact that they don't fit is, in itself, a puzzle piece."

"You lost me."

"I kind of lost me, too. So let's boil it down. What does Wolfredian want?"

"Mirplopalooza."

"Which he sees as what?"

"A solid investment and a collector's wet dream."

"Maybe. Or maybe that's Woody's bafflegab. He keeps dealing us out while saying he's dealing us in. Does that say reliable partner to you? Does that say square deal? Comes the moment of truth, we'll find out, but precedent says, Look out. We've been nothing but his yo-yo since day one."

"The kind of toy you eventually toss away."

"Yep."

Confusion is the soul of understanding.

Whatever the hell that means.

Yet despite all the confusion, I felt pretty damn good. I was out on the edge again. If nothing else, the air here was fresh. Maybe the edge was where I belonged.

Couldn't think about that now. We'd arrived at the front range of urban blight, a wall of dead businesses all along the west side of F

Street. Defabricated franchises. Gas stations with the tanks removed. Warehouses storing nothing. And at the end of the line, our destination, a derelict rectangle of tired stucco called the New Town Tavern Casino.

This sort of "casino" once proliferated in the lesser neighborhoods of Las Vegas. They were never much more than dive bars with short banks of slot machines, back-to-back blackjack spreads comprising the pit, a one-TV sports book, and a frayed-felt Texas hold'em table in a musty alcove tarted up with chipper signage: WELCOME TO R FRIENDLY POKER ROOM—CAN WE DEAL U IN? Such clubs stood or fell on the trade of shot-and-a-beer regulars for whom the first drink of Monday morning was just the last drink of Saturday night, and when these drunks and nickel-slot compulsives go south, as they will in a down economy, they take the clubs with them. Shells remain, like this shell here, boarded up and powered down, sunk into the sort of seed dormancy that the deserts know quite well. One good flash flood of prosperity would bring them back again, but who knows when the rains will come? Maybe never. Maybe this town turns into a ghost town covered up with sand and neglect for a thousand years, until some bright-boy archaeologists stumble across it and try to figure out what it all meant at the time. Meantime, in this time, the dives stay dark.

This one had failed worse than most. Evidence of fire could be seen on the soot-streaked exterior walls. Someone had used the club's sign for target practice, so that a casual glance would place you at the NEW OW TAVER SINO. "Are you sure this is the right address?" asked Allie. By way of answer, I showed her the text message on my phone. She compared it against the faded numbers over the padlocked front door and said, "Let's check around back."

We rolled into the parking lot behind the joint, where I saw a familiar black Segue parked in the shade of a tired acacia. On the rear wall of the club, a cinder block propped open an emergency exit door. Allie and I exchanged looks. "You ready?" I asked.

"Bite me," she barked.

"Yeah, that's the Miriam Plowright I know and love."

She jerked open the car door, stepped out, and slammed it behind her. I got out, too, squinting into the shadowed back entrance to the club. The thought crossed my mind that if Wolfredian were on a revenge tip, what could be more complete payback than erasing Woody's flesh and blood? And where easier than inside this busted fun house, far from prying eyes? But I didn't feel Jay's presence here, and not just for not seeing his big-ass Buick. The more I mulled it, the more this seemed to be Louise's off-the-reservation presentation, and the prying eyes we were away from, I suspected, were as much Jay's as anyone's.

Miriam Plowright, meanwhile, had taken her icy mien and strode it over the threshold into the club's dark interior. I skittered after, manifesting the nervousness of the guy who'd brought the meat to market and was hoping, for the sake of getting Dad out of Dutch, that the deal would go down clean.

Red Louise met me at the entrance, fronting me and patting me down. Was she looking for weapons? Bugs? Both? She'd find neither, of course, and what did she expect? For the several times she'd already hit me, could she not assume that I was committed to being a good boy? Yet she went about the enterprise fully ungently. I think she smacked my Johnson on purpose.

Then she turned to frisk Miriam, who bristled at the prospect and shot me a look like, *Really? I have to put up with this bullshit?* My eyes replied with a silent plea for her cooperation. Louise intercepted the transmission—I'd made no effort to hide it—and her eyebrows arched. She seemed to think that somehow this scored a point for her. Miriam relented and allowed herself to be searched.

As my eyes adjusted to the gloom, I started to get a sense of the space we were in. It was bigger than it looked from the outside, with plenty of room for slot consoles and table games. These were long gone, of course, but you could still see their footprints etched into the tired carpet, a gacky brown affair strategically patterned to hide the beer, barf, and blood stains endemic to a disaster area like this.

Satisfied that we were packing no no-no's, Louise led us to a card table and four folding chairs in the middle of the room, presided over by a thrift-store floor lamp with a long extension cord running off into the dark. As we sat, my mind flashed back to IKEA, and I silently christened the products: Messa, Seet, Brīt. At the same time, I recognized this as the completely wrong setting for a money pitch. Usually, you'd set up shop in a suite of offices and lay on the glass and chrome, the spreadsheet projections, expert opinions, and glossy brochures. This place, with its whiff of mold and mouse droppings, was hardly likely to inspire investor confidence. So either we're looking at total amateur hour or something altogether else.

I was thinking amateur hour. I decided to ping the target a little. "Where's Jay?" I asked.

"Wherever he is," said Louise.

"Isn't..." I essayed a certain helpless confusion. "Isn't this his deal?"

"Now, where'd you get an idea like that?" asked someone who wasn't Louise or Miriam or me. And out of the gloom stepped little Martybeth Crandall. She clomped over on tall wooden sandals and flounced into the empty seat across from me with an air of breezy confidence. I heard her sandals hit the floor.

Ever had your Johnson toe-frisked? Me neither, but there's a first time for everything.

I introduced Martybeth to Miriam. It seemed like the thing to do. Meanwhile, I processed her presence, trying to determine what it meant that Martybeth and Louise were jointly rendering Jay's whales. Martybeth must have read this on my face, for she said, "Poor Radar, you're confused."

"I am a bit, yes."

"That's because you believed me, *Dim,*" said Martybeth. "It's not Jay who's running this show, it's us. We." She indicated herself and Louise.

Without even looking at Louise, I could tell that Martybeth's line of chat irked her, for the chirpy muffin top seemed to be giving away too much too soon. Sure enough, Louise applied the brakes. "We'll get to that later," she said, by which she meant never.

"Come on," said Martybeth. "He already knows—"

"I said later."

Martybeth clammed up. This told me where the power lay between them. Also, to have open conflict in front of the mark was not the slickest play in the playbook, which reinforced my assessment of amateur hour. I started to feel slightly more comfortable in the situation. Granted, Red Louise could kick my ass six ways from Sabbath, and that's not counting any hurtful hardware she might be packing. Yet, hard as she liked to come across, she seemed out of her depth.

Martybeth's agitated attitude confirmed this. She cranked her gaze from face to face, checking everyone out, just dead avid to be in the middle of this...scene. I'd seen this response before in many a mook: Give them the sense that they're on the edge of outlaw activity and they get all jangly. But Martybeth was doing it to herself. Her chest rose and fell in rapid heaves. She drummed her fingers on the quilted vinyl tabletop, returning an echoey tattoo. That was the adrenaline talking. And it was saying, *Wow, wow, wow!*

Allie did what Allie does: she stayed cool, sitting with clasped hands, waiting for Louise and Martybeth to sort themselves out. In normal grifter circumstances, this would be called letting the game come to you. Here, it was a Plowright gloss applied atop Allie's natural crystal poise. Perhaps she'd resumed recalling her state capitals: *Olympia, Phoenix, Pierre.* But one thing about this Plowright character, she didn't suffer fools, and if these ladies didn't pretty quickly (as Mirplo would put it) cut to the cheese, Miriam would start to do a slow burn.

The moment opened. Louise and Miriam found each other's eyes and locked on. This was interesting combat, a battle of wills between two women with strong ones. And while this was Louise's meeting—she'd called it and should be expected to run it—she seemed to be waiting, and wanting very much, for Miriam to speak first. Like that would score another status point. But I knew it wouldn't happen. Allie was immune to status, and she could win a staring contest with a rock.

Which put things back on Louise. Having squeezed Martybeth into silence, it now fell to her to make the pitch. She had much to overcome: this setting; the manifest ill will of Miriam Plowright; and her own partner's edgy impatience. Of course, she thought she held the ultimate trump card in Woody. I wondered how she'd see fit to play it.

I waited.

Sometimes waiting is all you can do.

28

The Ace of Hostage

It was warm in the dead club, the day's heat penetrating the ceiling to cook the dusty air and boil the smell of old smoke out of the carpet and walls. The sound of a car radio blared in through the plywood windows, rising and then falling as a driver sped past on the street outside. A fly landed on Allie's arm. She did not twitch it away.

At last, Louise gave up and started talking. "These are unusual circumstances," she said. She opened a space where Miriam could insert agreement, but Allie left that space blank. Louise stumbled over the silence and carried on. "Normally, we only offer this opportunity to certain casino guests." She waved a hand to indicate the surroundings. "And normally not here, of course."

"What, this place?" I said. "It's all ambience." Louise favored me with a glower that seemed to say my editorial input would not be necessary, and Martybeth rather more strongly made the point by scrunching my junk with her surprisingly prehensile toes.

Louise returned her attention to Allie. "Miriam," she said. "May I call you Miriam?"

"No."

Louise was taken aback. "Very well... Ms. Plowright. Since you apparently control Vic Mirplo's—"

"Just Mirplo," I interjected.

"What?" snapped Louise, a crack in her cool.

"It's just Mirplo. He doesn't use his first name anymore."

Louise smiled sweetly. "Radar, I'm not going to say this again. Shut the fuck up." And with that she got into her pitch. Despite the vulgar preamble, I thought she did rather well. Better than I'd have expected: smooth and textured, with just a few verbal fumbles where she momentarily lost her place in the patter, which I quickly recognized as a customized version of the old Pump and Dump, a boiler-room scam wherein you artificially inflate the price of a stock or other financial instrument, create an investment frenzy, and then get out before the bubble bursts. Such snaggles inevitably rely on claims of proprietary knowledge—"company's perpetual-motion prototype to win patent"—dressed up in financial humbo gumbo, and this was no exception. The Gaia, Louise told us, was the target of a covert hostile takeover. This was common knowledge within the organization but not so common that one could exploit it without being popped for insider trading. An informed outsider, however, could make a short-term investment and a big killing. Martybeth here mentioned the Gaia's current share price and the proposed buyout price, a tantalizingly large differential. This seemed to be her only contribution to the pitch, and I could see her working hard to get it right.

Louise then delved into the particulars: How much she and Martybeth would invest, how much they'd want from Miriam, and how they'd split the take. In classic con fashion, they were prepared to trust Miriam with their money, provided only that she show them some earnest money—a million dollars was the standard ask—to justify their faith. Red further sweetened the pot by proposing a generous "finder's fee" for every one of Miriam's clients that she steered their way.

"Whose end would that come out of?" Allie asked.

"The clients' of course," said Louise. "They're going to make so much money, they won't even notice."

Louise applied several more coats of bafflegab, filling in the procedural blanks and fielding Miriam's questions. I listened to all of this with half an ear, relaxing my perception to let my radar do its work. Of course I knew it was all lies, but I wondered which level of lie, and why.

After all, Jay knew me to be in the game. Surely I'd see through the Pump and Dump. Therefore, either he didn't know or didn't care about this pitch. Trouble was, based on available information, I couldn't tell which. My mind wandered to a reconsideration of these greasy surroundings. The burned-out bar, I realized, actually helped legitimize the play, for where better to propose criminal conspiracy than in such a sneaky redoubt? It got those outlaw juices flowing. Made the deal seem more real. Well, it would to the casual mark. Even without the hidden stake raiser, a little card called the Ace of Hostage.

I tried to imagine how a normal mark would react. Would he be taken in by this well-below-board opportunity? Maybe. It certainly sounded enticing, the way Louise spun it out. Yet the more I listened, the more convinced I became that this was her debutante spiel. She pitched well enough, but there was an element of rote she couldn't hide. Add a few missteps, her less-than-instant answers to Miriam's questions, and Martybeth's stilted contribution, and the whole thing screamed opening-night jitters on someone's borrowed script. Would that matter to the mark? That person would be a high roller, a gambler by nature. The promise of a nosebleed ROI could easily suck him in, especially if he had a big gambling jones to support, and if he'd been eased in here in the first place by a casino host he trusted.

But none of this applied to Miriam Plowright. She was no whale. She was a tight-ass professional, financial advisor to a respected (albeit vaporware) list of clients. She had a fiscal responsibility to them—a responsibility that didn't extend to cutting sketchy deals in wretched ex-bars with newbie confidence tricksters. There was nothing at all in her character, credentials, or backstory to suggest that she'd shade the law for the right price, and not much in Louise's pitch, no matter how prettily presented, to persuade Miriam otherwise. So she couldn't possibly say yes.

But, alas, she also couldn't say no.

Louise knew this. She deduced it from the pure fact of Miriam's presence. Red knew that the pitch, whether right down the middle, high and outside, or all the way to the backstop, was largely irrelevant, just a layer of words spread over a ransom play, with her and Martybeth in tacit conspiracy with their third partner.

Me.

My mind went back to Kingman, and the words I so flippantly flashed while I was getting Woody's bailout cash. *"I suppose you think I'm just throwing good money after black sheep,"* I'd told Louise. *"I promised Mom I'd look after him."* I was just horsing around, but suppose she took my horseplay to heart? She saw how much cash I had, saw how easily I let it go. Then, when Jay ordered her to nab Woody, she saw her chance to go freelance. Put the right words in Martybeth's ears, who put them in mine (and here I thought Dim Ysmygu had been so clever). Then arranged our late-night light-heavyweight brawl, and softened me up with blows. After that, all that remained was for a properly motivated Hoverlander to put Plowright in an investing mood. Red knew I'd do my best, for she held the aforementioned trump card, the Ace of Hostage.

I was ghosting her now, seeing things from her side of the table. She'd ordered me to produce Plowright, and produce I did. But Plowright was only there to listen, yes? Consider an investment opportunity. She had the right to say no, yes? Maybe. But I'm a demonstrably persuasive guy. Presumably I'd persuaded her in advance that the deal was kosher, North Vegas hellhole assignation aside. Why had I done this? To get Daddy dear in the clear. And how had I done it? Hoverlander magic—who cares? From that side of the table, the seats on this side of the table didn't even get filled unless I had Miriam's cooperation locked up going in.

So what happens next? People shake hands and all agree to meet at the appointed place and time with the called-for bag of cash. There some ad hoc sleight of hand will transpire, and the next thing Miriam knows, she's holding a great big bag of nothing. What can she do? Go to the law she'd just put herself on the wrong side of? Nope, she'll just have to swallow the loss (maybe spread it painlessly among her clients, disguised as fee increases). And in the aftermath, all she will do is regret falling in with Vic Mirplo and his cunning, charming con-man comrade, who, she will ultimately conclude, must've been working with these two Gaia *chavalas* all along.

All that left was the shaking of hands and making of plans. Before we could get there, though, Uncle Joe bawled from my pants pocket, "He shoots, he scores!" Everyone jumped, and I told myself it was really past time to change that ringtone. A glance at the phone revealed a text from Mirplo: *Dragonfly flys. 4king awsum!* Well, I'm glad someone was having a good day.

Because mine was about to slide sideways.

Allie leaned back from the table, arms above her head. I could hear her vertebrae pop as she stretched. "It's a very interesting proposal," she began. "For the record, you do know it's illegal, right?"

Martybeth started to speak, but Louise cut her off. "We've spoken to lawyers," she said. "It's a gray area."

Allie nodded dubiously. "A gray area."

"In any case, you'd have deniability."

"Uh-huh." Allie rubbed her chin. This, of course, was a sign of introspection, and it landed on Louise with the intended effect. She started to doubt.

"We could increase your fee, you know."

"Yes, I imagine you have some give in that department. But still... bags of cash delivered to undisclosed locations. Good-faith money. This isn't how I'm used to working."

"Well...," grasped Louise, "be flexible."

Said Allie, "I'd love to be flexible. You're practically offering me free money."

"Yes!" said Louise, a little too loudly. She backed it down a notch. "Yes."

"And even two months ago, I'd have jumped on it. But now, with Mirplo..."

"What about Mirplo?" asked Louise, warily. I think she was starting to recognize that name as the ongoing fly in her ointment.

"You know, he's about to get big. Really big. And then he'll be in the public eye."

"So?"

"He'll be scrutinized. *I'll* be scrutinized."

"Your other clients—"

"I'm letting them go. Mirplo has asked me to lead his management team." Allie allowed Miriam an uncharacteristic smile. "I'm putting all my eggs in that bountiful basket. So you see"—she gave a commiserating shrug, the kind you give when you're delivering your definitive no—"much as I like free money, I really don't need it now. And I definitely don't need the risk." She essayed another smile. "Deniability aside."

By now I could see the *rookie* written all over Louise's face, as it cycled through a predictable set of expressions, mostly of the surprise and dismay variety, and none anywhere near the neighborhood of happy. She'd been so certain of this deal—it was a lock, right?—and now she was falling fast, scrabbling at thin air like a cartoon animal going over a cliff. She shot me a cold look and said, "Mr. Hoverlander..."—Oh, now suddenly I'm Mr. Hoverlander? See, that's a stumble. That's a broken play—"did we not discuss the hidden benefits of this deal?"

Hidden benefits, yeah. Like keeping my father alive. This was my cue to go a little nuts.

I took it in stages.

"Ms. Plowright," I said. "Miriam..." (See? That's a broken play.) "I thought you understood that the presentation was just a formality. Last night—"

Miriam cut me off with a laugh. "Last night, you were a grade B lay with a grade D scam. You want to know why I came out here today? For a laugh."

"Now look, that's just not fair. This thing is legit. The numbers—"

"Oh, legit," mocked Plowright. "The only number I'd trust about you is your shoe size." She stood up. "I'm out of here."

"Wait!" I said, standing, my voice now breaking into shards of anxiety. "What about my, you know..."

"Your dad? Your *dad*?" She turned to Louise and Martybeth, really working hard to suppress her glee. "Do you know what this yabbo told me? That you two kidnapped his father and were holding him hostage to this deal." She turned back to me. "That's when I knew it was all nonsense, by the way."

"But it's true," I protested, plaintively.

"Oh, you don't say. Really, truly true? Well, that explains why you're so desperate to sign me on to this clownish deal." She patted my cheek, a gesture I visibly found infuriating. "Look, pretty boy, this isn't my first chicken dance." She waved a hand at her surroundings. "This den of iniquity." She glanced at the girls. "These two laughable insider traders." Then back to me. "Your endangered dad. It all adds up to a con game, and not a very clever one. And then the good-faith money? Honey, if I fell for that, I'd deserve to get ripped off. So, bye-bye." She went to pat my cheek again, but this time I grabbed her wrist with my hand, and held her arm there in midair. "Let me go," she said.

"We had a deal," I growled. "We came to terms."

"You came to terms. I was jerking your chain."

I raised my free hand in threat.

"That's enough," said Red Louise. "If we can't reach an agreement like sensible people, then we'll find another way."

Her other way, unfortunately, involved her Glock.

29

Stash My Sh*t

It wasn't intended to happen like this. Allie, having double-crossed me, was intended to endure my vituperation for a while, then lose her patience and reply with ire in kind. Then would ensue an escalating frenzy of recrimination, insults, even grappling on the floor (though with this gacky carpet, I was now not so sure). Eventually, our fury would spend, Miriam would evacuate in a self-righteous huff, and I'd devolve, in Louise's eyes, into a total dickhead loser who couldn't even save his father's life. By such means we'd achieve our twin goals of finding out where Jay was at with this play (not a part of it) and categorically easing ourselves out. Later, Louise would discover that Woody'd slipped the noose on his own, but by then she'd have put us off her mental map. All because Allie and I would get so convincingly evil on each other. It was the best part of our script, but we never got a chance to play it.

A gun is the ultimate improv.

Now Allie and I would have to improvise likewise. She made the first move. "This doesn't concern me anymore," she said as she wriggled her wrist free from my hand and turned to go. Louise nodded to Martybeth, who sidled over and placed herself in Allie's path. In other circumstances, you'd have viewed this as comical, a distaff Mutt and Jeff, little Martybeth giving away a good six inches to Allie yet defiantly thrusting her sweater pies at the taller woman, itching to take her on.

Allie weighed the consequences of starting a brawl. No doubt she could whip Martybeth—one good shot to the sweater pies—but such sudden movements tend to trigger others, notably ones involving triggers. Best to keep things on the talking tip for now. Allie didn't give ground—Miriam never would—but she let her shoulders sag just a little, to indicate that she wasn't going to try to bull her way out, at least not yet. She looked back at Louise and said, "Well?"

"Sit down," said Louise. "Both of you."

We sat. Louise remained standing, her gun angled down and away, but casually ready. I tried to gain a sense of her competence with firearms. It affects how things go. "You do know how to handle that thing, yes?" I said. "I mean, when it comes to not accidentally shooting people."

"If I shoot you," she said, "it won't be an accident."

Louise became preoccupied with plotting her path forward. I ghosted her available scenarios. She could let us go, of course, but that didn't rate high on the likeliness scale, not when she (thought she) still held the Ace of Hostage. Plus, there are technical terms for people like us if you let them go running around loose: complainants; witnesses. At the extreme other end of alternatives lay the possibility of making us both dead and similarly tying up the loose end of Woody in due course. This also rated long odds against, for unless these two were terribly adept at cover-up, which they probably knew they were not, then killing us must necessarily turn into a gun-and-run situation, with Martybeth and Louise on the lam like Thelma and same. But flight works better with cash in hand, and to kill us now, without landing a payday, was to accept the worst possible outcome. Louise struck me as a lesser-of-evils type. And in that instant, I knew she'd try to sustain the play.

Which she did. She flipped a chair around backward and straddled it, bringing her face close to Miriam's. "Okay," she said, "here's what's what." She cocked her chin in my direction. "He wasn't lying about his father. I have him stashed, and no one gets him back until someone meets my price."

"So the insider trading thing . . . ," said Miriam, dryly.

"Don't get smug, sister. You were smart enough to see through that, but not smart enough to keep your wisdom to yourself."

"In which case," said Miriam, "I'm just an innocent bystander."

"You were. Now you're an interested party."

"Not that interested."

"Completely interested," said Red. "Because you're no longer ransoming his father's life."

"No."

"No. You're ransoming his."

To her credit, Allie managed the most convincingly derisive laugh I've ever heard. Man, if she ever meant that laugh, I'd want to kill me myself. There followed chapter and verse about the many nasty things that Louise and Martybeth were welcome to do to me for dragging Miriam into this mess. She was very convincing. I felt cold.

"Well, if that's how you feel," said Louise laconically, "then I guess you can go. But just so you know, we know you spent last night with him."

"So I fucked him. That doesn't mean I'm going to fuck my clients for him."

"Yeah," said Louise, "it doesn't. But I planted a camera."

With evident glee, Martybeth flipped open her smartphone, hit a couple of keys, and started a silent video playback. I saw Allie lying the length of me, and me running my fingers down her spine like tiny skiers jumping the moguls of Mount Back.

"That doesn't look like fucking," said Louise. "That looks like making love. So whatever you two have going on between you, we think it's more than just casual sex. Maybe you're working both sides against the Mirplo. But that's yesterday's news. Today's news is, Miriam plows up a million dollars by tomorrow afternoon, or she can kiss her lover, or conspirator, or whatever, good-bye."

Allie played a desperation card. "I already told you I don't give a rat's ass about him."

"Then that's his bad luck. But we'll give you a chance to have second thoughts." Louise gestured me to my feet with the gun. She groped in my pockets for my car keys, tossed them to Allie, and said, "Now go."

Allie went.

I stayed put.

I knew a guy once, a proper gentleman who hated profanity like a cat hates baths. When we got in trouble together, which we did fairly regularly, he would say, "Well, aren't we fornicated now?"

Man, he didn't know what fornicated was.

They tied my hands behind me, which I hate, and gagged me, which I really hate because it steals my voice, the spinach to my Popeye. Then they walked me to the Segue and belted me into a back seat, which is a really effective restraint when your hands are tied, because what are you going to do, push the release button with your nose? Try it sometime, let me know how that works out for you. They didn't blindfold me, and I know not why, for isn't that part of the Shanghai trifecta? But anyway they didn't, so I had a side-scrolling view of Las Vegas as we headed northwest through its suburbs, then its outskirts, to the verge where the buildings stop and the desert starts. There we entered a failed commercial development where nothing stood but a Stash My Sh*t storage facility. It wasn't much, just a line of concrete lockers with roll-up steel doors, alone and forlorn, on a broad, cracked slab of asphalt. In these befallen times, the manager's office was closed and shuttered, with a sign that read, FACILITY SELF-MONITORED, USE AT OWN RISK.

Louise parked the Segue, and I waited in the car with her while Martybeth got out, presumably to open a unit and prepare it to receive its guest. I tried to catch Louise's eye in the rearview mirror with a series of friendly, nonthreatening gestures, mostly of the kitten eye and raised eyebrow variety. She conspicuously paid no attention. After a moment, Martybeth returned, taking unsuccessful pains to hide the worried look on her face. Louise opened the window, and Martybeth whispered to her, a wholly ineffectual security measure when the man in the back seat reads lips.

"We've got problems," I saw her say. "He's gone." I couldn't see Louise's response, but I read the tension in the back of her neck, down behind the ponytail. "Just gone," continued Martybeth. "Come look."

Louise went with Martybeth. I lifted myself as far as the seat belt would allow and craned my neck to watch them walk together to one of the storage units. They stood there inspecting it, at a loss. I could just barely make out the source of their consternation: somehow, a bottom corner of the door had been pried up. Not much. Enough for a man to wriggle through, especially a spry one. A nearby shank of rebar might have played a part. I found it inspiring to see the evidence of Woody's resourceful escape. Here I'd been having a little pity party for myself (you're never in the best of moods when you've been hijacked), but in that moment I figured that if there was something to this business of being "a Hoverlander," then maybe I'd manage, too.

They came walking back toward the SUV, Martybeth looking hangdog and Louise radiating fury. It sucks, I guess, when your criminal mastermind plans go blooey.

"We should have left him tied," I saw Louise say.

"How would he pee?"

"He could've pissed in his pants."

"Sweetie, that's cruel."

Sweetie? Okay, that's news. I wondered if Jay knew that his staunch softballer switch-hit.

"Whatever," said Louise. "We still have this one." Meaning me. "And we won't make that mistake again." Then she smiled. I did not like the look of that smile.

For, as it turned out, excellent reasons.

An hour later, just after dusk, I'm locked in the dark, bound and gagged, but butt naked so I can pee any time I like into this here conveniently placed slop bucket. Such consideration. A feature of all the finest hotels. I think they took particular delight in stripping me bare, but if I was meant to find this humiliating, it really just annoyed. Of rather more concern was the comprehensive use they made of duct tape, encasing my hands and feet in giant balls of the stuff, securing my elbows and knees, then cinching the whole enterprise together so that all I could do was lie on my side like an abandoned bike or rise briefly and awkwardly to my knees. They taped my mouth as well. No yelling for help for young Radar. (Not that anyone would hear me out here—*Last Stash My Sh*t for 500 Miles.*) A slit and a straw gave me access to a bowl of water, but food would have to wait.

Well, wait for what? Presumably for Allie to pull together my ransom, and that grieved me, for there went the bankroll for Operation Citizen. It further grieved me, naturally, to find myself in such a fornicated situation in the first place. I had completely underestimated Red Louise. As for Martybeth and her distaff affections, I plain never saw that coming. Radar's radar was seriously on the fritz—had been, in fact, since Woody first waltzed onto the scene and drove a wedge between me and my plans. Now look at me. As a function of failed focus, I'd hit a new low. Between my ambivalence toward Woody and my half-assed determination to go straight, I was never fully committed to the snuke nor fully committed to turning my back. Throw in the problematic relationships with my beloved, my jackalope, and the rapidly morphing Mirplo... Grifters shouldn't have relationships. It makes us lose track.

Speaking of relationships, if Martybeth and Louise were lovers, then what did that make Martybeth's come-on to me? A purely professional move? Ouch, my feelings.

The hours passed. I think I nodded off.

"He shoots, he scores!"

What?

"He shoots, he scores!"

Yutzes! They left my cell phone in my pants, and left my pants...

where? I tried to echolocate the sound of Vic's voice, but it bounced indiscriminately within the bare concrete box. Then I remembered that my phone also lit when it rang and . . . yes, there it was, a faint pulse of light, diffused through denim, in the far back corner. But how to get there? You'd be surprised how big a ten-by-twelve storage space can be when it's pitch-black and your only means of movement involves struggling to your knees, flopping forward, rolling over, then getting back to your knees and repeating that clumsy dance.

Of course the phone stopped ringing just as I reached it. Not that I could've answered it anyhow. Feeling now truly forlorn, I took what comfort I could in having found my jeans. At least I had a pillow.

"He shoots, he scores!"

Oh, now that's just mean. The caller must've thought so, too, because the phone cut off after one ring.

Then it rang again, and just as quickly cut off. Then it rang twice, then silence.

Well, this went on for a while, and it gradually dawned on me that someone was trying to send me a message.

Someone who knew Morse code.

30

....–.. .–.. –––

Allie knew Morse code; we'd messed with it together that night so long ago at that Mexican bar, when Operation Citizen began. They say you can identify Morse senders by their "fist," the characteristic way they send a string of dashes and dots, but I imagine that the cell-phone ringtone method wreaks havoc with an operator's fist. It certainly takes forever. With one ring representing a dot and two rings a dash, you're looking at fifteen phone calls just to say ....–.. .–.. ––– (Hello). Hope your battery's charged. Anyway, I figured it was Allie, especially when the first phrase I deciphered was .. – ... / .– .–.. .–.. .. . (It's Allie).

Of course, Allie couldn't know my circumstances: Someone else might be listening in, someone who knew Morse or could coerce me to decode. Therefore, her message was crafted as music both to my and my captors' ears, basically stating that she'd soon have the cash in hand and was prepared to trade, straight up, one million dollars for one Hoverlander. Everything, she averred, would go according to the script. The use of the word *script* was key, because it assured any eavesdropping antagonists that she was glatt kosher but also alerted me that someone, somewhere, presumably Woody, was improvising new plays for the playbook. I'll tell you one thing: For the first time since this whole thing began, I felt faith in my father. I just knew—gut knew—that he wouldn't let me down. I'll tell you another thing: By the time silence ensued, I was goddamn sick of Uncle Joe. Gotta change that ringtone. Really. First chance I get when my hands are free.

I spent some time attacking that goal, for I'd discovered by feel (using my cheek) that the interior walls of the storage locker were cross-braced with rebar, and if that's where Woody got his, then there might be a raw edge left where he'd jimmied a piece free. So I flop-and-rolled my way around the perimeter, pausing at intervals to investigate the wall with my face. By the time I'd done two walls, I was pretty exhausted and had to take a break to flop-and-roll back to my water bowl. I flailed around like a bobbing bird until I hit water, then sucked up a few mouthfuls through the straw taped into my gag. This is not the normal way one drinks, of course; some of the water went down the wrong pipe, and I coughed it back up into my mouth. So unpleasant on so many levels.

Halfway along the third wall I found what I needed: a jagged end of metal, either Woody's doing or some other, unrelated mishap. Trouble was, it was too high to get my hands on. My only choice was to lie on my back, stick my feet up, and have at it.

Okay, easier said than done. *Much* easier said than done when you're naked in the dark, your legs move as one cumbersome unit, and lying on your back actually means lying on your heavily wadded hands on your back. It was like bedding down on a bowling ball. Nevertheless, I gave it my best effort, and through a combination of sawing and hacking, soon made some inroads into the great glump of tape binding my feet.

I'm a whistle-while-you-work type. Always have been. Give me a goal, something to focus my energy on, and my mood inevitably lifts. That happened here. I fell into a certain rhythm—saw, hack, flex, wrest, rest, saw, hack, flex, wrest, rest—and found that the effort soothed me. I hadn't forgotten my dire nocturnal straits. Even if I managed to cut myself loose, I was still alone in a dark place, with a million-dollar price tag, crazy chicks who would probably try to kill me at some point, the unresolved threat of Jay Wolfredian, and the equally unresolved question of whether Woody could, as claimed, button up his old enemy. I figured I was still a good four or five big moves from clear of this thing—assuming I got clear and didn't, in fact, get dead.

And I never felt more alive.

Call me perverse, I don't mind. But there in that storage locker, scraping duct tape off my bound feet, I realized that the grift was graphite for my life, the dry lubricant that kept everything running smoothly. Forget about leopards and forget about spots, just keep your eye on that sign over there, the one that reads, "Love what you do. If you don't love it, you won't do it well." Even this ridiculous scenario appealed to me. It stimulated me and commanded my powers. I desperately wanted to get out of the current bind, of course, but at the same time, if I were being truly honest with myself (and hadn't bedrock honesty been the whole point of Operation Citizen?), I equally desperately wanted to get into some other subsequent bind and maybe just a bind or two after that. At that moment, I attained clarity. A grifter I was, and a grifter I would remain. I hoped and trusted that when it came to it, I could make Allie see things my way. She was my betrothed, after all. We should try to walk the same path.

Then, suddenly, *sproing!* The last sticky shred of duct tape gave way and my feet fell free. This let me attack the tape around my knees, which freed rather more quickly than my feet, and after that it was a simple matter to shred the rest of the hogtie. Soon I could stand upright again, and man, that felt good. Primordial. Like I'd just come down from the trees.

My hands took a surprisingly long time to unwrap. Maybe there was a lot more duct tape, or maybe I was just getting tired, but in any case, the effort extended through the long, slow hours of the night. Eventually I noticed a weak gray light rising—daylight, crawling in under the rolling metal door, most notably through the part that Woody'd pried up and the girls had hastily banged back into place. I knew I could go out the same way. *Just get these hands free,* I thought to myself, *and I am outta here.*

Finally the tape gave way and I pulled away the tape on my mouth, too. And there I stood, jaybird naked, but for the gooey adhesive residue clinging to various body parts. In the growing light, I headed to my clothes to put them on. First, though, I stopped at the slop bucket and had myself a good, long piss. It seemed like a piss of triumph.

Until the steel door rolled up, and Louise and Martybeth caught me relieving my horse in midstream.

And that's what we call bad timing.

Suspiciously bad, in fact. A suspicion instantly borne out by Martybeth, who smugly waggled her smartphone. I didn't bother looking around for the infrared pinhole camera they'd planted; like the one in my hotel room, it would be small enough not to be seen. It must've amused the hell out of them to watch me struggle through the long hours of the night, and meanwhile, they were building quite a collection of Hoverlander porn.

Keeping me covered with her gun, Louise waved Martybeth to my pile of pants. Martybeth plucked out my cell phone and tossed it to Louise, who eyed it suspiciously. "I don't suppose you want to tell me what this was all about."

"Wrong number." I shrugged. "Very persistent."

"Uh-huh." She dropped the phone to the floor and ground it beneath the heel of her work boot. Farewell, Uncle Joe. So much for changing my ringtone.

"Get dressed," said Red. "You look ridiculous." This was true, but tell me who doesn't when they're naked and gooey, only half peed, and everyone around them is in clothes? As I skivvied into my jeans, she said, "Hurry up. We have a long drive."

"Why not save us all the long drive," I asked, "and kack me here. Price of gas and whatnot." I looked around and spotted the Segue. "And you must measure the mileage on that thing in feet."

Louise came up to me and stood close. "Know what your problem is, Radar?"

"Irritable bowel syndrome?"

"You think you're funny. And you think that matters."

"What can I tell you? Laughter is the best medicine. It works a treat against gunshot wounds."

"Don't worry," said Martybeth. "No one's going to hurt you, not if your girlfriend holds up her end." From the way she said *girlfriend,* I could tell she meant Allie, not Miriam. Red knew it too, and threw her partner an angry hiss. Loose lips on that one.

"You two," I said, "really need to get on the same page if you're planning to make a career of this." I smiled at Martybeth. "How'd you find out?"

"Find out what?" asked Martybeth, futilely slamming the barn door behind the cow.

"Never mind," I said. "You know what you know. Anyway, happy endings all around, that's good news. So let's get going." I extended my wrists to Louise in surrender, naturally assuming it was duct tape time again.

"Oh, no," said Louise. "We're way past that." She shot me a fierce grin.

Then gave me a shot of something that put me to sleep.

I awoke curled up on the deck of the Segue's cargo area, staring into the back of the back seat. Shaking off the sedative, I tried to sit up and found it a struggle. This I attributed to the unpredictable effects of off-label prescription tranquilizers, until I realized that my constraint was more physical than chemical: a choke chain of no small girth, circling my neck, thick and weighty, and secured by a heavy nylon lead to a tie-down on the deck of the Segue. *Now he was a dog on a leash, and they have no free will.*

"Cute," I muttered, when I could muster a voice.

"I thought you'd like it," said Louise. "Utilitarian and, one hopes, not too painful. How do you feel?"

"Like my brain's been turned inside out."

"That'll pass. My advice: enjoy the ride, and invest faith in the faithfulness of your friends."

Faith being too abstract a concept to process just then, I rested my brain on available visual information, gleaned through the Segue's side and rear windows. We were far out in the desert, the sort of blank, endless desert that Nevada does better than almost anywhere. The Segue was traveling north across an immense endorheic basin—a salt flat—pluming a spray of fine, white dust in its wake. Hundreds of other such plumes dotted the dry lake, all made by cars and trucks bombing along at speed, channeling Craig Breedlove. Many of these, I could see, were tricked out with psychedelic paint jobs and ambitious artistic add-ons, or towing trailers of odd shapes and designs. It made for a festive parade, which, as the lake bed narrowed into a canyon mouth at its northern end, merged and funneled into a festive traffic jam.

The smoked glass of the Segue's windows filtered the ferocious desert light as I studied the steeply angled canyon walls. Desperate vegetation clung to cracks in the rocks, demonstrating nature's marvelous eptitude at making the best of a hellish situation. Then again, someone had built a road through this place long ago, so that's human eptitude, too. Did they think they'd find gold here? Probably. They think they'll find gold everywhere; it's how guys like me stay in business.

The road rose with the canyon, traversing a rocky streambed that may not have run with water for five or five thousand years. The walls closed in as the canyon narrowed, and I imagined the scene as seen from above: a line of amazingly funked-up vehicles penetrating the desert like a funeral procession on LSD. And all roads led to Mirplopalooza. Just ask the signs by the side of the road, or the drivers or perpetrators of any of the hundreds of art cars with Nelson mandalas on their quarter panels or plywood shark fins on their roofs. The theme of the show was "Be the Show," and this crowd had enthusiastically bought in.

The road climbed up the canyon to a ridgetop, where a line of prefab ticket booths slowed traffic to a walking pace as each vehicle stopped to hand over cash or printed tickets. Chipper ticket takers greeted each carload with enthusiastic approval for their artistic efforts. When it was our turn. Louise rolled down the window and a multiply pierced kid leaned in. "Welcome to Mirplopalooza," he said. "Be the show." As he took money from Louise, he glanced back and noticed my leash-and-chain ensemble. "Nice," he said. "I like it."

Great. Now I'm art.

The kid waved us on. We drove around a small hill and descended into the basin beyond.

And I was moved. Just like a train.

31

Mirplopalooza

Some places in the natural world, you look at them and can't imagine how they possibly came to be. Your rational mind offers a scientific explanation: tectonic this; oxidized that. Your spiritual mind argues otherwise: "Well, God's no slouch with aesthetics."

God, nature, ancient astronauts wielding laser chain saws, whatever, they sure did good work here.

A wall of red cliffs leaped a thousand feet from the desert floor, topped at the plateau with a line of small pines that ran along the lip like stunty green teeth. Striations of color ranging from pale coral to deep sanguine bespoke the variable presence of iron in the original sandstone. Laser chain saws (or erosion) had carved away the base of the cliff, leaving it with a vertiginous overhang. The cliff formed a soaring curtain of stone that ran halfway around a flat basin of sand, itself giving off a soft glow the color of sunset. Opposite the cliff curtain stood a line of stone towers,* a dozen pink pinnacles of tuff, each bony finger topped by a knob of harder stone—basalt, most likely. Some had lost their capstones and eroded down to nubs, not much more than head high. Others rose majestically, and these had been fully Mirploed: wound around with sheets of linen and strung between

*True fact: geologists know these as hoodoos, the most bogus-sounding real name for anything I've ever heard in my life.

with flags of shiny Mylar that flapped in the breeze and refracted light like oil slicks in sunshine. Kites filled the air around the spires, hand painted with strange flying beasts, some loosely based on myth—your dragons, your griffins and such—but most pure Mirplovian invention, and you didn't know exactly what you were looking at, but you knew what it meant: The good guys were the good guys, the bad guys were the bad guys, and say, fellas, who's up for a kite fight?

Between the stone fingers and the red cliff lay the broad expanse of the basin, bare as an airfield, and aptly so, for there stood a fleet of helium balloons tied to stone anchors on the desert floor. These were Mylar too, but hardly like you'd find in the hospital gift shop. For one thing, they were huge: giant floating sausages. For another, they had control surfaces—stubby wings and rudders—plus propeller packages aft and stilettolike spikes up front. Like the kites, they rocked the livery of heroes and villains, and once again you had no trouble knowing who the good guys were. Teams of young men and women tended taut tethers as someone somewhere tested the blimps' remote guidance systems, making them fight their handlers like fish on a line.

From walls of loudspeakers, music filled the basin, a sonorous blanket of tranquility that reminded me of new-mown grass, of nap time in kindergarten, of the night before Christmas. I recognized Vic's signature tonalities, and found my spirit rising to the sound. It changed, though. Subtly and by degrees it shifted through neutral into uncomfortable, then heaving and joyless; ultimately, a dirge. Intellectually I understood that this was the mere manipulation of major and minor chords, of finding certain disharmonic combinations that strike the ear the way clashing reds and greens strike the eye. But when is music understood intellectually? I suffered until it stopped.

Attendants directed us to a parking area apart from the basin, and here a party had broken out, as arriving festivalgoers poured out of cars, vans, and buses wearing costumes of every level of complexity, from thrift-store throw-ons to grandiloquent Rio regalia. The most ambitious displays were not so much costumes as constructions. Here you'd see a walking castle, and there its counterpoint, a trebuchet that fired balls of dye-soaked sponge, so that the castle became, over time, its own terrible history of conflict. And more than a few guests wore the homage of elaborate papier-mâché Mirplo heads. Whatever he was selling, these avid fans seemed to have bought in bulk. And credit the infosphere for getting the word out so well and so quickly; back in the day, it took legwork and luck to create such fads and ride their fast-burn trajectories. Hits, as we know, have a life of their own, but it never hurts to goose them with a little flash-mob APB.

Judging from available evidence, Mirplopalooza was a hit.

I, meanwhile, was still a dog on a leash. After we parked, Martybeth opened the cargo door and tugged me out of the Segue by my neck. To my choke chain she now added garlands of red peppers, face-painted whiskers, a sombrero, and a faded wool poncho. "If anyone asks," she said, tugging again on the nylon line to show my neck who's boss, "you're a Chihuahua. Say *sí*."

I said, "*Sí*." As a costume concept, it was wholly hokey, yet you had to admire the job it did of hiding a kidnap victim in plain sight. I hardly stood out, for I wasn't the only visitor in light bondage drag. And whatever protest I might voice would be interpreted as just an overamped actor getting carried away with his role.

Between the parking lot and the balloon harbor lay the heart of Mirplopalooza, an explosion of tents, soundstages, food stands, carnival games, and strolling entertainers. Given the "Be the Show" sentiment of festivalgoers, you'd be hard-pressed to figure out where the paid entertainment left off and the penny public began. But the public was certainly forking over. Witness the abundant souvenir stands, where hawkers hawked Mirplovian artifacts: CDs, prints, models of the installation, T-shirts, hats, books of poems, even a quickie novel, self-published, self-illustrated, and each copy a signed original. And the stuff was selling. Mirplo the Golden Goose? *"I'm telling you, Radar, you gotta get in on this art shit. Easiest goddamn money you'll ever make."* To all appearances, yes.

Martybeth led the way, threading through the crowd with me on her leash. Louise trailed behind, one hand thrust deep in the pocket of her cargo pants, and she didn't figure to be fingering a good-luck charm. But was her gun a bluff? I mean, what if I just yanked the lead out of Martybeth's hands and took off? Would Louise have the nerve to shoot me down as I ran? I decided not to find out. The thing about going all-in is, you have to not care whether your opponent calls your bet or not. In this case, a call would grieve me deeply.

Out of the teeming throng of stilt walkers, jugglers, henna tattooists, and strolling troubadours came someone wearing the full-body costume of a ferocious Kodiak bear. He loomed quite close—feinted toward Martybeth, in fact, so that she flinched and gave ground—and he reeked of clove cigarettes. So Honey was here. And Woody? Was he likewise orbiting close? And how would I know if he was? A harlequin to begin with, he could be anyone in this gymkhana from Madame Lola Reads Your Fortune to the guy with the tofu hot-dog cart.

I caught a glimpse of Zoe striding through the crowd with purpose, consulting her Geoid and barking into the microphone of a wireless headset. I read her lips as she said, "Places, people. He's two minutes out." She headed off toward the balloon area, and my attention went with her until an ungentle tug brought it back to Martybeth.

"This way," she said. We flanked a bank of Jon's Johns and followed a row of craft stalls to a big round tent, a yurt, really, but updated with postmodern eco-fabrics and emblazoned with the logo of the Gaia Casino. We were just about to enter the tent when suddenly...

...everything stopped.

The bands onstage ceased playing. The vendors stopped vending. The strolling acrobats and clowns turned serious and still. Even the trash pickers stopped picking trash. Like robots with drained batteries or zombies under mind control, every single event staffer went slack. It wasn't mind control; more likely Zoe's command, transmitted first via Geoid or radio and then out among the masses through a series of hand gestures or prearranged signals. Moving in a loose choreography, the hirelings all shifted to gain lines of sight to the sky overhead, an open invitation for the patrons to do likewise. Martybeth tried to tug me into the yurt, but I stood my ground. This I wanted to see.

And here it came, an ultralight aircraft motoring in at a stately pace, pushing a high, whining engine sound before it. As it reached the festival grounds and circled there, low above the gawking crowd, it revealed itself to be an Aeroprakt Foxbat, but stunningly reimagined as a dragonfly, with the undersides of its boxy wings painted to emulate that insect's gossamer double-blade configuration. A long, trailing windsock created the illusion of a posthensile abdomen. Two metallic green crosshatched bulbs—the dragonfly's compound eyes—covered the cockpit and obscured any possible view of a pilot inside. Manifesting Vic's passion for duality, the dragonfly was at once inspiring and distressing: lyrical, poetical, yet potentially monstrous. I contemplated all the good-guy/bad-guy kites and balloons and understood that this creature completed the picture in a fundamental way. In the morality play of Mirplo's imagining, here, at last, was the protagonist. And yes, he was right, it's all art, including planes.

The ultralight described lazy figure eights overhead. There was a nacelle or pod slung low under the Foxbat's monocoque fuselage. Evidently remotely controlled, it opened now like a tiny Enola Gay and spewed forth a stream of... what? Dragonfly eggs? Light, fluffy somethings that swirled in the plane's prop wash, then drifted down behind it in a diffuse pink cloud. People scrambled to gather them, for no more reason than folks chase beads thrown from krewe floats at Mardi Gras. I plucked one out of the air and found it to be an origami bird—a tiny, tiny Albuquerque Turkey—handmade, lemongrass scented, signed, and absolutely stunning. Prompted by I know not what urge, I turned to a stranger and gave my treasure away. I saw others in the crowd likewise inspired to this small generosity. *Art is something that moves you.* Maybe it moves you to act.

The ultralight now spiraled upward, like a hawk riding a thermal, and flew off toward the red cliffs. It crested the line of toothy pines and disappeared behind them. The engine sounds softened and died as, apparently, the plane touched down. Nobody moved. Long moments later, just as impatience began to ruffle the crowd, a figure appeared on the cliff top, dressed in coveralls and holding a helmet. You knew it was Mirplo. You could tell by the swagger in his walk.

A chant broke out, softly at first but quickly growing louder: "Mir-plo, Mir-plo, Mir-plo!" Fans pumped their fists in the air in time with the chant. When it got loud enough to reach Mirplo's ears, he acknowledged it by putting on the helmet and spreading his arms in benediction.

Or for a swan dive.

And as five thousand people watched, none more surprised than I, Vic Mirplo plunged off the cliff.

32

Gospel Drop

Half a heartbeat later, Vic's BASE jump parachute opened, and he floated down beneath its big Mirplo logo like an origami bird, coming to rest out on the sandy flat, near the balloons. The surge of delirious fans in that direction suggested that the myth of Mirplo was about to get kicked into higher orbit.

Louise had had enough. She impatiently prodded me into the tent, Martybeth hustling along behind, lest I accidentally throttle myself. The yurt was spacious, party-size, big enough for a portable bar with keg taps and well drinks, and half a dozen play-money gaming tables. Hundreds of Gaia-logo zipper duffels lined the perimeter, two and three rows deep, presumably filled with Gaia-logo swag and ready for distribution to the masses when the hospitality tent opened for business come nightfall.

Louise kicked a plastic folding chair in my direction (the Jeff, an IKEA bestseller) and ordered me into it. Martybeth stood behind me, keeping the rope slack and, oddly, stroking the back of my head, smoothing the grain of my hair. Something so weird about this chick. Was she gay? Straight? Bi? All evidence indicated, *Reply hazy, try again.*

We waited.

I passed the time by thinking about Mirplopalooza. For a first-time venture, it was manifestly a grand slam. I saw it getting bigger and bigger in the years to come, the sort of cash cow that a savvy investor could milk and milk and milk. If Jay saw it the same way...

The tent flap fluttered. Allie stepped in.

She'd shed the Plowright drag and reverted to simple loose jeans and a pockety blouse. I liked her much better this way.

Martybeth said, "Why, Ms. Plowright, you've changed."

Louise didn't bother with such niceties. She skipped right to "Where's the money? I don't see it."

"Oh, it's here," said Allie. She indicated the formidable line of swag bags. "I stopped by earlier and put it in one of these."

Louise sputtered her anger. "If you think I'm going to waste my time searching a hundred—"

"Relax," said Allie. "I'll tell you which one it is, once Radar's safely on his way." Louise just rolled her eyes. "No, huh?" said Allie. "Okay." She pointed to a bag in the back row. "It's that one. The one with the TSA lock." She produced a key from a pocket and dangled it in the direction of my locked collar. "We'll swap keys."

"No," said Louise. "You'll give me *your* key and I'll check out *your* bag. If what's supposed to be there is there, then you can take this shit-for-brains and get out of here."

Allie shrugged, caught between bad choices. She tossed Louise the key. Louise handed it off to Martybeth, who clomped over to the bags, grabbed the one with the chartreuse Transportation Security Administration lock, and unlocked it. She looked inside. "Holy crow!" she said.

"Just count it," said Louise. "And make sure it's real."

Well, this Martybeth did, dumping a hundred bundles out on a blackjack table, counting them out in groups of ten, inspecting them, and placing them back in the bag. By the time she was done, she was drunk with money. I've seen this before. The look, feel, and smell of cash stirs something primal in people. It makes 'em a little nuts. I think it made Martybeth wet.

"It's all there," she said at last. She licked her lips. "And it's all real." She relocked the bag and hugged it to her chest like a teddy bear.

Louise pulled out a key of her own and freed me from my choke chain. I quickly shed the peppers, hat, and poncho. Let someone else be the show.

"Let's go," said Allie.

"No, let's stay," said someone who wasn't any of us: Wolfredian, entering the tent with two hefty sidewheels along his flanks.

To Louise this was clearly an unwelcome interruption, but she worked hard to keep her ire in check. "Jay," she said, "we had a deal. I get this, you get the other thing."

"Yes, but I decided I want both things. Martybeth?" Martybeth continued to clutch the bag. She either didn't know what was going on or didn't want to acknowledge that she did. Jay crossed to her and lifted the duffel bag straight up and out of her arms.

So now I had some new information, and it wasn't good news. I thought the ladies had gone indy, but it turned out that Louise, at least, had been operating with Jay's blessing—blessing now revoked. As Louise was the one with the gun (that I knew of), I guessed Jay's authority trumped that. Sigh, women's lib, sold a bill of goods again.

But new information brought a new conclusion, again not good news, because Red's hastily improvised snatch job now seemed to have been neither hasty nor improvised. It anticipated Miriam's rejection of the Pump and Dump, even when that looked like a deal Miriam had to accept. It's like someone knew we'd try the trapdoor double cross at exactly the point we did. Someone who knew it wouldn't work.

And who's got that kind of foresight?

Who indeed? Shall we recite it together in rhyme?

You must've known
Sooner or later
Your dad would be
Your fornicator

Looking at me just then, you'd see me becoming jangly, agitated, furious at how I'd been mooked. Allie had warned me. Mirplo had warned me. Hell, *I* had warned me. What could I have said in my defense? That I was so desperate for a father's love I'd grasp at the straw of it even when I knew the straw wasn't there? That I took his many acts of contrition as contrition and not acts? Or how about this: that I secretly *wanted* to get played, just to prove that the absconding scoundrel was exactly guilty of the charges I'd historically filed against him? In that instant, it all fell apart, the need for approval replaced by a murderous rage. At least that's how it struck Wolfredian, who deployed his side-wheels a little closer to the loose cannon, should I decide to go off.

For his part, Wolfredian seemed to find my rage reassuring. He no doubt had a picture in his mind (an old and cherished one) of Woody as someone who would lay waste to lives to get what he wanted. To betray one's own son—steal his *bankroll*—all to close a money deal, fit perfectly with that picture. Despicable, yes; double-crossing, sure; but with his eye firmly on the bottom line, no matter how many bodies got strewn in the wake. Jay must've felt his jones—lock, stock, and Mirplo—to be legitimately in his grasp at last. And what could be expected from me now but the petulant protests of a broken son, trying desperately to take someone, *anyone*, right down with him?

With that, my fury boiled over into words. I poked a savage finger at the duffel bag. "That's his damn gospel drop, isn't it?" I said, using grifter slang for good-faith money. Wolfredian didn't answer, just smiled tightly. He would have seen the Mirplopalooza projections by now. He knew about the long-term lease and the year-over-year growth estimates. I recalled how Miriam Plowright had raised this subject back in the sports bar, only to have Mirplo strategically quash it. That's tantalizing, true, but Jay would still want to see the thing for himself. Was he dazzled by the fan base, the souvenir sales, the identified flying objects? Maybe, but it still wouldn't be enough, because he knew Woody and would ever have to consider the source. How could the source prove his good faith? Ripping off his own son—and using the boy's own cash for the gospel drop—would put that fear to rest forever. It may have been how Woody pitched Wolfredian in the first place: "My son's got this deep, unprotected pocket. What say we go after it? We'll have to jump through some fairly funky hoops, but his money might not be the only benefit." Thus does the timely carrot of Mirplopalooza get dangled. From Jay's point of view, he gets it both ways. He gets to watch a father crush a son—certain satisfaction in that—and that very act of destruction eliminates his last doubts about Mirplo. "I suppose it makes sense," I said, defeated. "Stealing your good-faith money from your own flesh and blood. I can just imagine how you two kissed and made up after his stay in your little storage-shed hostel."

"He wasn't as upset about that as he might have been," conceded Jay.

"Why would he be?" I said ruefully. "Eyes on the prize, right? Let bygones go by. Was that when he told you Miriam was Allie?"

Jay gave a terse nod, from which it was easy to backpredict that at some point after Woody's rendezvous with us in Villa 23, he would have made his state of liberty known to Jay. He'd have expressed his understanding for Jay's move—a kidnapped father assures the cooperation of the son—and made it clear that no hard feelings would interfere with their intended win-win. The ultimate sellout: let a guy kidnap you and then let him off the hook for it. And to authenticate this amity, you hand over your son's girlfriend, too, blow the lid off the Plowright identity. Of course, it was already half blown, thanks to Louise's hidden camera trick, but still, Red could've bought Miriam and me for one-night stand-ins—unless she already knew otherwise. So Jay had sent the girls to the doomed Pump and Dump with their backup kidnap plan already in place. Though later they were surprised not to find Woody at Stash My Sh*t. Why didn't Jay tell them Woody was out? Need-to-know basis, I guess.

So Woody sold us out. And was Jay sold? If yes, then he was about to barf a serious chunk of change into Mirplopalooza. All thanks to Woody's master manipulation of a mark who came into the play armed to the teeth with suspicion.

That's not just repeat business, that's art.

"You can't trust him, you know." I was stating the obvious, in words that came out of my mouth so thick with grief that I could see Jay dismissing them as bafflegab.

"Can't trust whom?" asked a new voice, and now, as if on cue (and who's to say it wasn't?), here came the old jackalope himself, striding into the tent like the king of the county fair. For once he wore no camouflage, and that made sense, for there now remained no call to play dress-up. Or you could say that at this point his Cheshire grin was all the outfit he needed. He carried a Geoid under his arm. Jay waved his sidewheels out of the tent, then took the Geoid from Woody as if he'd been expecting it, which, of course, he had.

"Any problems here?" asked Woody.

"None," said Jay.

Woody pointed to Allie. "She coughed up, no fuss?" Jay nodded. "Motivated by love," said Woody without a trace of irony.

"Only now Jay says we don't get the money," said Martybeth petulantly. "And if we don't, who does?"

"Don't worry," said Woody. "Everyone's going to do fine. There may be some adjustments along the way, but trust me, darling, you'll be more than happy with your taste."

Martybeth seemed satisfied with this, but to me it looked like an assault on a small mind with a blunt instrument, and Jay's smirk confirmed it. Perhaps Louise picked off that sign, for she said, "We'd better be. Unhappiness spreads."

"Yes," agreed Woody, stepping up to me. "And here's where it seems to be pooling. Hello, Radar. Can you honestly say you're surprised?"

"By your level of duplicity, no. But by some of the finesses, yes."

"Like having Jay set Martybeth and Louise up as independent agents?"

"Yeah, that distracted me."

"As it was intended to do."

"Plus slip my California Roll right up into your gospel bag."

"Intended as well."

A guy in my position—so used, so badly betrayed—could be expected to show a fair chunk of irk, and I wasn't shy about spewing mine. "So," I asked Woody, a grim challenge in my voice, "what price did you finally set?"

"Price?"

"On Mirplopalooza. Three million? Four?"

"Three point five."

I turned to Jay. "He's ripping you off, you know."

"I did my diligence," said Jay. I could tell my words carried no weight with him, except to reinforce his feeling of holding all cards.

"Uh-huh. And if I told you that Mirplo was a golem constructed just to get you on this particular hook?"

"Nonsense. You've seen the crowds. The kid's a hit. The next hundred-million-dollar pop star."

"If he's still around. Guy like that, the flake factor runs pretty high."

Jay patted the Geoid. "He'll have his incentives." I caught a glimpse of an online banking screen.

"Give it up, Radar," said Woody. "We three businessmen found a way to do business. Long-term business. If it comes at the expense of your hurt feelings, well, you can add them to your growing collection."

"So it was all bullshit," I said sadly. "You must be pretty disappointed. You raised a sucker for a son."

"How am I supposed to answer that, Radar? Anything I say will just hurt you more."

But still I wouldn't leave it alone. I was that angry and that desperate. I turned to Jay. "You know his measure," I said. "He mooked me from birth, but he's got a pretty decent track record with you, too. Did he tell you about the Kagadeskas, the other fakes?"

Woody tried to cut me off. "Radar, shut up."

"Or what? You'll steal my bankroll? Ruin my life? Can't break the same egg twice, man." I turned to Wolfredian. "But you sure can pick the same pocket." I fixed my gaze on the Geoid. "It looks like you're ready to make a buy there. You go ahead if you want to. I don't really expect you to believe anything I say. I'm probably just trying to throw whatever monkey wrenches I have handy. But whatever. Fair warning, that's all I'm saying. Fair warning."

Jay stared at me for a long moment. Then he chuckled. "Beautiful speech," he said. "Excellent monkey wrench." He fingered the Geoid. "I knew about the Kagadeskas. I sold them on to someone even less suspecting than me. As for Mirplo, I like the kid. He's the real deal. I think I'll take my chances." He stabbed a spot on the touch-screen surface with authority, then handed the pad back to Woody. "It's done."

I sagged against the portable bar, visibly staggered by Woody's triumph: He'd skinned Allie and me out of a million and touched up Jay for more than three times that. Hand it to the old goat, he knew his game.

Just then, Vic's voice rose outside the tent. "Step aside," I heard him say. "This is my meeting." A moment later, he threw back the tent flap and strode in. "Goons," he said. "They're funny."

Vic had changed clothes again and now wore gleaming sequined satin cowboy gear and a big Stetson so white it glowed. "This better not take long," he said. "I have a sunset show to do, and in case you don't know, sunset won't wait." His eyes found, and fixed on, the Geoid, and he wore the same expression Martybeth had when she counted the cash. Lust. "Set?" he asked.

"Set," said Jay.

Now Vic noticed Allie and me. "Oh, hi, Radar," he said. "Hi, Allie. Great to see you here. I guess you know this is good-bye. But it's been real." I could hear the icy finality in his voice and knew that his transformation was at last complete. Gone were his innocence and bright-eyed sense of wonder. The man who stood before me had placed ambition above all. He was determined to be *Mirplo!* at the expense of everything, including old friends. He spotted the duffel bag at Wolfredian's feet. "That's the gospel drop?" he asked. "My walking-around money?" Jay nodded. "Cool."

"Wait," I said. "What?"

Vic grinned grandly. "You wanted to start over, right? Clean slate? And what could be cleaner than no ill-gotten bankroll to sully your past?" He nodded to the duffel bag. "Congratulations, Radar. Today, officially, you're a citizen."

How do you like that? Mooked by a Mirplo.

You see something new every day.

33

Balloonageddon

I heard a low growl from my right. It was Allie, giving voice to her rage. But impotent rage, for it was evident to everyone that there was no play to make here. She and I clearly had to swallow this outcome, cut our losses and move on. Money's just money, right? But it was *our* money, hard-won (well, hard-scammed), and she seemed in no mood to give it up without a fight. Correspondingly, when Jay picked up the gospel drop by its handles and flipped it through the air to Vic, Allie dove for the bag like a blitzing linebacker, picked it off in flight, and hit the ground with a thud and a spray of sand.

"What the nuck?" yelled Vic. He jumped on Allie, but she wriggled free and stood up, holding the bag tucked under her arm. They were both breathing hard, with matching mad looks in their eyes. The rest of us were momentarily frozen, suffering the familiar temporary paralysis caused by unexpected action.

"What's your problem?" shouted Allie. "You had your own money, and plenty of it!"

"Maybe it's not about money," said Vic.

"Then what?" I found myself asking.

"Oh, think about it, Radar. You just think about who you are and the way you are, and think about how your arrogance sits with the people you think you're so much better than. Let me know when the light dawns. Begrudger."

"This is about that? Vic, I've got nothing but respect for your—"

"Shut the nuck up!" He put his head down and charged at Allie. She easily sidestepped him, but he grabbed her as he hurtled past, and they went down together in a pile of swag bags.

I advanced to help Allie but found myself checked by Louise's gun—and Jay's grin. "Let it play out," said Jay. I picked off the look that passed between those two and understood that I'd been right all along: You don't just go watch a random woman play softball; you watch your *lover* play softball. In that instant, my heart went out to poor Martybeth. She wasn't gay, straight, bi, or anything but a big amorphous mass of emotional desperation. Just one of the minor players in a snuke who gets hurt more than they deserve because they hold so few useful tools for defense.

Meanwhile, Vic wrestled the bag free from Allie, but he lost his grip and it went skittering in among others. They both threw themselves after it. Allie reached it first, her fist closing around the green TSA lock as she bounced to her feet and put her back to the wall of the tent. Vic came after her but stopped abruptly when her hand flashed from one of her pockets and a box cutter appeared, blade out.

Allie slashed out with the blade, and Vic flinched.

But he wasn't the target.

Instead, Allie deftly sliced open a floor-to-ceiling seam in the tent. She stepped through, ready to run—then explosively fell backward, straight-armed by the great, brown paw of an exceedingly lifelike and faintly clove-smelling Kodiak bear.

"Damn, Honey," I said, "I thought you were on our side."

Honey removed the costume head and fixed me with those luminous brown eyes. "I told you from the start whose side I was on." He indicated Woody. "He says guard a tent, I guard a tent." To Allie he said, "Sorry for the hard hit. This getup steals motor control. Give me the bag." He reached down to take it, but she wouldn't let go. In her fury, she kicked his legs out from under him and he toppled sideways. They wrestled for a moment, but the outcome was never in doubt. He was stronger and, with the bear suit, much heavier. He basically just lay on top of Allie until the fight went out of her. Eventually he stood up, clutching the locked duffel in his paw. Woody took the bag from Honey and brought it to Vic, who grasped it with both hands.

Allie sat on the floor, panting, defeated. Without a struggle, she let Louise take the utility knife away.

Vic turned to me, his eyes glistening with triumph. "You're such a wet," he said. "It was fun mooking you." Then he turned to Allie. "Not you," he said. "I liked you. You're better than he deserves. Say hey to Boy for me." Then he addressed everyone with utmost Mirplovian grandiloquence. "And now, friends...fans...if you'll excuse me, as I said, sunset won't wait, not even for me." He adjusted his Stetson on his head at a jaunty angle and, swinging the swag bag like a schoolboy, left the tent.

I saw the smile on Jay's face. There stood a satisfied man. I could imagine some past conversation among the conspirators in which either Woody or Mirplo had pitched going after the California Roll. It must have appealed to Jay not just as a way to reduce his own cash outlay but also to test his allies. Yes, Jay seemed well pleased. He invited us to join him for the show. I don't know which he thought would be more fun, watching Vic's performance or watching Allie and me suffer through it. But he insisted. And his sidewheels wouldn't take no for an answer.

Vic Mirplo stood stock-still in the middle of the balloon basin. The setting sun bathed him in golden light and stretched his shadow out behind him. Spa music played. A dance ensemble swirled around him like flowing water. When the music and dance ended, a helicopter came flying in from the south and dropped to a low hover over Vic. A length of purple netting unfurled, spooling out below the chopper to dangle like a ship's rigging just above Vic's head. Still holding the duffel bag, Vic did a buccaneer's leap into the netting and cocooned himself inside it—upside down. As the chopper lifted, I saw him reach a hand into the bag and withdraw a broken bundle of hundred-dollar bills, which he set free to flutter down among the crowd. How to win friends and influence people.

As we sat together in our reserved seats, Jay said smugly, "At that rate, his walking-around money won't last long." He wore the contented look of an impresario who'd locked up the star act of a generation. Slot this act into the Gaia's main theater, and Jay could write his own ticket straight to the chairman's desk. Who cared what sort of nitwit behavior the star indulged in, so long as his show dropped jaws?

And this one did.

The helicopter airlifted Vic up to the cliff top and deposited him there among the pines. Just then, the massive sound system let loose with a sharp squeal of attention-getting feedback, and everyone looked to follow the sound. Immediately on its heels came a blast of percussion that resolved itself into the signature beats of Japanese *taiko* drumming. It started out loud and got louder, undershot with bass notes so profound they made the ground shake. The drumming gave way to the single tenor drone of a great Irish warpipe, which held and held and held, then shattered in a glissando of falling notes unrecognizable as that of any particular instrument (and therefore probably synthesized) that landed in a lake of full orchestration. All at once the air was alive with music of richness and sophistication, rife with tension and conflict. The dancers started up again, moving in complex choreography, a feast for the eyes. Vic, meanwhile, had left the line of pines; he was nowhere to be seen.

Next, a series of firecracker-pops explosively untethered the balloons. Controlled from below by dozens of young functionaries cradling Geoids, the dirigibles formed up in a lazy promenade. The controllers' fingers danced on the pads, and the airships overhead danced in kind. I didn't know the Geoid could serve as a radio controller, but I wasn't surprised; with the proper peripherals, it could doubtless walk my dog.

A draped and decorated scissor-lift cranked up from ground level to a height of fifty feet, and there stood Zoe, resplendent in rich crimson robes, hair dyed to match. Her own Geoid in hand, she presided over the show like a conductor. You had to wonder how much of Mirplo's achievement could be attributed to her. Behind every great man stands a techie queen?

The music morphed again, dipping down into long, low frequencies that made the sand on the basin floor bounce, and that's some subwoofing there. This gave way to something like a Sousa march filtered through cellophane, at once stirring and incredibly banal, a call to arms that made a mockery of calls to arms. The balloons separated into armadas of good and evil and moved to opposite sides of the basin, one near the hoodoos and the other in the lee of the cliff wall.

The crowd stood spellbound, and I noticed Jay mentally counting the house. Measured in demonstrable fan devotion, his investment was looking better by the second. Now a hum rose from the sound system, and it seemed to be the signal for a certain balloonageddon to commence.

The dirigibles closed on one another in attack phalanxes, then broke into a panorama of slow-motion dogfights. The name of the game appeared to be to engage your foe broadside and spike him with your stiletto tip. The operators' faces turned tense with concentration as small twos and threes of balloons coordinated their efforts, forming teams that could attack the enemy and defend each other's flanks. When one balloon speared another, the victim exploded in a shower of metal confetti, as if to convey that death may be pretty, or at least shiny. The Mylar corpses that landed in the crowd were raised above many heads and marched about like fallen gods. This seemed not to have been planned, just an enthusiastic, spontaneous response to noble sacrifice. Whatever Vic had tapped into here, it was primal stuff; folks had lost their minds.

Art is power, is what it is.

The two sides struck a rough balance, so that every time good or evil seemed to get the upper hand, its adversary adapted, changed tactics, regrouped. This may have been intended to show that morality needs strategy or that good and evil regress to the mean. Or something else, I don't know. Ask Vic.

He must be around here somewhere.

The dragonfly ultralight suddenly appeared above the cliff tops, clearing the pines on takeoff, then looping far around to the west. Now it returned, flying in out of the sun. It thrashed among the balloons, using nothing but prop wash to scatter the order of battle and create chaos. Then it climbed high, circling, surveying. Crimson sunlight caught the facets of the dragonfly's bulbous compound eyes and shot reflected flashes of red-green fire into the crowd.

The battle rolled on, good fighting evil for mastery of the sky. And now the black hats began to gain the upper hand as they relentlessly parlayed a small numerical advantage into a big one. The engagement, it seemed, would be over soon.

Or maybe not. For just then the ultralight descended from high orbit and made strafing runs on the evil balloons. You couldn't see anything being fired—bullets, darts, St. Elmo's Fire—but every time the plane lined up on its target, the target exploded. This mystified me until I glanced at the operators and noticed them fingering their Geoids at strategic instants. Interesting. The balloons were rigged with self-destructive charges. I suppose that said something about something—the futility of war?—but I couldn't form the thought. The spectacle had wiped my mind clean of most notions save the perplexing conundrum of whether Mirplo had made art or art had made him.

Soon all the evil balloons had been destroyed, and when the last one fell, a cheer went up from the crowd. The dragonfly flew a lazy victory lap around the arena, waggling its wings in acknowledgment of the crowd's support.

Then blasted every remaining balloon—all the surviving good guys—clean out of the sky.

Well, people were shocked. You could read it in their faces, hear it in their gasps. They'd been seduced into supporting their heroes, been rewarded with victory, and then, in the throes of their euphoria, seen even the victors summarily and arbitrarily wiped out. There was bafflement. How could a just and loving dragonfly do such a thing? The crowd became restive, unruly. I shared their unease. On a gut level, below reason, I felt betrayed.

The ultralight flew low over the crowd. The nacelle opened for two seconds and a small flutter of paper puffed out. Characteristic rectangles. Big Bens.

Blood money? Maybe. It altered the group mood in an instant.

Where the money fell, people went predictably nuts, stampeding, competing for their share of the windfall. Meanwhile, the dragonfly swooped and weaved here and there, releasing more cash in long or tantalizingly short bursts.

One of the bills wafted down into our midst, and Wolfredian snatched it. He examined it with a practiced eye, then pocketed it. "Look at that," he said. "Return on my investment already."

The battle was already a memory, for the frenzy of free money changed everything. Money is like that. It trumps good and evil. It trumps almost everything.

The music stopped. The dragonfly droned out beyond the hoodoos and lined up for another run over the crowd. Down on the basin floor the only sound was the undifferentiated growl of feral clashes for cash. The ultralight gathered speed. The dragonfly entered the basin. The nacelle cracked open, and a huge stream of hundred-dollar bills ribboned out.

Then...the ultralight's engine quit.

It started again, sputtered, then died for good.

And in the sick silence that followed, the plane drifted across the basin, describing a low, sinking parabolic arc. It smashed into the red cliffs about halfway up, exploded in a ball of flame, and vaporized at once.

This time there was no BASE jump and no parachute with a Mirplo logo. Just a minimal cloud of debris that rained down, including many charred hundred-dollar bills.

34

Memorial Gardens

Allie and I held a service for Vic in Memorial Gardens, an ecumenical resting spot on the southern edge of Santa Fe. I'd toyed with the idea of romancing him into the Santa Fe National Cemetery as a war veteran, but to what end, beyond slapping a bogus exclamation point on the end of his life sentence? While such chicanery might have tickled Vic, I think Memorial Gardens would probably please him more. It was so nondenominational as to be completely noncommittal, its approach to eternal repose as hodgepodge as Vic's constantly slurving definition of art. I don't know, somehow it suited.

We had a simple marker placed beneath a palo verde tree, red sandstone to clash with the tree's green blooms, then went back and forth for a while on what to inscribe on the stone. I wanted something Mirplovian, something like NUCK THIS or NOW I'M REALLY BORED. Allie preferred the modern allegorical RUST NEVER SLEEPS. In the end we settled on I'LL BURN THAT BRIDGE WHEN I COME TO IT. Next we sent word to the Santa Fe art community, announcing the day and time of Vic's memorial. Zoe didn't come—apparently she preferred to mourn in private—but quite a crowd turned out to eulogize, as they saw it, an artist of vision and great promise, tragically cut down in his prime. They admired that he died for his art.

I spoke a few words. I had intended something grand, perhaps a proposal to turn the site of his first studio into a monument after all, but in the end I just echoed Woody's observation about the slender thread by which we all hang, and encouraged those who love each other to love each other a little harder and make it known while there's still time. Allie held my hand. Boy lay at my feet. It seemed like the right thing to say.

While others chipped in with words of affection for a man they knew less well than I did, my mind wandered back to the aftermath of the accident.

There had been chaos. In the horror of the instant, people started screaming and swarming, going off in all directions at once. It's the small moments I remember.

Like Martybeth instinctively clinging to Louise, who shoved her aside with such open hostility that Martybeth finally understood how and why she'd been used.

Or Jay looking flatlined, though I knew that the color draining from his face was less about any sudden and tragic deaths than about a sudden and tragic nosedive in income projections. It took no genius to calculate that Mirplopalooza without Mirplo was just palooza.

Or Woody dodging the sidewheels and slipping away into the crowd, which struck me as exactly and precisely the right thing to do, so I grabbed Allie and we did the shade and fade, retreating across the festival ground, lost in the teeming mob.

Or the human tide sweeping us past the Gaia hospitality tent, where I caught a glimpse of Honey waddling around, portly in his bear suit.

Or the ride we thumbed out of there with a vanload of Mirplomaniacs from Reno, or the series of regional flights we caught from there back to Santa Fe.

Or when I started crying.

It shouldn't have ended like this. We had a good plan, a righteous plan to snuke a most suspicious mark by shoving his own suspicions back down his throat until he choked on them. First we spellbound him with the spectacle of Mirplopalooza, then we drowned his doubts in all that conflict between Woody, Vic and me—played right into his smug security that "the enemy of my enemy is my date to the prom." I like to think I played my ire well enough to bury all of Jay's suspicions in the angry, desperate efforts of a hurt and heartsick son trying to destroy his father out of spite. But credit really had to go to Vic, not just for his acting ability—changing his game face as the situation demanded—but really for injecting Mirplopalooza with legitimate artistic energy. True, I had heavily hedged that bet by hiring not just the event staff, but all the festive festivalgoers as well. Mirplomania, bought and paid for from the start; no wonder it looked so good to Jay. Next year's affair, not thus artificially propped, would have flopped, but by then Jay's money would have been long gone, distributed among us all from the joint account that Jay'd paid into. At that point, what could he do about a fickle public turning its back on last year's fad? Mirplo would've given it the good ol' college try, but you can't catch lightning in a bottle twice. Probably by the third year, Jay'd realize his investment was crap, cut his losses, and quit. Then Vic would've been free to pursue whatever flights of fancy next tickled him to try.

That was the plan.

But the plan hit a wall, disintegrated and burned, along with my best friend.

Along, also, with our million bucks, which Allie said was a mistake: There was supposed to be a switcheroo.

This she told me the night we got back from Nevada. We were sitting on the front porch of our cottage, still in shock. We'd retrieved Boy from Zoe's dad and, sensing the mood of the moment, he lay between us in solemn repose.

"We had a bag swap on," Allie said. "It was Vic's idea. When I told him you'd been kidnapped, he thought we could pay your ransom and still keep it."

"He knew about the Gaia duffels?"

"Sure. Remember, he's the one who sold Wolfredian on doing the hospitality tent. He must've seen the swag when the casino loaded it in."

"So you two set up a switch."

"We three. Woody was in on it, too."

"He was, huh?" I got a sinking feeling, the same one I always got when Woody was in on things. Because Woody already knew about the kidnapping. Fed Jay the idea, in fact. "How'd it work?"

"Easy. I just signatured one bag with a TSA lock and planted another one, a dummy, in with all the rest. I made the switch during my scuffle with Vic."

I could see it. I could almost replay it in my mind's eye. Vic and Allie go down in a hail of swag bags. Allie grabs a second locked bag and loses the first among the others, with plans to come back and collect it later. The ol' switcheroo. Except...

"Why didn't you go back for the money?"

"Because it wasn't there."

"What do you mean?"

"Remember when Honey hit me? We fell down and rolled around. I was trying to move him off the play, but he must've thought I was giving him cover. He switched the bags back."

"But why?"

"Maybe he didn't know the switch had been made."

"But it makes no sense. Why bother swapping at all when Vic's supposed to end up with our cash anyhow, then kick it back to us later?"

"Well," said Allie, "because..." Her voice trailed off. After a minute, she said, softly and with no conviction whatsoever, "Belt and suspenders."

"Come again?"

"Belt and suspenders. Extra protection. That's what Woody called it when he called the play."

"I thought you and Vic called the play."

"I thought so, too. But now I'm not so sure. You know how your father is. When he gets talking, everything seems so reasonable, you kind of lose your mind."

"So," I said, "Vic ended up with the money and decided to spew it all over the festival ground." I thought back to the performance. "But that didn't seem like improv. It really seemed planned, part of the show. Its whole point, really."

"Maybe it was," Allie thought for a minute, then said, "Maybe... Radar, I don't like to say this, but maybe that was Vic's move all along: Steal our money and Robin Hood it out to the crowd. An employee bonus, like. Or a statement."

"What statement? 'Art irritates life'?"

"Something like that."

"I don't buy it," I said. "For that to be true, he'd have to have been double-crossing us for real and not for show. It wasn't Vic."

"Then who?"

"Well, who else?"

"Woody," said Allie. "But how?"

I replayed Honey's and Allie's struggle in the tent. Yes, Honey had come up with the bag: the real one, not the dummy one; unless...

I snapped my fingers. "Of course! Allie, Honey didn't switch the bags back, he switched in a third one! Then bootlegged the money out later. No wonder he looked all portly. He had a million dollars' worth of bear fat."

"But we saw the money fall from the plane."

"We saw *some* money fall from the plane. Who's to say how much?"

"Maybe not much," agreed Allie. "Maybe just enough to make us think it was all of it."

"Right, like salting a gold mine."

"Vic did have some cash," she mused. "The high-roller roll you had him bring to Vegas."

"Which maybe he put in the plane beforehand."

"So it all comes back to Woody. At the end of the day, he snuked us right out of our stake."

And when we checked the joint account? Yeah, he'd snuked us out of that, too. Is anyone here surprised?

The thing plagued me, though; it did. Maybe I put too much trust in Radar's radar, but I just couldn't believe Woody would do me like that. The evidence was there. The facts stacked up. The narrative was completely consistent. But I didn't vibe it. Deep down in my gut, the explanation wouldn't take hold. Still, what could I do? Woody was in the wind, and Allie and I were left holding the bag. A great big bag of nothing.

We started looking for straight jobs. Our hearts couldn't have been less in it if they'd been surgically removed and shipped to South Africa. Still, we managed to land something. Allie caught on at an arts council, writing grants. Honest grift—I knew she'd be good at it. Me, I got a job groundskeeping a golf course, suitably mindless work, driving a rider-mower all day and listening to books on tape.

In my quiet moments, I mulled Vic's death, trotting out every rationalization I could think of. *He made his own choices. He never had to say yes. And he didn't have to go to such ridiculous extremes.* But I never could shake the feeling that Vic's blood was on my hands. It was me. All me. I made him fly too high. If I hadn't, he'd still be holed up somewhere doing horrible things to dolls and stuffed animals, making a modest name for himself. It wouldn't have been a bad gig. Anyway, worthy of a Mirplo.

A month passed.

Zoe came to see us. She didn't look too terrific. Her dyed hair had grown out, her brown roots emerging neglected and ignored, and she'd devolved her dress to sweatpants and a dirty shirt. Her skin was dark, though, for she'd been spending lots of time outdoors. "I've been walking," she explained. "That's all I do is just walk."

She told us she was selling Vic's stuff, and did we want to buy any of his tools or supplies? I said all I wanted was *The Albuquerque Turkey.*

She shook her head sadly. Wolfredian already bought it.

What a vulture the man was, picking over the bones.

And that wasn't all. Zoe said he'd arranged to buy it all, every last piece Vic had produced in his short career. I guess he thought of it as a consolation prize, cornering the market of the doomed.

"Who organized the sale?" I asked.

"Your dad," said Zoe. "Somehow he controls the estate."

Well, why did that not surprise me? *My damned old man's still snuking us all, even after the fact.*

I made it a point to be at Zoe's the day a fat van rolled up to cart Vic's works away. Jay had sent Red Louise to oversee the operation, and she wasted no time getting the moving crew humping their loads. When she saw me, though, she stopped and—literally—cracked her knuckles. "You're not going to do anything stupid, I hope."

Actually, I think she hoped I would. "Where's Wolfredian?" I asked.

Louise snorted. "Like he's got time to trek out here. There's other whales to fry, you know." She reached into her back pocket and pulled out a piece of paper. "You'll probably want to see this." It was a document giving Woody control over Vic's art. Possibly bogus, but what did it matter? Control is control.

I stayed through the load out, making sure that, if nothing else, Vic's stuff was properly packed for travel. This was his oeuvre, his legacy, and while I hated seeing it in Wolfredian's hands, I'd have hated worse to see it damaged or destroyed. There was lots of it, too, more than I'd imagined. Guess Vic had mastered that whole "procrastinate later" thing in the end.

At last Louise was ready to go. She couldn't resist a parting shot. "You're looking at this wrong, you know. Jay'll make your friend immortal. Tragic young deaths sell big. Swear to God, in the end that flake'll earn more dead than he would've alive."

That's when I hit her. Hard enough to break her jaw, but also my hand.

I don't know if that made us even. It sure didn't make us friends.

35

Where Charlie Does Brunch

A week later, we get a postcard.

On the front is a photo of a cowboy astride a giant jackalope, herding cattle, with the caption, "Roundup Time." On the back, in Woody's familiar hand, a riddle of sorts:

Q: When is Las Vegas not Las Vegas?
A: When Charlie does Sunday brunch.

"Don't buy into it, Radar," said Allie. "He's just messing us around again."

"It looks like he's inviting us to brunch."

"Where?"

"In the Las Vegas that's not Las Vegas. The one in New Mexico."

The one just an hour and change down the road from Santa Fe. The one with a restaurant called Charlie's Spic & Span. Did we go? Of course we went. I wanted answers. I figured he owed me that much, and figured he figured so, too, else why the postcard?

We arrived on Sunday just before noon and found Woody seated in a booth by the window, placidly eating pie. The distant and obscure meeting place had suggested sequestering, so I was a little surprised to see Woody casually and normally dressed, no more disguised than the ranch hands at a nearby table or the old woman in the next booth over. I sat down opposite him, with Allie by my side.

Oblique as ever, he opened with, "Try the pie. It's prune."

"Prune pie?"

"House specialty," he said, his mouth full. "It's better than you think."

"What I think," I said, "is you'd better tell us what happened to our money."

"Oh, it's right here," he said. He moved his leg under the table and shoved something solid against mine: a laundry bag, large and overstuffed. Allie bent down to explore the contents. She came up with her eyebrows arched.

"Cash," she said softly. "A whole damn lot of it."

"Yeah, sorry about the bank account. I had to sweep it clean before probate stepped in."

"You couldn't let us know?"

"I'm letting you know now. I wanted to make sure Jay was buttoned up first."

"And you couldn't warn me I was going to get kidnapped?"

A shrug and a smile. "True believers sell best."

"And is he?" asked Allie. "Jay, I mean: sold."

"Completely. He bought the collected works at yard-sale prices. He's thrilled."

"And the Mirplopalooza money?"

"Of course he doesn't get that back. A deal's a deal. But he thinks he'll make it back in the posthumous Mirplo market. Personally, I don't think he'll find the market all that strong. The kid was kind of a flash in the pan."

"Dad," I said, "don't speak ill of the dead."

Woody eyed me thoughtfully. "You know," he said, "I think that's the first time you've called me Dad." He kicked the bag with his foot. It made a resonant, dull thud. "Anyway, that's your share of the get, with an extra twenty-three thousand out of my end. You didn't think I forgot about that, did you?" He grinned entirely inappropriately. "Oh, plus your million. Sorry I had to play a little fast and loose with that. You figured out how it went down?"

"Yeah, we figured out how," I said. "Still haven't figured out why."

"Well, you don't want to leave that kind of cash in the hands of a Mirplo."

I repeated quietly, "I told you not to speak ill of the dead."

"I'm not," he replied.

"He's really not," said the old woman in the booth behind us—in the voice of Uncle Joe!

"Vic!" I dove straight over the banquette and landed upside down in Vic's lap. I jarred my broken hand and suffered a shiver of pain, but I didn't care. Then Allie was in there too, squirming around and burying granny in her affection. No doubt we looked mad to the ranchers, but they politely focused on their sopaipillas and left us to our antic reunion.

"I think," said Woody blandly, "that we should take this party elsewhere."

Elsewhere turned out to be a campground at Storrie Lake State Park, where Vic and Zoe had holed up since Mirplopalooza. We all sat together on the treeless shore and watched windsurfers skim across the reservoir while Vic filled in the blanks of his staged demise.

"I started to get nervous," he told me, "after you were kidnapped."

"I'm glad that made you nervous."

"No, that wasn't it. Jay called me into a meeting. The night before Mirplopalooza. Laid out his plans for my career. *My* career! Can you believe it? The yutz wanted to manage me. And low taste? I swear to God, Radar, he'd have me painting velvet Elvi."

"So you decided to fake your own death."

"When you think about it, I had to. Our business is all about selling nothing for something, you know? If I give him Mirplopalooza and then keep doing it, I'm just selling something for something, and what kind of sense does that make?"

" 'Our business'? Vic, I thought you were an artist."

"Yeah, it was fun, but... man, a lot of work."

"How'd you pull it off?" asked Allie. "Did you have to re-rig the ultralight?"

"No, man, it was remote controlled from the start."

"What about your flying lessons?"

"I took 'em. Then I stopped. That shit's dangerous."

"So when the helicopter dropped you off on the plateau?"

"I just started walking."

I turned to Zoe. "And you worked the whole thing from the Geoid?"

She nodded. "I had to write an app."

"You can do that?"

"I can now."

"I tell you, Radar, the girl is gifted. She's got a future in the grift." I thought about her haggard appearance and her well of sorrow when she came to see me and lured me out to her place for my last act of surrender. Vic was right. The girl had game.

I asked Woody, "Why didn't you tell us? Why couldn't you let us know?"

"Well, I didn't see either of you until we got to the tent. And anyway..."

I cut him off. "I know, I know," I said. "True believers sell best." Woody just beamed. So glad I could please my papa. "You could've told us after."

"I asked him to wait," said Vic.

"Why?" asked Allie.

"Okay, I'm gonna tell you," said Vic, "but before I do, let me ask, how has the last month been? You liking your jobs?" Allie and I exchanged looks. We both shook our heads. "Well, there it is," he said. "You kids were so bent on going straight, I had to give you a taste of it so you'd know how stupid it was."

"*You* had to?"

"Radar, look, think about where you were before. You'd made some money, built a bankroll, and then you didn't have to grift anymore. So you were ready to get out of the game. I couldn't let it happen."

"Are you saying you set this whole thing up?" asked Allie. "To convince us not to go straight?"

Vic just smiled. "And how did you like the ride?"

My thoughts went back to my night in the storage locker and the revelation about following my path. I don't know where Allie's thoughts went, but the next thing I knew, she was punching Vic hard on the shoulder.

"You're a bastard," she said. "You know that?"

"Tell me I'm wrong, then."

"No," she said. "No, you're not wrong."

"You know what art is, really?" said Vic. "It's what you do because you want to, not because you have to."

And that kind of closed out the conversation. There were some matters still to be resolved, like what Vic would do next, who he'd become, how he would cover his tracks. But he wasn't worried about that. As he saw it, he'd been reincarnated without the hassle of having to die, and would happily go where the wind blew him next. Sure he was giving up his brand—*Mirplo!*—but figured that was a small enough price to pay for getting Allie and me back on the snuke. I guess you call that friendship.

Woody's plans were more prosaic. He was going down to Phoenix to hustle golf with Honey. They didn't really have to, considering the money they'd just made, but they'd do it anyhow. Maybe just to stay sharp. Or maybe because Vic's right: Art's what you do because you want to, not because you have to.

So it looks like I'm going to stay an artist. And we all know what kind.

36

Jackalope Prologue

Much later, I found out about this:

It's a cool morning in June. Vic Mirplo, starting artist, has dropped in to see his good friends Radar Hoverlander and Allie Quinn in their Santa Fe home. He's been worried about them lately. At first he thought it was just noise, all this talk about embracing the straight life. But now they've got this adobe abode and catalogs from trade schools—hell, there's no telling where this nonsense might lead. They're on the verge of squandering their gift, and that, Vic reckons, is not to be allowed. He wants to talk sense to them, but they're both so stubborn, he fears he'll have to show, not tell.

Radar and Allie aren't home, but there's a postcard stuck in their door, a funny one with a picture of a jackalope. Mirplo reads the message scrawled on the back.

Saw you on YouTube, son.
What do you say to a grift?

There's a phone number, too.

It's worth a shot, thinks Vic.

He pockets the postcard and reaches for his phone.

Acknowledgments

I'd like to thank my agent, Betsy Amster, who kept the faith, and my new and formidable editor, Christine Kopprasch, who directed traffic with grace and aplomb. Sometimes the puzzle seemed more like a ticking time bomb, but we clipped the right wires in the end. Thanks always to my wife, Maxx Duffy, there through thick, thin, and all points in between. Thanks to everyone who loved *The California Roll* and took the time to tell me so; you inspired me in dark days. And thanks to the scoundrels and scalawags of the real world, who never run out of inventive new grist for my mill.

Remember, folks, if it seems too good to be true, it is.

About the Author

JOHN VORHAUS wears many hats: novelist, poker expert, international creative consultant. When not basking in the sunshine of his California home, he travels the world, teaching and training writers. He swears by Radar's words: "Love what you do. If you don't love it, you won't do it well." Visit him online at www.johnvorhaus.com.